Madeline Martin is ~~~~~~~~~~~~
Author of historical r~~~~~~~~~~~
and turns, steamy ro~~~~~~~~~~~~
and the men who are strong ~~~~~~~
She lives a glitter-filled life in Jacksonville, Florida,
with her two daughters—known collectively as the
minions—and a man so wonderful he's been dubbed
Mr Awesome. Find out more about Madeline at her
website: madelinemartin.com.

Also by Madeline Martin

How to Tempt a Duke

Discover more at millsandboon.co.uk.

HOW TO START
A SCANDAL

Madeline Martin

MILLS & BOON

First Published in Great Britain 2020
by Mills & Boon, an imprint of HarperCollins*Publishers*
1 London Bridge Street, London, SE1 9GF

© 2020 Madeline Martin

ISBN: 978-0-263-27715-9

MIX
Paper from
responsible sources
FSC® C007454

This book is produced from independently certified FSC™ paper
to ensure responsible forest management.
For more information visit www.harpercollins.co.uk/green.

Printed and bound in Spain
by CPI, Barcelona

To my mom,
who has always been my biggest supporter.

I love you beyond words and am grateful for you
every single day.

Chapter One

June 1815—London, England

Lady Violet Lavell had been summoned to the Earl of Hollingston's study, which never boded well, and was settled precariously upon the chair her eldest sister had once dubbed the 'squeak seat'.

Her father cut an imposing figure with his large, square-shaped face and eyes that held the potential to bore into one's very soul. There were moments of tenderness, of course, but now was not one of them.

'You have four older sisters who are married with children of their own and a brother who has spent his life preparing to assume the title in addition to having his own family as well.' Lord Hollingston's brown eyes lifted from a piece of paper. Several stacks of paper, that was.

'All my children have gone on about their lives,' her father continued. 'With one exception.'

His stare jabbed into her as though she was one of the hapless butterflies pinned into frames on his wall. 'You,' he said.

She shifted on the chair before she could stop herself.

Squeak.

Drat.

'You are three and twenty, Violet,' he continued. 'Nearly "on the shelf" as it's said these days. Yet you certainly spend money as if you are still seeking a husband.' He tapped the stack of papers with his fingertips.

Her bills, no doubt.

'You have no plans for an unexpected windfall, do you?' He lifted his brows.

Actually, she did. But certainly nothing she meant to share with him. Not just yet, at least. Not until she built up the readership of her *Lady Observer* column in the *Society Journal* to the point where it generated a decent income. And by 'decent income', she meant the ability to afford more than a new dress once a year and a few sweets each month.

She sat quiet as a mouse, unmoving on the dreaded squeak seat.

He took her silence as surrender to his sound logic and proceeded. 'Violet, I have indulged your desire to remain unwed long enough. It is high time you were married.'

Violet's heart knocked hard in her chest. 'Please do not make me, Father.'

He pinched the bridge of his nose, then laboriously lowered his hand back to the desk. 'I anticipated that might be your response. If you refuse to wed, I'm afraid I will have to insist that you retire to the country.'

Violet nodded slowly. Retire to the country. It was not ideal, but she would readily take it over marriage.

'As it happens, your sister is seeking a governess and would appreciate assistance with the children until she finds one.'

Squeak.

Drat.

'Which sister?' Violet asked quickly to cover up the groan of springs.

Please don't let it be Sophie. Please don't let it be Sophie. Please, please, please, be anyone but Sophie.

'Sophie,' her father answered.

At that, Violet's insides withered with dread. Sophie had four children. They were an unruly, spoiled lot, resorting often to screaming fits as well as biting and all manner of awful habits.

Violet shuddered. 'They've been through four governesses already. This year.'

Lord Hollingston's expression was implacable. 'Which is why I suppose she requires another.'

'I would prefer not to, please,' Violet said as prettily as was possible.

Her father remained unmoved. 'Your only option, I'm afraid, is to either wed by the end of the Season, or retire to the country and assist Sophie.'

Violet's mouth fell open. 'Papa, it is most likely only three weeks until the end of the Season. Perhaps a month at most.'

He steepled his fingers. 'So it is.'

'Might I have the summer to think it over?' The chair cried out beneath her, but she didn't care. 'Perhaps next Season—'

'You've had six already.' He spoke drily as his fingertips found their way to tap against the stack of bills. She didn't have to look to know they were from the modiste, the milliner and other various shops she frequented.

She had needed that clothing. In order to glean gossip for the *Lady Observer*, she had to move freely among the *ton*. How was such a thing possible in an old frock?

'There will be no negotiation.' Lord Hollington got to his feet and indicated the door.

She had been dismissed with the worst of choices laid out before her.

He walked around the desk and followed her out of the study. 'I am not doing this to be cruel.' His tone was gentler. 'You cannot simply exist in life like this, Violet. You need purpose.'

She pressed her lips together. She did have purpose. The *Lady Observer* occupied all her free time. Except no one knew she was the author of the column and she didn't care for them to know. Instead, she simply nodded and made for the stairs. Her feet hesitated as she got to the landing and considered her options.

Going up the stairs would lead her to her chamber. Walking down the hall in the opposite direction, however, would lead to the kitchen where Cook had made the most delicious pastries earlier. Violet knew well enough that Cook made more than would ever possibly be eaten in only one day.

She shouldn't, she knew.

Except that she could practically taste the sweet, tart strawberry jam against her tongue. Her teeth longed to press down into the flaky dough and meet the delicate crunch and pop of the sugar crystals that glittered over the top like frost.

Yes. To the kitchen. She shifted.

'I wouldn't bother.' Lord Hollingston lifted his gaze over the top of a paper he held in front of his face as he walked. 'Your mother anticipated you might be emotional over this and had Cook lock away all the pastries.'

Emotional? All of them?

She tried to swallow her sorrow, but still a squawk emerged. It was bad enough to be given such dismal choices. It was entirely another to be deprived of consolation.

Tears blurred her vision.

'Good evening, Violet.' Her father's gaze swept up the stairs, a silent order to proceed to her chamber.

She nodded, unable to speak, and backed away from him, this time climbing the risers as she was bid.

As her feet trudged upwards in a slow march, she concocted an article in her mind.

Scandal-sheet writer disappears from society rather suddenly. Speculation abounds, but rumour has it she's gone to take on the menial task of unpaid governess to her sister's four children. A scandal, indeed!

Not that anyone would truly even notice if she was gone. What was one less wallflower floating in the background at a ball? The knot in her throat tightened and she almost burst into tears right there.

She couldn't, just *couldn't*, act as governess to Sophie's children. Not when countless others who had far more experience and patience than she had given up the task as hopeless. But marriage…

Well, she couldn't do that either. She pushed through the door to the bedchamber and glanced at the silver-tissue gown on a dressmaker's form propped at the side of her room. To some it might be considered a fashionable form of decor.

For Violet, it was a painful reminder. Of what

she had lost, of how she had failed. That she always needed to try harder. A surge of anger overtook her.

A pox on trying harder.

She shoved past the gown to the small box in the drawer behind it, the one filled with toffees. She snatched one up, unfurled the crinkly wax wrapper, popped it into her mouth and practically moaned as the decadence of sugary confection dissolved against her tongue.

She shouldn't be doing it, she knew, but could scarcely help it any more than she could stop breathing. After all, food was a way of remembering for her. Well, for remembering and for forgetting and, at that moment, she wanted to forget it all.

Even if it was fleeting.

A sob choked out around the sweet in her mouth, a pitiful sound to be sure. She put her face into her hands and gave way to the desolation ringing hollow in her chest.

What was she to do?

Seth Sinclair, the Earl of Dalton, entered the town house located on Grosvenor Street for the first time in nearly six years. In his absence, the old brick front had been stuccoed over, the layer of plaster smoothing out all the chinks and seams.

He had left as a second son with little purpose beyond his purchased military commission. He now grudgingly returned, fresh out of a major battle, as an unqualified earl who would rather continue his life as a soldier. Especially when he'd been only months away from being promoted to major, a rank he'd worked damn hard to achieve.

Gibbons was still the same, the old butler not looking a day over ninety as he always had. Pleasure flushed the aged man's cheeks as he offered a warm welcome.

Despite the external alterations to the town house, the interior was unchanged with a shining marble floor in a checked pattern and a pale green silk brocade on the walls. Paintings from centuries of Sinclair ancestors stared down at him with bland expressions. Disappointed with him, no doubt. Most Sinclairs generally were.

Though everything was as it had always been, Seth did not have the sense of having returned home. But then Dalton Place never truly had felt like a home should. At least not for him.

His feet echoed on the hard floor as he made his way back to the morning room where Gibbons had informed him his mother was taking tea. Seth stopped in front of the grand double doors, loathing the trepidation tightening the back of his neck. He had sent his mother a missive to inform her of his impending arrival. No doubt she was expecting him.

'Seth?' Lady Dalton's voice came from the other side of the door, pitched with what almost sounded like desperation.

He opened the door at last and stepped inside. His mother had already risen from her favourite blue-velvet sofa and stood poised with a foot set forward as if she'd meant to go to the door herself. Though it had been over a year since William's death, she still wore a black gown, indicating her full mourning.

Of course she did.

Had Seth been the son to have died, doubtless she would be outfitted in a pastel sprigged muslin.

'Are you injured?' she whispered.

For that one moment—that wrenching and sadly fleeting moment—she actually appeared to care. He hated the wrench in his chest. After all these years, he should be beyond hope.

'No, I'm not injured,' Seth replied steadily. Many of his brethren at Waterloo, however, had sustained debilitating injuries of those who had the good fortune to even come away with their lives.

But he couldn't think of Waterloo. Not now. Not when it had been less than a fortnight since the battle and the stink of gunpowder and blood still clung to his nostrils. Not when the images left were lodged like nightmares in his mind.

He clenched his teeth.

His mother straightened and, all at once, her expression smoothed. 'You are home then? For good.'

'I'm selling my commission,' he replied. He had to, lest he be tempted to return. The life of a soldier had suited him far better than one wiled away tediously in drawing rooms and Almack's. 'I am home.'

She nodded and considered him for a long moment. No doubt comparing him against William. Seth would come up short. He always had.

Her forehead crinkled and he almost thought she might express some concern for his well-being during the six years he had been away fighting. First on the Peninsula, and then at Waterloo.

Many of his fellow soldiers had died in that time. Though Waterloo had easily claimed the most lives, wreaked the most carnage.

The beginnings of sweat prickled along his brow. He clenched his hand into a fist.

Stop thinking of it.

'It's been over a year,' his mother said, emotion clogging her voice for the first time in perhaps Seth's entire life. She swallowed. 'It's been over a year since William—' Her words choked off and she dabbed at her eyes with a handkerchief she pulled from her long, black sleeve. 'You didn't attend his funeral.'

'I was escorting Napoleon to Elba when it occurred and was then required to attend the Vienna Congress.' Seth kept his response absent of emotion despite the ire nipping at his nerves. 'I didn't even receive notice of his death until well after the funeral had passed.'

'And yet still you did not return home.' Her words were accusing as her tears fell in earnest.

'I was fighting for England,' he countered.

'You were fighting for glory,' she scoffed and pushed past him, not bothering to close the door behind her as she left.

Seth sighed into the empty space. That had gone exactly as poorly as he had anticipated.

'Seth?' a soft feminine voice spoke up from behind him.

He turned to find his younger sister, Caroline, standing in the open doorway. She was no longer the little girl he'd left behind, but now a woman of nineteen, recently come out. He'd missed her debut, too, though he'd read about it in the papers some months later when they were finally delivered.

'Caroline, I'm sorry I wasn't there for you,' he said.

She raced over the thick Turkish carpet and threw her arms around him. 'You've nothing to apologise for.' She squeezed him fiercely. 'You're home. That is all that matters.'

Home. The word was so easily thrown about. But it wasn't his home. It wasn't his title. He didn't even have his own bloody valet. Everything had all belonged to William. Seth was merely a figure standing in place for a ghost.

He gave a half-hearted smirk. 'You may be the only one pleased with my return.'

Caroline released him and stepped back. She'd grown into a lovely woman. She had the same dark eyes and hair as him, but where his features were hard lines and sharp angles, everything about her was soft with femininity.

'It's been terribly difficult on Mother.' Caroline glanced behind her and lowered her voice. 'The solicitor who was handling our affairs stole all her jewellery. Mother tried to keep it quiet, but…' Caroline pressed her lips together. 'Word got out. It was quite the scandal to weather.'

Seth winced. 'And I wasn't here.' For the first time, he truly did regret his absence from London.

'You were fighting for our country.' Caroline gave a little shrug. 'And you're here now. That is all that matters. I'm so pleased to have you home, Brother.'

'I intend to fully take on the earldom and see to all our affairs. Neither of you will ever have to worry again,' he vowed. And by God, he meant it. No matter what it took, he would do what was necessary to be every bit as good an earl as William had been.

Or at least he'd be the best he could.

Chapter Two

Though Seth had attended the Duchess of Richmond's ball prior to the battle breaking out, returning to such opulence so soon after having been mired in dirt and gore practically left him reeling.

The ballroom glittered with an undeniable splendour. Beeswax candles emitted a golden glow, made brighter by the backing of opulent mirrors. Hothouse flowers were arranged into perfect displays giving splashes of colour throughout and sweet music floated effortlessly beneath the hum of conversation.

It was all such a beautiful waste. Soldiers had gone without pay, sacrificing their lives while the *ton* nibbled on food they didn't intend to eat and threw money about with reckless abandon. Profligates, the lot of them.

More than the unnecessary extravagance of it all, what struck Seth again and again was how clean everything was. It was the same at his home with the polished wood furniture and the dust-free notions and floors.

His life as a soldier had been one of fighting and death. Sometimes this had brought injury, other times hunger. There had been wet chills from rainstorms, oppressive humidity that hummed with insects and thick, sucking mud.

Never had there been luxury.

Not like this.

Though he looked very much as though he belonged in his surroundings with his black tailcoat and silk breeches, he felt worlds apart. He glanced down at his hands encased in white gloves. His cuticles and fingernails were still stained with the grime of war despite his inherited valet's valiant attempts. The hours that Bennet had worked to make Seth look presentable had made him feel like the town house—chipped, broken brick smoothed over with an attractive facade. It didn't mean the cracks weren't there any more, only that they were covered up.

'Dalton.' A hand clapped him on his shoulder and sent him spinning around.

The Marquess of Kentworth grinned at him. 'I dare say it's been ages since I've seen you about. Still looking quite the soldier, I see.' He indicated Seth's red waistcoat.

The colour had been intentional. Seth could no longer wear his uniform. He'd given up that honour when he decided to sell his commission.

But by God, he could still wear the colours of a proud soldier.

'Rawley, look who is among us once more.' Kentworth tapped the arm of the man beside him.

Viscount Rawley turned and gave a rare and broad smile. 'Lord Dalton. Good to see you've returned home safe.'

Seth inclined his head in thanks.

'Now I'll finally have someone to drink with me.' Kentworth winked at Seth. 'After the necessaries of the ball have concluded, what do you say we go and find ourselves some gin and a bit of muslin?'

While the offer would have been appealing years ago, Seth now shook his head. 'I'm afraid I cannot. I have a meeting with my new solicitor early tomorrow morning.'

Kentworth's blue eyes widened. 'I heard about the perfidious cretin who pilfered from your accounts while you were off fighting for England.' He scoffed. 'A shabby show of loyalty for one's King and country, I say. Truly despicable.'

'Did they find him yet?' Rawley asked.

'Find him?' Seth narrowed his eyes. 'He is still at large?'

Rawley smoothed a hand over his brown hair as though worrying it had somehow been mussed out of place. The action was one he carried with him from his youth and had apparently not yet dropped. 'It was my understanding that he absconded with nearly all of Lady Dalton's jewellery and was never heard from again.' He offered an apologetic shrug. 'I could be wrong.'

'No,' Kenworth confirmed. 'You're not. The wretch buggered off to who knows where.' He waved at someone across the room.

Seth's mind spun at the news. Not only had no one been there to protect his mother and Caroline from theft in his absence, no one had even seen to the arrest of the man who had done it. The notion was unfathomable.

But then, Seth had put the whole business of his family from his mind, hadn't he? He hadn't taken the time to reach out to friends and ask them to look after his mother and sister. He hadn't ensured someone was nearby to offer support should it be required.

No, he'd tucked away the news of William's death as though it was a missive he could read later. Except while Seth let the responsibilities of the earldom slip from his care, his family had suffered the consequences.

His stomach clenched. Such a failure was unforgivable. He would not make so grave a mistake again. Not ever.

He'd start making up for his transgressions immediately. Starting by finding the bastard who'd had the temerity to steal from the Sinclairs.

'Do excuse me.' Kentworth slapped a hand on Seth's arm. 'Meet me at White's later for a nightcap, then a trip to Kings Place. You won't regret it.' The Marquess lifted his eyebrows with the bawdy suggestion of visiting the area that housed his favourite brothel.

The ballroom had become thick with people. Someone bumped into Seth and murmured an apology.

Seth's head spun with sudden lightness. The crowd was too thick, too close, the lights too bright.

Seth shook his head. 'I have already told you that I cannot accompany you tonight.'

'Please,' Rawley hissed in a whisper.

Kentworth laughed at his friend. 'What does it matter to you, Rawley? You'll have a finger of Scotch, glance at your watch and be gone before my grandmother is in bed.'

Rawley gave a long-suffering sigh. 'It doesn't mean you won't harass me to join you.'

'Harass?' Kentworth scoffed. 'One day you might actually allow yourself to have some fun.'

With that, the two were off to chat with another university chum whose name Seth couldn't recall. The press of people was even closer now, stealing his air, making it overwarm.

The battle had been the same way. Worse. The blasts of gunpowder, the cannons detonating, raw firepower igniting the fields of Mont-Saint-Jean into a damned inferno.

He fisted his hand at his side and focused on the pressure.

Don't think of the battle. Not here. Not now.

He needed a distraction. *Any* distraction. He scanned the room, desperate for someone he might know that wasn't Kentworth.

A woman with dark brown hair in a blue dress caught Seth's attention. She was nestled among the spinsters and old women, tucked towards the back of the room, too beautiful, too vibrant to fade into the background as she was so obviously attempting to do.

The woman was one he would recognise anywhere—his neighbour's daughter and childhood friend, Lady Violet Lavell.

Death at a ball!
A beleaguered soon-to-be spinster has passed on from sheer boredom at the most gossip-free ball there ever was.

Despite her early demise, it was widely considered that her fate was a gracious deliverance from the burdensome obligation of becoming an unpaid governess.

Violet tapped her slipper in time to music she would not dance to and kept a pleasant expression on her face even as she penned the sardonic header to the *Lady Observer* in her mind. To anyone who might notice her, she simply appeared to be enjoying the orchestra playing for the dancers. But it was not instrumentals to which she tuned her ear.

It was gossip.

Salacious, enticing gossip. Whispered words dominated any ballroom and tonight's gathering was no exception. Unfortunately what was said was all redundant, information easily gleaned through the papers that prior week. She nearly issued forth a painstaking sigh.

Even watching those around her had proven to be lacklustre entertainment. No gentlemen danced with women they were not supposed to, no one appeared to have imbibed too much wine to the point of behaving foolishly. But then, supper had yet to be served.

She'd heard there would be beefsteaks with sautéed onions and a rich oyster sauce. How she loved a good beefsteak. It always made her recall the time she'd attended Lady Norrick's supper party and had the grand idea to begin the *Lady Observer*.

In any event, any food would be preferable to crayfish in jelly, which was also rumoured to be served that evening. The poor creatures were heartily unappetising in such a plating where they hovered, boiled red and suspended in jelly, with their beady black eyes gazing out at those who would eat them. She shivered and hoped she did not sit near that plate.

For the time being, she surveyed the ballroom

for a possible sighting of the Earl of Dalton. Gossip had indicated he would be in attendance.

Violet had not yet caught sight of his face in the crowd and found herself grateful for that small mercy. No, that was a lie. She was both grateful and disappointed. He was a charming man, enticing in every way she should find displeasing, but did not. No, she certainly did not.

Something in her chest gave a little twist, one she chose pointedly to ignore.

'Lady Sarah has been rather popular with the gentlemen,' a woman in a feathered turban whispered to the woman beside her.

Violet's ears perked up at the conversation— a refreshing deviation to the direction of her unwanted thoughts.

'I hear she is the newest pupil under that woman's tutelage.'

Violet feigned interest at something across the room and stepped closer towards the ladies.

'How a courtesan ever put herself in a place of edifying the young, impressionable ladies of the *ton* is beyond my realm of comprehension,' the woman with the turban replied in a haughty tone. 'It's disgraceful.'

Unfortunately, two ladies strode in front of Violet, engaged in a very enthusiastic, very loud, conversation on the latest trend of spencers. With a ripple of irritation, Violet abandoned her attempt to overhear the conversation about the newest student in Lottie's care.

For though they had not mentioned the courtesan by name, Violet knew her well. Or at least, knew of her. After all, it had been her own cousin Lady Eleanor—now the Duchess of Somersville—who had first gone to Lottie for assistance in wresting herself free of the dreaded moniker of Ice Queen.

After the scandal of her instruction was made known, Lottie's clandestine lessons became quite popular and very sought after, ironically by the very people who had bemoaned their affectations of its vulgarity.

For all the repugnance pervading the topic of 'Lottie's Ladies' as they were called, rumours continued to spread of noble daughters seeking her instruction. What was more, it was not unheard of for ladies to spread their own false tales of attending such tutelage when they had not, in the hopes of drawing the attention of male suitors.

Because the male suitors *were* interested in Lottie's Ladies. Very, very interested. To such an extent that any woman who was even said to be attending those unmentionable lessons was almost always married within a month's time.

The curiosity of what possibly could transpire in those meetings with the famed courtesan briefly flitted through Violet's mind when an idea slammed into her.

What if she went to see Lottie herself? Not to try to obtain a husband, but to glean information for an article. No, an exposé.

The *Lady Observer* was a column read by some of the *ton*, but not all. However, if Violet penned a story revealing what truly went on in Lottie's parlour, the *Lady Observer* held the potential of becoming a tremendous success. It would propel the *Society Journal's* subscriptions and they would pay her significantly more. She would make the *Society Journal* esteemed enough for every household to purchase one.

Which would give her the income and purpose that would hopefully impress her father to the point she would no longer be required to choose between such unsavoury options.

Violet was so overcome with delight at her idea, she did something she never allowed herself to do on an ordinary night at a ball. She went to the refreshment table to permit herself a small cake. Well, not so small.

In truth, she selected the largest one on the platter. One with a beautiful marzipan rose adorning its sugary frosted top. Before she could talk herself out of the indulgence, she plucked it from the tray and popped it into her mouth.

'Lady Violet.'

The voice made her go still. It was unfamiliar and it was masculine.

She pressed her lips together to contain the cake and covered her mouth as she hurriedly chewed.

Of all times for someone to approach her. A man, no less.

Heavens.

'Forgive me,' the man said. 'I didn't mean to interrupt.'

She shook her head and waved her hand as if it was no bother. It was, though. Very much. She never allowed herself those small dainty treats from the refreshment table. Indeed, she'd hear about it from her mother on the way home.

She hastily swallowed what she'd intended to savour, turned towards the gentleman who had so rudely curtailed her enjoyment and froze. Even the cake lodged itself uncomfortably midway down her suddenly dry throat.

Mr Sinclair.

No, that wasn't right. He was no longer Mr Sinclair. He was an earl.

Lord Dalton.

She put her fingers to her mouth to cover an unseemly gulp and hastily brushed at her lips in case any crumbs or frosting remained. He watched her with a half-smile, as handsome as ever.

Perhaps even more so.

His dark hair had a habit of being unruly, but rather than giving him an unkempt appearance, it lent him a boyish, rugged charm. His time at war had chiselled his face and his body, carving with time and experience what had once been soft with youth. And it only made him all the more alluring.

More than the appeal of his appearance, however, his eyes were always what had left Violet totally and utterly captivated. With irises so dark one could not make out the pupil, his was a gaze that held all the emotion his features repressed. Right now, that stare was bright with interest and genuine delight.

At her?

Truly, it was unfair how intensely attractive he had always been. His were the good looks that made one recall every deficient attribute in themselves by comparison.

Soon-to-be spinster, nearly on the shelf, dies from the sheer handsomeness of newly minted Earl upon his return from war.

'Lord Dalton,' she said at last. 'Forgive me.'

'I intruded upon you,' he replied.

At least they could agree on that.

'What are you doing among the spinsters and old women?' he demanded.

Violet's eyes widened. 'They might hear you.'

'They know what they are,' he said, but did so with at least a lowered voice. 'Why is your husband not sweeping you across the dance floor?'

She wanted to close her eyes and truly fade back into the wall until she turned entirely invisible. But such a thing was impossible. Instead, she squared her shoulders and met his gaze despite the heat burning her face. 'I am unwed.'

He lifted a brow. 'You can't be serious.'

This is where she ought to say something witty and poignant. Except that she had dulled the point of her humour over the years, grinding it away in an attempt to slip unseen into the background where she would not be noticed. No doubt she'd come up with a charming reply somewhere between three and four in the morning when it wouldn't serve her a whit of good.

Instead of an intelligent reply, she offered a helpless shrug and inwardly rolled her eyes at the action. Could she be any more of a dullard?

'It's been six years since you came out,' he said. 'That would put you nearly on the shelf.' His gaze reflected something she didn't care for. Was it disgust? Pity?

In that moment, she was able to remember more than just how his handsome looks stole her attention and how his flirtation made her pulse stutter. Times when they were children and he had crushed her spirits with words that sliced deep. Like referring to her as hearty or commenting that she wasn't skinny like other girls.

The angry hurt swirled around the small cake in her empty stomach and snapped some steel into her spine.

'Perhaps it's because I'm so *hearty*,' she shot

at him. She wished she had been completely calm when she said it, that her heart wasn't hammering with frantic, erratic beats when she ripped those painful words from her memory, but she'd be lying.

His eyes narrowed at her. 'I feel as though you're being cryptic.'

'I assure you, I'm being quite blunt,' she replied. 'You said that to me when we were children.'

He lifted a brow. 'You remember that?'

She met his eyes. 'I recall many things you said to me when we were children. And even when we were older.'

A muscle ticked in his cheek, and he shifted his weight from one foot to the other in a show of apparent discomfort. 'I believe,' he said slowly, 'that I was rather an idiot in my youth.'

'And you're a better man now?' The disappointment of that night slammed into her anew, tearing open the old wound she'd thought long since scarred over. He'd held her heart by a string then, dangling it, toying with it. And she'd so readily handed him the end of that string, so eager for love, so desperate to be seen as more than a minor flirtation. Perhaps that was why she'd been so easily swept off her feet later.

'I certainly hope to be a better man.' Lord Dalton's gaze softened and he regarded her with such earnestness, such heartfelt emotion, that her defences relaxed.

'You're home now, then?' she asked. 'From the war?'

Though she hadn't meant the question to be a barb, the skin around his eyes tightened briefly, almost a flinch.

'I am,' he replied. 'I do hope I'll be seeing more of you now that I'm returned?'

The inflection at the end of his statement turned the words into a question. An invitation. She would do well to break out a whetstone and sharpen her wit back to rapier precision. For even with her shield up, it was always best to be armed when it came to a man like Lord Dalton.

Chapter Three

Seth had nearly forgotten how beautiful Lady Violet was. She fixed him with her ice-blue gaze. Her eyes had always been lovely, pale blue like a winter sky, ringed in a darker, deeper blue set beneath her black, expressive brows. The effect was stunning, especially with her long, dark lashes.

Though he shouldn't, he let his hope that she might be interested in seeing him more often hang for a moment between them. Surely he didn't deserve the attention of a woman like Lady Violet Lavell. Not when she was so beautifully pure within and he was so horribly damaged.

She tilted her head and offered him a contemplative look as if studying him in a manner he rather liked. Earlier that day, he'd been irritated at Bennet for the hours of attention he'd given Seth upon his return from Waterloo. Now, however, Seth was grateful for his valet's efforts.

'Perhaps,' she replied at last.

'A bit coy for a wallflower, aren't you?'

She flushed prettily. 'Perhaps I'm full of surprises.'

It had doubtless been meant as innocent banter, seasoned with a dash of flirtation, but, good God, how it set his mind wondering. Every thought that flitted through his mind was entirely too wicked for the likes of a ballroom. 'Indeed,' he simply replied.

He considered her for a moment, really taking her in for the first time since seeing her. The blue silk of her gown was overlaid with a bit of gauzy thing that had ribbons sewn all over it. But that wasn't truly what caught his interest—it was the hint of her body beneath, her voluptuous curves.

She'd always enticed him with that body, the one society forced her to try to hide beneath the high-waisted hideous gowns in fashion. Now, though, the lower-cut bodice of her ballgown cradled her generous breasts, full and sensual where the gentle, creamy swells teased him.

It took nearly every ounce of his control to keep from letting his gaze fall to her bosom.

'How the devil are you not married?' he asked aloud the question that he probably ought to have kept silent.

'Not every woman wants to get married.' She lifted her chin in a prideful manner, in a way that suggested she defended her position often. She always had been one to play up her false bravado. But then, didn't they all?

That was one of the things he'd always liked about her, how very real she was. It made her instantly likeable and wonderfully relatable.

'Of course every woman wants to get married or men's lives wouldn't be as difficult, attempting to thwart matches and debutantes.'

He shouldn't be having this light-hearted conversation with her any more than he should allow himself to be swept away by her. Not when he had his family to care for and his demons to tame.

She gave a little laugh at that and he couldn't stop the surge of victory swelling through him at the warm sound. She had a beautiful smile, her lips full and pink, her teeth white and straight. He'd fantasised about kissing her when they were acquainted as youths those years before the wars.

That was a lie, actually.

He'd fantasised about doing far more with her than just kissing.

The orchestra tinkled to life in preparation for a set.

'Would you care to dance?' he asked.

Her smile faltered. 'Forgive me,' she said in an apologetic tone, 'but I don't dance.'

He should take her rejection and walk away. But he remembered the young woman she'd been and how her eyes had always lit up when she danced.

'Nonsense. Yes, you do.' He waved aside her protest and offered her his hand. 'I've danced with you several times in my life. You performed adequately with your feet moving in the appropriate steps and in perfect time with the music.'

Her brow lifted in a bemused expression. 'How flattering.'

'You were quite graceful as well,' he offered. 'As I recall.'

Though he gave the praise flippantly, he felt the words in his bones. Or at least some part of him that was below his waist. He'd very much enjoyed dancing with her in those earlier years. Her eyes had a way of sparkling at him every time they came together and some of the more vigorous steps in the dance had made her breasts give an enticing bounce.

'I'm sorry, I…' She shook her head even as her gaze found the dance floor, her expression longing.

False bravado indeed. Why wouldn't she give in to her desire to dance?

He was certain it had something to do with how she'd nestled herself among the wallflowers. A brilliant violet standing out boldly in the garden no one paid mind to.

'Perhaps the next set, then?' he offered in an attempt to give her time to yield to her own desires.

A drum was struck in the orchestra, a deep resonating tone that thwacked him dead in the chest.

All at once, he was marching towards the enemy at Waterloo, heart hammering in time with

the pulse of that bloody drum, energy and anticipation crackling all around him.

Sweat prickled at his brow.

This. This was what he had dreaded the most
in striking up a conversation with Lady Violet.
He curled his hand into a fist and squeezed in an
attempt to gain control of his thoughts.

When the devil had they started incorporating
drums into the orchestra at a ball? Or was it for
this victory celebration commemorating the defeat at Waterloo?

It didn't matter. All that concerned him was
how his mind had flickered back to things best
left forgotten and how his skin suddenly prickled with sweat.

Lady Violet's mouth moved, but he didn't possess the wherewithal to understand a single word
emerging from her lips.

The drum sounded again and echoed in his
brain.

*The first shot. The shouts that followed. The
cannons. God, the cannons.*

He gritted his teeth.

The drum pulsed again. Its rhythm echoed in
his temples and drowned everything out except
memories he could not push away. Being shoved
by Brent and how it had sent Seth sprawling. The
cannonball that would have ended Seth's life if
Brent hadn't so bravely saved him.

That cannonball.

Bile rose in Seth's throat. His cravat was too damnably tight. He wanted to dig his fingers into the bound silk and rip it from his neck.

Except he was in a ballroom where etiquette prevailed. Where men were men and not cowards whose minds were plagued with the horrors of war.

Lady Violet regarded him, as though expecting him to speak.

He shook his head. 'Forgive me,' he said. 'I can't...' He backed up and bumped into someone.

It was all he could do to mutter an apology, to keep from letting the breath escape his chest in heaving gasps. He was a man, damn it. A soldier. He was no coward to fall prey to these memories that haunted him during the day. Especially not at a simple ball.

He managed to keep his gait slow as he made his escape to the door leading out to the veranda. The cool night air was a balm against his blazing skin and the darkness eased his aching head.

The reprieve did not last long.

What kind of a man was he to buckle under thoughts? They were only memories, after all. He'd spent years in battle. Years.

But none had been like Waterloo.

A shiver raked over his skin.

Waterloo had been bloody. He'd lost more men in that one battle than in the whole of his career. Men exposed to fighting for too long did not always fare well in the long of it. He'd seen them himself. Soldiers with hollowed eyes and gaunt expressions, their minds shattered by memories.

Was he becoming such a man?

He leaned against the stone railing overlooking the garden and dropped his head forward. Perhaps it was a good thing he had been forced to sell his commission. As much as he'd dreaded facing the unfamiliar obligations of an earl, they might be the very things needed to save his sanity.

He lifted his head and glanced behind him, through the glass-paned doors and into the ball-room. Violet was in there somewhere, abandoned by him in the middle of their conversation.

He pulled in a deep breath and forced himself to make his way inside once more. To face the social responsibilities of an earl and to face his error with Violet.

Except she could not be found, not even among the wallflowers.

Violet made her way up Fleet Street with her maid, Susan, and a sack of coins secured in the confines of her reticule. Her collections from the print shop were larger than anticipated. Of all times to receive such a boon, she was most glad for it now—when she had true need of funds.

She had secured an audience with Lottie for that evening, well past the time her parents would have retired, an hour that seemed to come earlier as they grew older. It would be easy to sneak past the servants, secure a hackney, and make her way to Lottie's residence at Russell Square in Bloomsbury. Surely the money Violet had collected, as well as what she'd been setting aside, would be sufficient to afford her a proper number of lessons.

A giddy flicker of excitement rippled in her chest at the idea of putting her plan into motion. She, Violet Lavell, muted wallflower, plump spinster, would be attending the highly coveted lessons with Lottie.

Two gentlemen were approaching them in the opposite direction and she nodded politely as she and her maid passed.

Yes, she could have had the carriage bring her directly to Fleet Street rather than pretend to have turned down the road while out shopping. Except the carriage driver was not as discreet as Susan.

Part of Violet—a tiny, minuscule part of her—wondered what Lottie's edification might do regarding her interactions with the men of the *ton*. Or, at least one in particular.

Lord Dalton.

No sooner had the thought entered her mind than she tried quickly to push it away. He had been rude the evening before, abandoning her after having invited her to dance. Granted, he had not looked well.

Regardless, he was a man who did not keep his promises. Not six years ago. And not last night when she changed her mind and was finally giving in to the temptation to accept a dance for the first time in nearly six years.

Then he'd walked away.

Just like the night of her debut.

But she wouldn't think of him and his dark, soulful eyes or how the way he looked at her made her knees go soft. She wouldn't think about how he'd returned from the war with a hardness to his masculinity she shouldn't find appealing. Which she did. Oh, she did.

She was so busy not thinking of him that she actually heard his voice in her thoughts. 'Lady Violet.'

Violet could have rolled her eyes heavenwards if she weren't on the streets of London. Would she never be free of Lord Dalton's grip on her?

'Lady Violet, may I walk with you?'

That voice was apparently not in her head. Her cheeks went hot as she glanced over her shoulder to find Lord Dalton walking towards her at a brisk pace.

Susan caught her eye and suppressed a smile. The maid had been with Violet long enough to understand the impact of Lord Dalton on her mistress.

'What are you doing on Fleet Street?' He caught up to her and offered her his arm. He wore a black jacket with a brown waistcoat and buckskins. The latter fit him perfectly against his snug thighs and muscular calves, as if the entire fad of wearing the more casual clothing had been designed entirely for him.

Heavens, if every man wore buckskins like he did, even Almack's might be willing to soften their dress code.

Violet pulled her musings, and her stare, from his well-made legs and held up a folded copy of the most recent instalment of the *Society Journal*, which had been turned to the *Lady Observer* column. 'You've caught me.' It was the excuse she always had prepared in case she did get caught on Fleet Street, an occurrence that had not happened until that very moment. 'I was at Fleet Market and figured I might wander down this road to obtain a paper.'

He peered at it as though she held up a dead rat. 'A scandal sheet, Lady Violet?'

She let the flirtation in his tone burn her cheeks in an effort to allow herself to look slightly remorseful at the guilty pleasure. 'Well, it is rather a nice day to be out walking.'

And that was her folly. For even as the words were emerging from her mouth, she glanced up at the grey sky as flecks of rain spattered at her face. 'Or rather, it was nice earlier.'

'It was storming earlier,' he offered with a smirk.

'I meant, after that.' Her reticule was terribly heavy and cutting into her wrist. She fiddled with the strap while considering a way to spin the conversation on him. 'It's quite fortunate to run into you in any event. I'd intended to thank you.'

He looked at her, wary, clearly smelling the trap she'd laid at his feet. 'Thank me?'

She hummed in soft agreement. 'For the dance last night.' It was snide of her, yes, but she wasn't feeling especially generous. The wonderful thing about being beyond caring about marriage was not having to always tiptoe so delicately around her words.

'Ah, yes.' His brow furrowed slightly. 'Forgive me for my abrupt departure. I'm afraid I suddenly felt rather unwell.'

His gaze was so earnest with remorse that she was left feeling very much like the idiot in the conversation this time. Whatever witty retort Violet might have had at the ready died on her tongue. He would never have looked thusly, so sincere in his youth when he'd been wild and unrepentant.

Maybe he had changed.

'You did appear unwell,' she offered by way of apology. 'I trust you are quite recovered.'

'I am in better spirits.' He gave her a genuine smile that nearly knocked the low-heeled slippers from her feet with its charm. 'Especially now.'

Heavens, but he could turn on his allure when he wished to.

'I believe this is your carriage, is it not?' He stopped.

Regret pinched at her. Though the sprinkling

of rain had increased as they strolled and the humidity in the air promised a proper and thorough storm, she could have spent the rest of the afternoon at his side. 'It is,' she conceded. 'Thank you.'

He didn't wait for the footman to scramble down from his perch. Instead, Lord Dalton put his gloved hand to the handle of the door and opened it for her, first assisting Violet into the small cabin and then Susan. This set both ladies flushing with pleasure as he bid them good day and snapped closed the door once more.

'Well,' Susan said with an exuberant exhale. 'He seems to have changed.'

'Indeed he has.' Violet peered out the window at his departing figure.

'And he appears to be rather taken with you.' Susan lifted her thin brows at Violet as her hazel eyes twinkled with delight.

Violet scoffed. 'A war hero returning home to an earldom and a ballroom filled with available debutantes would hardly pull a spinster from her shelf and dust her off for the wedding of the ages.' She sighed. 'I don't see that tale headlining any articles of the *Lady Observer*.'

Susan appeared nonplussed. 'It's not impossible. I'm sure your cousin the Duchess's situation seemed just as hopeless. More so, perhaps.'

Violet adjusted her skirts rather than watch Lord Dalton sweep past the window. 'It's of little concern regardless,' she said. 'I have no intention to wed.'

Susan did sigh at this, a soft resigned sound. 'Pity, that. You'd be a fetching pair if I do say so myself.' Silence fell over the carriage before her voice continued. 'If it wasn't for Lord Fords—'

'Don't,' Violet choked out. 'Don't say his name.'

Susan immediately pressed her lips together to still her words. It didn't matter. Violet needed only hear his title and her folly the night of her come out rushed back at her.

Lord Fordson. He'd happened upon her when she was freshly wounded from Seth's dismissal and her mother's disappointment. He'd filled that first dance of her debut that Seth had left open, as well as another towards the end of the ball.

Afterward, they'd gone out on the veranda for a bit of fresh air and received far more than a little rosiness in their cheeks from the outing. Violet had been wholly taken by him, by the way he'd gazed as her as though she was the only woman in the room. He had made her feel worthy of love. He'd made her feel beautiful.

All the way up until the next day when he did not call. He hadn't as much as sent flowers. When next they saw one another, he avoided her. It had taken a moment for her to realise he was intentionally edging away from her, but once the understanding dawned on her, it came with a fresh wave of hurt. And the truth of exactly what a fool she had been.

It still cut now, even six years later.

Now, Violet looked up too quickly in the carriage and caught Lord Dalton's gaze on her as they rolled away. Her heart, silly and stupid as it was, gave a little leap.

And though she could not bring herself to even hear his name any longer, Violet found herself agreeing with Susan. It was indeed a pity Violet was not going to wed, but it was certainly nothing that would change.

No matter how tempting the man.

Chapter Four

After Seth delivered Lady Violet to her carriage, he made his way back to his own where it sat idly on the street waiting for him to return. He'd insisted on stopping so he might attend to Lady Violet whom he'd seen walking with her maid in what promised to be a violent summer storm.

He'd meant to smooth over what he'd rumpled the night before. Judging from the faint colour touching her cheeks when he saw her into the carriage, he'd succeeded.

His intention in speaking to her had been to apologise and now he had done exactly that. There would be no further need to speak to Lady Violet in the days that followed. He would leave her to her life of feminine pursuits—watercolour paintings and shopping and the like. And he would continue salvaging what bits of his life he could scrape into a semblance of wholeness once more.

'To White's,' he told the footman.

The man, Burton, was a slender soldier who'd fought alongside Seth in the Peninsula. He'd previously worked as a builder prior to becoming a soldier. Unfortunately, the bullets to his leg had shattered his bones and left him with a terrible limp, one that rendered him unemployable. At least, to all but Seth.

He'd hired Burton as well as Harold, a burly soldier who had lost an arm and could no longer work with horses as he'd done before his time as a soldier. One arm or two, there was no one in all of London who cared more for the chestnuts than Harold. The man tended to the beasts as if they were his children. What's more, Harold was a genius with maps. If it weren't for his inability to gently stop a carriage, he might be the most perfect driver there ever was.

While Seth had no desire to be an earl, he would at least concede that it allowed him the opportunity to offer employment to those society would otherwise cast aside.

'While I'm at White's,' Seth continued, 'I'd like you to pick up a paper called the *Society Journal*.' He regretted the request as soon as he'd made it. Whatever Lady Violet found interesting within those printed pages ought to be of no concern to him. He set a foot upon the small stair leading into the carriage and hesitated. 'For Lady Caroline, of course,' he added.

Burton's lips quirked in a ghost of a smile. 'Of course, my lord.'

* * *

The ride to White's was short. Regardless, rain began pattering at the windows, fat droplets that melted against one another and ran down the expanse of the glass pane. Had Lady Violet decided to pursue a lengthier walk, she would have got soaked.

What a shame that would have been.

An image of her dripping wet immediately sprang into his mind. Her hair falling around her shoulders, tousled and damp, her gown clinging to those luscious curves, the fine, thin fabric made practically transparent by the thorough dousing. Rain would sparkle on her creamy skin like diamonds and those blue, blue eyes of hers would practically glow in contrast to the grey sky above.

Oh, yes, what a shame indeed.

His body responded to his imagination, growing warm and, well, rather hard. The carriage stopped abruptly, knocking him from his thoughts and giving him a solid thump on the back of his head. Served him right for thinking of Lady Violet again. Even the fates were telling him to leave her be. She was not for him. Or, as was more likely, he was not for her.

He rubbed at the sore spot as Burton pulled open the door with an apologetic smile.

'He's getting better at the stops.' The footman winced as he noted Seth rubbing at the back of his head. 'I think...'

Seth lowered his hand. 'I did stay in my seat this time.'

Burton grinned. 'You see, m'lord?'

Seth didn't bother to nod as he removed himself from the carriage and made his way into the opulence of the most exclusive gentleman's club in all of London. In the past, Seth would never have dreamed of belonging to such an elegant establishment. Now though, as the Earl of Dalton, there were plenty who sought to sponsor his membership.

Money, of course, had a role to play in all of it. Money *always* played a role. And Seth had a considerable amount. A ridiculous amount, really. Enough to summon notice.

All in all, it was still a gentlemen's club and one he hoped could provide a strong lead as to what had become of the solicitor who had stolen from Seth's mother.

He had a name, at least. Mr Charles Pattinson, Esquire, as well as the description of an older chap with thick dark hair and fine white teeth. No doubt he had exerted his charms on Lady Dalton which had led to the embarrassment of her having been duped. Why else would she have allowed him to get away without repercussion?

Viscount Rawley stood by a window on the second floor of White's with a cup of tea in his hands as he gazed out into the street in quiet contemplation. A quick glance confirmed his counterpart, Lord Kentworth, was decidedly absent. What good fortune.

'Good afternoon, Rawley.' Seth approached the studious man.

The Viscount turned with a friendly expression and the two exchanged the usual pleasantries, health and the weather and all that, performed with careful haste on Seth's part before Kentworth could invade on the conversation.

When the usual polite chatter fell away, Seth broached the topic he'd most wanted to discuss. The missing solicitor.

Seth scanned about once more to confirm Kentworth was not nearby. 'I was wondering if you might be able to assist me with providing a contact to locate the solicitor who took advantage of my family in my absence.'

Rawley's forefinger tapped at his teacup in consideration and slowly nodded. 'I have a man for such a thing.' He, too, looked over his shoulder, as though concerned Kentworth might interrupt. 'He's a former Runner who now operates on his own. He's devilishly smart and hasn't failed me yet on any matter I've brought to him. What's more, he's discreet.'

Seth nodded. 'Perfect.'

'I'll have him reach out to you.' Rawley went silent as a pair of men strode past them and did not speak again until they were out of earshot.

'You're forewarned, he can be rather rough around the edges.'

Seth was undeterred. 'After so long being a soldier, that is certainly the least of my concerns.'

'What have we here?' Kentworth's voice filled the conspiratorial space between them.

Years ago, Seth had enjoyed the good times shared with the Marquess, but now the man's boisterous presence rankled at Seth's nerves.

'You missed quite the time of it last night.' Kentworth lifted his glass in silent salute. 'The ladies love a man with war scars to show for his efforts.'

Seth offered a stiff nod in an attempt to be polite despite the lack of consideration on the other man's part.

'You should come with me tonight, I'll be—'

'I'm afraid that's impossible.' Seth braced his feet wide on the soft carpet. A soldier's stance. 'I have matters to see to the following day.'

'Matters that no doubt require a clear mind and good rest.' Kentworth rolled his eyes and nudged Rawley with his elbow. 'He's sounding like you.'

Rawley merely lifted a brow.

'Seeing to one's estates and family is a noble occupation,' Seth responded.

'Stewards.' Kentworth took a swallow of brandy. 'They handle the lot of it. Well, them and solicitors.' He paused, tilted his head and cast an exaggerated grimace in Seth's direction. 'Well, most of them, that is.'

Sweat sheened Seth's palms. A sleepless night filled with horrible memories was exacting its toll.

'Kentworth,' Rawley said in a low tone.

'Don't, Rawley.' Kentworth pushed at his friend's shoulder to put him off. 'What happened to you?' He frowned at Seth. 'Rawley's always been a puddle of mud. But you… You used to be able to drink more than me, you'd take two ladies when I took only one, you didn't care a whit for anything. And now look at you. Your *joie de vivre* has died.'

Rage whipped hot and reckless through Seth in a wave that immediately overwhelmed him.

'No, my men died,' he bit out. 'In front of me.' Images flashed in his mind, broken and violent.

Red and white flickered at the edge of Seth's vision.

Blood. Chaos. The acrid odour of gunpowder. The screams…

'Sounds as though you need a tup more than the rest of us.' Kentworth chortled and lifted his glass.

Seth flew at him, pinning him against the wall, forearm to neck. 'A tup won't remove what I've seen and it won't bring those men back.' He pushed himself harder against Kentworth. The glass fell from his hand and landed on the soft carpet with a *thunk*.

'They were good men,' Seth growled into Kentworth's face. 'They were hard-working. Brave.'

'Lord Dalton.' Rawley spoke quietly as he put a hand lightly on Seth's shoulder.

The Viscount stepped back to reveal the sea of faces turned towards them, aghast with horror. Seth uttered a curse and released Kentworth, who rubbed at his cravat.

'I'll handle this,' Rawley said quietly. 'I think it's best you take your leave.'

Seth nodded and backed away. He put up a hand as he did so, in silent apology, in acknowledgment for what he'd done. He hadn't been back for a week and already he was on the cusp of most likely being blackballed from White's.

The quiet room erupted into a buzz of voices as he departed. The incident had rattled him. His own reaction had rattled him. It was more than the sleeplessness that had led to him exploding as he did, it was the awfulness in his head, the way he could never clear the smell of blood and smoke from his awareness. It was the paralysing fear that the horrors he'd witnessed had left his mind broken.

Despite what he'd been through, despite the years he'd aged and the man he strove to be, he was still an idiot and he was still making mistakes. He was an earl now, however, and his errors no longer only affected him. It was his family who would suffer.

At least the visit to White's had revealed what he needed: someone to aid him in finding the runaway solicitor. Seth would make certain he did not err in bringing the bastard to justice and making right the wrongs he had caused his family by leaving.

The sky had opened up into a veritable deluge by the time Violet arrived at her town house on Grosvenor Street. She declined the proffered umbrella, put the *Society Journal* over her head and dashed through the rain to her home, nearly tripping over the cat in the process.

The cat?

She spun around and squared off against the offended animal, both gazing with incredulity at the other. Her with dripping hair and a sodden newspaper and it with... Was that a bonnet?

She blinked.

It blinked.

'What—?'

The thing hissed abruptly and tore off, causing Susan to let loose a startled shriek.

'Good thing you were wearing a bonnet,' Violet called after the large cat. 'Or I might have dripped water all over you.'

Small footsteps tapped over the marble entryway. Violet turned towards the sound and was met with the sight of a little girl with blonde hair, large blue eyes and a slightly upturned nose. Violet blinked again.

'May I help you?' she asked. 'Are you lost, perhaps?'

'I'm Felicity.' The girl folded her arms over the frilly front of her pink smock. 'Lady Erstworth's eldest daughter.'

Lady Erstworth. Violet wanted to clap a hand over her face and groan. *Sophie.*

'Oh, yes. Felicity,' Violet exclaimed with as much brightness as one could when dripping with rain water and having recently tripped over a well-dressed cat. 'Goodness but it's been so long since I've seen you. I scarcely recognised you. Is your mother here?' Dread shivered along Violet's damp skin. 'And your sister and brothers?'

'Just me.' Felicity gave Violet an expression that mixed scepticism with blatant irritation.

Only Felicity, then. Thank heavens. Even if she was the worst of the bunch. Being the eldest, she was a ringleader of sorts, encouraging naughty behaviour and revolts.

The girl peered around the corner where the feline had fled. 'Was that Hedgehog?'

'It was a cat,' Violet replied helpfully.

Felicity rolled her eyes. 'I'm perfectly aware that he's a cat. His *name* is Hedgehog.'

Violet pursed her lips. 'Why ever would you do that?'

'Do what?'

'Name a cat Hedgehog.'

Felicity strode across the entryway, her shoes clacking noisily, and peered around the corner.

'Because his body is grey, but his belly is fat and pink. Like a hedgehog.'

'Ah, well, when you explain it like that…' Violet handed Susan the sodden newspaper with an air of apology.

Susan silently wished Violet luck with a look and departed to dispose of the ruined news sheet.

The butler, Wilson, took Susan's place and collected Violet's gloves and hat. 'Lord Hollingston would like to see you in his study, if you please, my lady.'

Violet almost groaned aloud. That was all this day needed. First the meeting with Lord Dalton where she'd acted like a mindless dolt, then nearly running down a poor cat with a rather unfortunate name, followed by the disagreeable meeting with her niece. And now, the squeak seat. Again. For the second time in only one short week.

Violet swallowed her chagrin and nodded in thanks to the butler.

Clothes still damp from being caught in the rain and on the lookout for an errant beast scurrying about the carpet, Violet made her way to her father's study. He was waiting, his elbows perched on the expansive desk on the opposite side of the tyrannical chair.

She tried to give a happy smile and act as if everything was perfect, which, of course, it wasn't. 'Hello, Papa.'

He lifted his eyes at her, his face impassive.

Drat.

His expression didn't bode well. Her spirits sagged like sails whose wind had suddenly died.

'Wilson said you wished to see me.' Violet entered the room and hesitated before the squeak seat.

He gestured for her to sit down. She complied, bracing herself for its protest.

And protest it did, in a grating squawk of irritation and pressure of her ample rump upon its surface.

'You recall Sophie's eldest daughter, Felicity?' Lord Hollingston lifted his bushy brows.

'I do,' Violet replied.

'She's come to visit. For you to become better acquainted with her prior to removing yourself to the country this summer.'

'Oh, yes.' Violet kept her face from showing any of her emotions. 'I saw her. As well as Hedgehog.'

Lord Hollingston's composure rumpled in a furrow of his bushy white brows. 'Good God, she brought a hedgehog?'

'It's a cat.'

He held his hands wide, opened his mouth, shook his head, and continued. 'Your mother and I would like for you to spend some time cultivating a relationship with your niece while she is in town.'

Violet pressed her lips together to still her protest, then thought better of it.

If she had only weeks of freedom left, she would not spend them beleaguered with a condescending child and a cat adorned in frippery.

'I had hoped to spend the remainder of the Season enjoying my time in London.' She widened her eyes in the way that always worked on her father. 'After all, it will be my last opportunity to do so.'

Her father stared at her for a long moment. 'Violet, you have a choice to make. Whatever the devil you choose, I'd like you to know it well before you settle on your decision.'

A smile nearly erupted on Violet's face at his word selection. She tried to squelch it and instead sent the chair crying out in displeasure.

His forehead crinkled in question.

Violet swallowed her laugh. Or at least attempted to. 'Did you just call your granddaughter a devil?'

Lord Hollingston sat back in realisation and his lips quirked as a snort of a chuckle escaped him. 'Well, it would appear I did. But you well know that is not what I meant.'

'I know, Papa.' Violet grinned at him.

'Go on, you imp.' He waved at the air playfully in dismissal. 'And know I'll not change my mind on this.' His final words were laden with seriousness that left no room for argument.

Violet closed the door and suppressed a sigh. There would be no escape from this task. An unhappy beast hissed from somewhere in the house and Violet steeled herself for the task at hand. After all, how awful could a seven-year-old girl and a bad-tempered, ill-named cat be?

Chapter Five

Violet discovered exactly how awful a seven-year-old girl and a bad-tempered, ill-named cat could be.

There had been a game of hopscotch that had gone horribly awry when Violet tripped over Hedgehog and went sprawling into the perennials. Inside the home was no better when a game of dressing dolls had changed focus and poor Hedgehog became the object of Felicity's styling. Following all that had been the upset tea table in the creature's haste to run off, leaving his dignity behind. Violet couldn't fault the beast.

And it was best not to even think about Felicity's attempt to bring the cat to the dinner table. Lord Hollingston, fortunately, was far more firm in his orders and Felicity had been forced to sullenly deposit her hapless feline in another room before a fine roast could be spoiled by a dusting of cat hair.

* * *

By the end of the day, Violet was heartily exhausted. If she didn't have plans, she would have collapsed in her bed and not roused until well after noon the following day. She did, however, have plans. Or at least one very grand one.

Her parents retired earlier than usual, not long after Felicity, coincidentally, which gave Violet plenty of time for Susan to help her into the domino and summon a discreet hackney to the back of the house.

Violet slipped into the carriage and noted a similarly discreet coach at the house beside hers, taking off in the opposite direction. She craned her neck to see the passenger. The chiselled profile confirmed her suspicions. Lord Dalton. And whatever he was doing apparently required that he leave through the back of his home in secret.

A changed man, indeed.

Perhaps it was for the best Violet had no interest in marriage. Surely there was nothing guaranteed but heartbreak. And she had already been well acquainted with that pain.

She drew the curtain closed over the window to ensure there was no possible way for her to be seen. Especially when Violet's parents were unaware of her intention.

Violet remained thus in her seat for the duration of the journey, stock still, heart pounding, until at last the hackney rolled to a stop. The door opened and the driver held out his hand before leading her down.

'Busy address, this is.' He gave a grin that bordered on a grimace and showed splotches of rot in his teeth. ''Specially when it's at the back o' the 'ouse.' His threat was thinly veiled and his intent apparent.

Violet took one of the precious coins from her reticule and deposited it into the driver's grimy palm without touching him. He winked at her and let her pass.

Not wanting to linger on the street or in his presence, Violet rushed to the back door of the town house where she'd been instructed to go. She had just lifted her hand to knock when it opened before her.

A butler welcomed her in. He led her through the clean, neat kitchen and into the drawing room where Violet noted the curtains had been drawn tight against any prying eyes. Only then did he take her domino, which she relinquished with shaking hands.

He bowed low upon receiving the item and left her to take in her surroundings. She'd only time to notice a harp in one corner set atop the Brussels weave carpet when the double doors opened and one of the most beautiful women Violet had ever seen stepped through them.

The woman's hair was thick and dark, glossy with becoming curls, her skin was smooth as cream with high, elegant cheekbones and a generous mouth. She had a slight tilt to her blue eyes which lent her a sensual, intriguing air.

Violet hadn't been certain what to expect from Lottie. She knew her to be a courtesan, but this woman was dressed in a lovely periwinkle-satin evening gown that opened at the centre to reveal a panel of demure white muslin. The sleeves were short, revealing slender arms and the bodice was low, but not indecently so. In fact, the entire ensemble was nothing more or less than what Violet would expect to see at any dinner party.

'Lady Violet?' the woman prompted in a soft, sweet voice.

Violet's cheeks flamed at the realisation she'd been staring. And who would not? Lottie was the epitome of what a woman dreamed of looking like. Her slender arms and impossibly small waist. Violet wouldn't have a body like Lottie's even if she starved herself and she knew that from experience.

'That's me.' She hated the timidity of her voice and how much she wanted to crawl inside herself to disappear from the presence of the lovely courtesan.

'I'm Lottie,' the woman said. 'I can see the resemblance between you and the Duchess of Somersville. You both have such flawless skin and expressive eyes.'

Violet nodded dumbly. All this had seemed

such a good idea from the outside. But being in Lottie's drawing room, staring at the exquisite beauty Violet could never dream of attaining, Violet felt the terribleness of it all come crashing down around her. She wanted to dash through those double doors and race the whole way back to Hollingston House.

'I know this is uncomfortable.' Lottie stepped closer. 'You're probably regretting your decision and wish to leave.' She gave an understanding smile. 'Please know that I put your privacy and the discretion of my tutelage at the forefront of everything I do. My staff is well paid and loyal and I take personal responsibility for every one of the ladies who passes through my doors.'

Her acknowledgement of Violet's discomfort relaxed some of the tension from her shoulders.

Lottie poured a glass of wine and held it out in offering, which Violet accepted with gratitude and sipped with more ease than she felt. The rich, ruby liquid was decadent, the alcohol like velvet as it warmed a path down her throat.

'Tell me, Lady Violet—' Lottie levelled her gaze '—why are you really here?'

All the tension clenched back into Violet. Did Lottie suspect her?

The woman reached out and gently rested her fingertips on Violet's arm. 'You needn't look so frightened. I merely wished to know what you hope to receive from our lessons together if I agree to take you on.'

Violet almost gasped in relief. 'I… I hope…' she stammered.

Truthfully, she hadn't put much thought into what she had expected to learn.

'The usual, I suppose?' Violet said in a very non-committal fashion and sipped at her wine.

Lottie smiled patiently. 'Every student is different. There is no "usual".' She regarded Violet appraisingly. 'You've been a wallflower for years with no mind towards marriage despite your beauty and the family you hail from.'

Despite her beauty.

Violet almost issued a bark of laughter at that and instead swallowed her mirth with a bit more wine. 'I am not noticed,' she managed to say.

Lottie studied Violet as though she was peering straight through the veneer Violet had long since donned. As though Violet was transparent and Lottie could look clean through her and put her finger on where the issue lay. 'I'm afraid I disagree. You are a woman who is not noticed because you do not wish to be,' Lottie said. 'You are aware that any instruction I might offer will encourage attention.'

'My father wants me to wed.' The truth burst from Violet. 'If I do not marry, he insists I retire to my sister's country estate to help care for my nieces and nephews. He thinks I require purpose in my life and this is how he means to see I have it.'

Lottie smirked, a wry twist to her pretty lips. 'Men often do not see women's lives as having purpose.' Her gaze lowered to the empty wine glass clutched in Violet's grasp. 'I have only one more question.'

Her words hung in the air while every nerve in Violet's body went taut.

Lottie looked imploringly at Violet. 'Do you want to be here?'

Violet's heart slammed so hard in her chest, she feared it might be audible. Was she up for the challenge? Could she force herself back out into the attention of others to properly pull off this charade?

'Yes.' Violet nodded with resolve. 'Yes, I want to be here.'

The concern on Lottie's face smoothed. 'Then I shall see you tomorrow evening for your first lesson.'

And there it was: Violet had secured a space in Lottie's highly sought-after, extremely secretive lessons.

Seth met the former Runner in a dodgy public house that smelled of hot bodies and smoky tallow candles and stale spirits, and sat apart in a shadowed corner where they wouldn't be disturbed.

The man, known simply as 'Nash', was entirely the sort of man Seth had predicted he would be:

grizzled, with a beard that hadn't been trimmed in some time, a straight, humourless mouth, clothing that looked as though it hadn't been washed in an age. He was the kind of man who could blend into a tough crowd and disappear. Unmemorable. At least until one glimpsed the sharp intensity in his eyes, bright with intelligence and heavy with a haunted expression Seth had come to know well. He'd witnessed it in his men, after hard battles or too many years on end without cease. Worse still, he sometimes even saw it in himself.

Seth handed him a leather portfolio containing all the information gleaned on the solicitor, Mr Pattinson, which sadly, wasn't much. The perfidious solicitor had managed to lay low for the duration of his time in London prior to weaselling his way into Lady Dalton's employ. Then again, a widowed countess who had recently lost her son was surely an easy target.

'No one knows where 'e's gone, eh?' Nash peered into the portfolio, his brow crinkling.

Seth leaned forward to be heard over the raucous crowd without having to speak too loudly. 'It's as though he's simply disappeared.'

Nash snapped the portfolio closed and curled the string around the supple leather. 'No one just disappears.'

'And that's why I have come to you, my good man.' Seth took a sip of the porter at his side. It wasn't a proper drink for a gentleman and certo right the wrongs of England. And indeed it was not Lord Hollingston who alighted from the carriage. It was a woman.

Seth sat forward in his seat. The mysterious lady wore a full-length black domino and a concealing mask over her face. Surely it was not Lady Hollingston, who watched the world with a tight-lipped frown of disapproval. And no servant would dare risk ruining the Lavell name by bringing scandal to their doorstep. Quite literally. Especially not servants as loyal as those serving at Hollingston House.

Which left only one potential lady who might be out at such a damning hour.

Lady Violet.

He remained fixed with riveted fascination as she rushed through the back gate and garden. The door opened before she even arrived, shooting a streak of light out over the moonlit grass. She slipped into the house and the door closed. Darkness resumed once more.

Lady Violet, out alone and wearing a domino. What was the little wallflower doing?

The thought teased at him throughout the night as he tossed and turned on his fine mattress that had taken several nights to readjust to.

There were many reasons a woman might don a mask and cloak in the dead of night. The gaming hells ladies frequented beneath the obscurity of anonymity, a lover whose arms she might secretly fall into. There were even salacious parties where couples loved freely among one another while wearing only those masks.

Suddenly there she was in his mind's eye, naked save for a fitted mask that framed her startling blue eyes and thick, sable lashes. While Seth had never been to one of those parties, he'd heard enough to know what went on. Enough to consider what she might do if they were in attendance at one together and she was entirely free to come to him.

That night, for the first time since his return from Waterloo, he wasn't tormented by images of his men dying, but ones that were far sweeter and left him hot, hard and aching the following morning.

Through it all, he could not liberate the thought from his mind: What if Violet was not as innocent as he'd initially presumed?

Chapter Six

❧

Violet had been playing with spinning tops for the span of a very long, very monotonous afternoon that involved a tedious amount of flicking her wrist. Lift the top, twist it to spin, wait for it to roll to a stop. On and on it went: lift, spin, wait, lift, spin, wait. And throughout the excruciating duration, Hedgehog darted about madly in an attempt to pounce upon the small, whirling objects.

It had been rather funny at the start. The first several dozen times at least. Then Violet began to feel rather sorry for the poor beast. Surely he was getting as tired as she.

'Would you like to play another game?' Violet asked.

Felicity stared at a final spinning top with a smile hovering on her lips in expectation. Hedgehog, adorned in a blue-sprigged cap with bits of lace at the edge, flew into the air with a sprightliness his corpulent frame would not suggest him capable of and landed upon the top with an audible *thunk*.

Felicity threw her head back with laughter. Her glee was such that Violet found herself chuckling at the child's mirth.

'I believe Hedgehog will grow weary if we keep making him run about,' Violet said.

Felicity reached for her cat and drew him towards her. He allowed the action with the bland expression of complete resignation at his fate.

'Are you getting tired, my dear one?' Felicity cooed.

The cat hung in her arms without moving. She hugged him closer to her like a doll and kissed the top of his head.

'We could change his bonnet.' Felicity fingered the lace edge of his current adornment.

Hedgehog issued forth a soul-deep sigh.

'I believe he looks fine as he is,' Violet said quickly to spare the creature another ridiculous hat. Felicity had been eyeing a feathered hat that looked as though it might drive Hedgehog to distraction.

'Do you think so?' Felicity lifted the cat into the air and scrutinised him. For his part, Hedgehog dangled from her hands by the undersides of his arms, his pink belly jutting out, exposed.

'Quite,' Violet replied. 'The blue flowers are very fetching.'

Felicity gave a quiet hum, suggesting she did

not agree with Violet's assessment. Regardless, she set him down where he promptly rolled on to his side and nestled against her knee.

Felicity scratched under his chin and the sawing purr of his contentment filled the room. 'Why don't you have children, Aunt Violet?'

The question was so bold, so beyond anything ever considered polite in a child that it took Violet aback.

'I'm not married,' she replied without thought.

'Why aren't you married?' Felicity looked up from the cat.

'Such questions are not proper for a child to be asking,' Violet scolded in a gentle tone. They were hardly proper questions for *anyone* to be asking.

'I'm hardly proper and we both know it,' Felicity stated matter-of-factly. 'Are you afraid to answer?'

Foolish irritation nipped at Violet's nerves. She shouldn't let a child get to her and yet she hated the challenge hanging in the air. 'Of course not. I simply haven't met the right man.'

'Do you want to get married?' Felicity fired the question almost as soon as Violet replied.

Violet hesitated in her answer. To be truthful and say no would doubtless result in a new barrage of questions. 'Some day I think marriage would be nice,' she lied.

Never would it be nice, especially when it would require that she empty the contents of her heart on to the table prior to any discussion of marriage. Even if she wanted to wed, no gentleman would want her. She was completely ruined.

Felicity's unwavering stare remained fixed on Violet. 'Mother says you haven't wed because you're too plump.'

Violet swallowed down an indignant gasp. 'I beg your pardon?'

'Men don't like plump women.' Felicity lowered her attention to Hedgehog once more and scratched her fingers over his bonnet just behind his ears. 'That's why Mother said I'm not allowed to eat more than one sweet at a time, lest I end up like Aunt Violet and be too plump to ever wed.'

'I see,' Violet replied. And she did see. So clearly that it made tears sting in her eyes.

She was being used as an example for her nieces.

Self-relegated wallflower who put off marriage after her debut deemed too plump to wed.

In the next instalment of the Lady Observer*: How not to attract a sought-after suitor...*

Now, that would be a headline.

Violet's throat felt thick suddenly and the threat of crying in front of her niece seemed like a very real and awful possibility.

'Please excuse me a moment.' Violet did not bother to wait for Felicity to acknowledge her statement or offer any indication she had heard her.

Violet didn't rush to her room where her footsteps would clatter noisily and give away her location in the quiet house. No, instead she sought her solace in the one place where she'd always sought comfort: in the garden.

Away from everyone, even the servants.

Violet let her head fall back against the closed door and breathed in the summer scents of the garden. Rich dirt mingled with the sweetness of sunwarmed grass and the delicate perfume of flowers in bloom. A balmy breeze brushed her face and drew her from the tiled steps, out into the narrow garden. She sank on to a marble bench under the shadow of an elm tree and let her ears feast on the blissful nothing around her.

Carriage wheels rumbled over the streets in the distance, a clattering of dishes came from within the house, somewhere a dog barked a high, pitching yap. She closed her eyes and let herself be pulled in by her senses, yielding to it for reprieve.

Another sound entered her awareness—the distinct click of a door being shut.

Her eyes flew open and she glanced back towards her town house, but no one was there. Movement over the hedge separating her property from the one next door caught her gaze and her heart went still.

Lord Dalton.

He was alone as she was. The same as when they were children and would speak together between the hedges. Sometimes even skirting the small gap between the foliage that never quite closed all the way between the two properties.

She doubted he remembered such childhood romps.

But she did. In fact, she recalled them fondly, with the exception of when he'd referred to her as hearty. Of course, that was all before his rebelliousness when he grew a bit older. It was then he alternated between pretending she didn't exist and flirting with her so keenly, he robbed her of breath.

Suddenly, she did not want to be there, to be seen by him. She carefully slid down the bench to put herself from the line of his gaze.

'Lady Violet,' he called. 'Is that you I see under the tree?'

Violet hissed a soft exhale. Not this. Not now.

But all the wishing in the world wouldn't change the situation for what it was: she'd been caught.

There was nothing for it but to swallow down her trepidation and speak to the man. She peered around the elm's peeling trunk and saw his dark gaze fixed on her.

Be still her pathetic heart.

* * *

Seth thought he'd been imagining things when he first laid eyes on Lady Violet in the garden next door. He stepped closer to the hedges separating their properties and found himself searching to see if the narrow gap between the dense green leaves was still there.

'Lord Dalton.' Violet watched him from the bench where she sat like a forest nymph.

She got to her feet and approached the hedge. 'What brings you into the garden?'

His mother. Her waspish words. A respite from the verbal assault. A reprieve from a conversation about—of all things—Almack's.

Because being outside cleared his head of the nightmares that threaded through the dark recesses of his mind like ubiquitous cobwebs.

He said none of this, of course. In fact, he should say nothing beyond bidding her good day and returning inside.

His curiosity at his neighbour's nocturnal activities, however, kept him locked in her presence.

He put his hands behind his back and stood at attention like the soldier he'd been. 'I don't strike you as the type to peruse a garden for its simple enjoyment?'

'You do not, my lord.' A smile teased at her lips.

'Then I may surprise you.'

She lifted her brows. 'Oh?'

'Yes, I often come out to admire the...' He

turned to a patch of pink flowers on long pale green stems. 'Uh...the...'

'Peonies,' she supplied.

'Yes, of course, the peonies.' He gestured to the white flowers. 'And the, uh...well, the...'

'Daisies.'

He nodded. 'Yes.'

'I never realised you were a connoisseur of flowers, then.' She nodded her head as though thoroughly impressed. 'Do you have a favourite?'

Ah, now there was an answer he readily knew. 'Violets.'

'Flatterer,' she chided. Yet, even as she did, her cheeks coloured with a pretty blush.

He'd had it in his mind to nudge their conversation towards the late-night carriage he'd seen, but then their eyes met and he thought better of it. There was something tender beneath her flirtation, something shy and perhaps wounded.

Suddenly, he recognised himself as the cad he was. No doubt she was still upset over his abrupt departure from the ball.

'I apologise again for not dancing with you,' he said earnestly.

Her eyes widened and her mouth fell open. 'Well, I suppose you were eager to join your regiment,' she replied in a halting stammer.

He paused, uncertain what the devil she was talking about.

Her cheeks went scarlet. 'I thought you were

referring to my debut.' She touched her hands to her face as though she could press away the flush of embarrassment. 'Forgive me.'

At her debut? He concentrated, driving his memory back six years, and recalled that yes, he had promised he'd dance with her first at her debut. Had he not?

'You don't remember.' A look of pain flashed on her face and she quickly turned her head to the side to break the connection between them.

Without thinking, he reached over the narrow hedge and touched her cheek to turn her pretty face back towards him. It was a mistake to do so. Her skin was soft and warm beneath his touch, no doubt scented with a delicately feminine fragrance. The slight connection made him want to touch her more, to lift her face up to his and kiss her deeply.

He half-hoped she would draw away, but she did not.

She allowed the gesture, looking up at him in supplication, her stare brimming with hurt. A hurt he had placed there.

And the worst part about it was that he'd been too foxed at the time to remember what had even happened.

'I was an idiot, as I've said.' His thumb moved against her jaw, stroking the smoothness of her skin. God, she was sweet. Tempting. Perfect. 'I'm not that man any more and never want to be again.'

She swallowed. 'It's fine.'

'It's not,' he countered. He had to make it right with her. 'Will you dance with me?'

He wanted to regret the words once they had left his lips, but he could not. After all, it would only be one dance. To put things right between them once more.

She exhaled a nervous laugh. 'Here?'

He laughed with her and dropped his hand from her lovely face lest he give in to the temptation to kiss her. 'When the next opportunity presents itself. Most likely at Almack's on Wednesday night.'

She gave him a shy smile that made him want to draw her towards him and wrap his arms around her. 'Almack's?' She put a hand to her chest. 'My, you have changed.'

He'd tried not to glance down at her bosom, but with her fingertips resting lightly on her fair skin, his gaze wandered of their own volition. Her breasts were high and round, supple skin rising over the modest neckline that made his imagination take over.

His stare lingered for only a second, a glorious, tantalising second, before he met her eyes once more.

'My mother,' he grumbled. But he stopped himself. He didn't want to talk about his mother right then, or the fight they'd had over her planned discussion with the patronesses of Almack's to get him permitted back in.

And though he shouldn't admit it, he was exactly where he wanted to be: in the garden, alone with Violet, and wishing the hedge between them wasn't there so he could pull her into his arms and kiss her. Even as he thought it, he leaned closer. The hedge dug into his waist and pressed at his stirring arousal.

'Dance with me,' he said. 'The next chance you get.'

If she rejected him again, he would not protest. In truth, even in making it right, he knew better than to dance with her. A dance couldn't be enough. Even though it ought to be.

He half-hoped she would say no, yet part of him wanted desperately for her to say—

'Yes.' She licked her lips. Pillowy soft and pink and wholly tempting.

He nearly groaned his relief in her reply.

God, he wanted to kiss her. To taste the sweetness of her mouth and sample the smoothness of her skin with his tongue. Especially along the length of her graceful neck and over the tops of those beautiful breasts.

He kept his gaze fixed on hers to avoid letting it drop to her bosom again. It was too easy to admit to himself how badly he wanted to cup his hands over the generous swells, to tease at her nipples with the pads of his thumbs until she cried out beneath him. He leaned further still, practically bending over the hedges to close the gap between them. Sharp sticks dug into his thighs and stomach, but he paid them no mind.

He cared of nothing but the woman in front of him.

There was a delicate powdery perfume about her. Violets. She smelled like her namesake and was just as lovely, just as delicate and sweet as the flower.

'Seth.' She whispered his Christian name, one she hadn't spoken since they were children. She said it in a breathy voice, one laced with intimacy and desire.

'Tell me to walk away,' he said.

She gave a shaky sigh. 'I can't.'

'Tell me not to kiss you,' he cautioned.

She licked her lips again, slower this time. 'I can't.'

He reached for her face once more, this time tilting it up towards his. Her lashes swept to her cheeks just as his own eyes closed. She was silk under his fingertips and fire in his veins. Had he ever wanted anything more to kiss this woman?

He lowered his mouth, expecting to encounter warm, sensual lips. But that was not to be.

Before the slight breath of distance between them could be fully closed, a door banged open, Violet was forcefully flung away from him and a high-pitched shriek pierced the air.

Chapter Seven

❦

One moment, Violet was locked in the anticipation of an impending kiss, her heart pounding, head spinning, and the next, she was sitting hard upon the grass in total bewilderment.

There had been a bit in between, of course. When a cat wearing a pink bonnet collided at an impossible speed against her shins with the force of a stone and sent her sprawling backwards. How ungainly.

'Don't let him run away,' Felicity shouted in a most unladylike manner.

Violet wanted to drop her face into her hands and die of the humiliation burning through her. Instead, she sneaked a glance upwards at Lord Dalton.

He stared down at her, his brows furrowed with concern. 'Good God. Are you quite all right?' He cast a chagrined glance at the hedge between them.

'Yes.' Violet floundered on the ground in an

effort to haul herself to her feet as gracefully as possible. There was no grace about it, however. Not when one wore several layers of skirts while attempting to extricate oneself from the grass without allowing any indecent flashes of unmentionables.

Dalton shoved through the small gap between the hedges, the very one they'd used as children. He *did* remember. It almost brought a smile to her face, except at that very moment he pitched forward and fell as well. Right alongside her.

He landed on his side with an *oof*.

Violet stopped struggling and immediately turned her attention on him. 'Are you hurt?'

'I assure you, after the years of fighting and battle, it will not be a gap in a hedge that will best me.' He righted himself in a far more fluid motion than her fumbled attempts and held his hand out to her. 'What the devil was that?'

'Hedgehog.' Violet put her hand into his and found herself gliding upwards with incredible ease, as though it were no effort on his part whatsoever to lift her to her feet.

'Found him,' Felicity cried out in victory somewhere in the garden.

'A hedgehog?' Dalton's hand remained locked with Violet's even though she was properly standing. 'It looked rather like a cat.'

Violet, self-consciously and yet reluctantly pulled her hand from his large, warm one and brushed at her skirts in an effort to smooth the crumpled muslin. 'He is a cat. His name is Hedgehog.'

Dalton narrowed his eyes. 'Is he wearing a bonnet?'

Violet turned to where he stared at Felicity carrying the rotund creature by its armpits.

'I almost lost you,' Felicity cooed. 'That was very naughty.'

Hedgehog glowered up at her from beneath a layer of pink organza this time.

'Yes,' Violet confirmed. 'He is wearing a bonnet.'

'The poor wretch,' Lord Dalton muttered.

Felicity marched her way over to them, Hedgehog swinging in her grasp. 'Aunt Violet,' she said in a chastising tone. 'You ought to know better.'

A chill trickled down Violet's back. Had Felicity seen her almost kiss Lord Dalton? The hellion of a child would tell all of London with boisterous tone.

If such a thing fell on the *ton*'s ears, it would be quite the scandal. And Violet was keenly aware of what a scandal could do to one's standing in society.

'I beg your pardon?' Violet asked in a manner she hoped did not reveal her horror.

'To be outside without your bonnet.' Felicity lifted Hedgehog in indication of Violet's face. 'Look at how red your cheeks already are. You'll have freckles soon for certain. Mother says freckles are most unbecoming.'

So great was the force of Violet's relief, she could have laughed aloud. It was such an innocent offence compared to the one nearly committed. The one Violet wished she could still commit.

Even now, she kept her attention averted from Lord Dalton lest the 'the sun' hasten the redness of her face further.

'Thank you for your concern,' Violet said. 'This is our neighbour, Lord Dalton. Lord Dalton, this is my niece, Lady Felicity.'

'My parents are Lord and Lady Erstworth.' Felicity's small chest puffed with importance. 'Do you know them?'

'I've not had the pleasure of an introduction,' Lord Dalton said.

Felicity nodded in understanding. 'They are very busy. I hardly see them myself. Isn't that right, Hedgehog?' She nuzzled the cat to her face and rocked him so his dangling feet swung back and forth. The look on his face was not one of amusement or joy.

'I think we should get Hedgehog inside,' Violet said in an effort to intercede on the creature's behalf. 'Lest he end up with freckles.'

Felicity peered under Hedgehog's bonnet. 'Do cats get freckles?'

She didn't wait for the answer before carrying the feline from the garden and into the house, leaving only Lord Dalton and Violet. Except this time, he was in her garden with her. Alone.

It was improper. And delicious.

Would he try to kiss her again?

She truly hoped so.

Alas, he did not. Instead, he stepped back to put space between them and his lips twitched in the hint of a smile. 'It was a pleasure, Lady Violet.'

It was a fortunate thing she could not get freckles from blushing or she'd be covered with them on every inch of her body by now.

'For me as well,' she said quietly.

He backed towards the gap in the hedgerow while facing her, as though he could not bear to look away. 'Wednesday night, then?' he pressed.

She ignored the nip of trepidation. After all, it was far from a marriage proposal. Her secrets could remain safe and she could enjoy at least one more dance before finally entering the futility of spinsterhood.

'Yes,' she replied. 'Wednesday.'

He glanced over his shoulder and pressed through the gap in the hedges. It apparently did not yield easily to him, for it took several jerking steps and a bit of a struggle on his part before he was on the other side.

He smirked at the wayward hedge, then bowed in her direction. 'I look forward to seeing you, my lady, without the barrier of shrubbery between us.' With that, he made his way back into Dalton Place.

tainly the glass was far from clean. But it was the kind of libation he'd often found himself enjoying during his time in the military, alongside his men.

An ache clutched at his heart. Too many of those men were now dead.

He tightened his grip on the glass.

'If anyone can find 'im, it'll be me.' Nash spoke with the confidence of a man who knew his worth.

A man who would get the job done no matter the cost.

Seth swallowed down the rest of his porter and got to his feet. The room had become increasingly crowded since he'd arrived. The hour was late, the ideal time to drink, gamble and visit brothels.

Six years ago Seth would have been meeting up with Kentworth, eagerly anticipating the night's sport—in whatever fashion it happened to be enjoyed. Now, exhaustion pressed on him and the only thing he looked forward to was morning, when another night of haunted dreams would come to an end.

He nodded a farewell to the Runner and took his leave. The ride home was swift, as it often was with so few carriages about. Curiously, there was one arriving at Hollingston House next door when Seth drew closer to his home.

He peered into the darkness. Lord Hollingston was a man well known for his morals. He cared for his children, remained faithful to his wife and served in Parliament with steadfast determination

She waited for him to go inside before replying, 'As do I.'

And indeed she did. Far too much.

She slowly walked towards her own home, preferring to relish the idea of the impending dance rather than face Felicity once more.

If Hedgehog had not scampered outside at such an inopportune time, would Lord Dalton have kissed her?

Violet was sure he would.

Would she have let him?

Of that, she was even more certain.

And it was what scared her most.

It also was not where she ought to be focusing her attentions. That evening, she would be attending her first lesson with Lottie and had to compose a list of discreet questions to ask. Violet would have to be strategic, not only to avoid arousing suspicion, but also to glean the most information as possible. The Season was drawing to a close and there was most likely only little more than a fortnight remaining.

For the first time since Seth's arrival in London, he felt lighter. Happier.

It had every bit to do with Violet and her promise to dance with him at Almack's. This time he knew there would be no drums in the orchestra. The patronesses of Almack's would never allow such a deviation from the social norm. Which meant he would be able to dance with Violet in peace, without terrible images nudging into his mind.

Then he would be able to stop seeing her. The dance would make up for having abandoned her the other night, as well as during her debut six years prior.

Resolved, he made his way to his study to tend to the daily correspondence and tried to put Violet from his mind. It would be too distracting to think about the shy way she'd looked at him when he'd leaned in to kiss her, and how that reticence had slipped away as her lashes fluttered in preparation for their lips to meet.

He sat down in the chair behind his desk. God, how he'd wanted to kiss her, to taste her lips with his own. And how dangerous it had been to attempt. Were it not for the cat, he might have ruined her reputation. Had anyone seen them in that garden, kissing over the hedges...

'Seth?' Caroline's voice came from the doorway to the study. 'Do you have a moment that we might speak?'

'Of course.' He pushed aside the correspondence so he could offer her his undivided attention.

She smiled her appreciation and approached. 'I know you aren't eager to be attending Almack's so soon upon your return and with so little time left in the Season. But Mother is only doing what she thinks is best.'

Seth bit back a retort. After all, Lady Dalton had suggestions for everything she thought was best. How he ought to vote in Parliament, as if he didn't have his own opinions, who he ought to dance with to attract the right quality of woman for a wife, how he ought to hold his brandy glass to make him look most debonair, how to tie his own cravat, et cetera, et cetera...

'I'd hazard to guess she did not do this with William,' Seth surmised.

Caroline sank slowly on the chair, clearly weighing her words before speaking. 'It was different with William.'

'I'm quite aware of that.'

'Will you please reconsider allowing Mother to speak to the patronesses at Almack's?' Caroline asked patiently.

She always had been the peacekeeper among them, the one who interceded on their mother's behalf with him and the one who went to her to make apologies for Seth. Not that he'd ever supported a single one of those apologies. It had been a role Caroline handled with grace and dignity, without ever making Seth feel like the horrible person he knew himself to be.

'She can speak with them today,' Seth replied.

'You see, there are a great many reasons why attending Almack's could benefit you—' Caroline stilled. 'What did you say?'

'I said she can speak with them.'

Caroline straightened. 'Oh. Well. That was far easier than anticipated.'

'Contrary to what others may believe, I want to be a good earl.' Seth glanced at the stack of correspondence. It was larger than he'd been expecting, but he would address it as he had the days before. One missive at a time. 'And that extends beyond our holdings and those we employ. I know I have been...difficult in the past.'

Caroline shook her head, brushing off his castigation. 'You weren't always so bad.'

'Now you're being kind.' He settled back and regarded his younger sister with a frank stare. 'Do you remember the night before I left to join the military?'

Caroline fiddled with the hem of her sleeve, as though finding it intensely fascinating.

It was all the response he needed. He hated the answer he feared she might give, but he had to ask the question regardless. 'Do you recall if I attended Lady Violet's debut?'

'That was all in the past.' Caroline smoothed at the lace on her sleeve. 'It needn't be brought up now.'

Was it all that bad, then? Seth grimaced. 'I'm relying on your good memory and honesty, Caroline. I confess I cannot remember much of that night.'

'That doesn't surprise me in the least. You were sufficiently foxed by mid-afternoon that day.' Caroline's mouth pulled down in a slight frown. 'I only remember because Mother made a point of grousing about you being in your cups and missing Lady Violet's debut.' She pursed her lips.

Seth winced. 'Go on if there's more.'

Caroline lifted a shoulder in a partial shrug. 'I was not yet old enough to be invited, so I cannot vouch if you were indeed in attendance or not. I only know Mother did not see you there.'

That gave Seth pause. *Had* he gone? He tapped his finger on his knee in thought.

'There is another matter I'd like to speak to you on,' Caroline said.

Wary, he lifted his attention back to her. 'Yes?'

'You said you wanted your care to extend beyond your property and those you employ, meaning Mother and myself, correct?' An anxious expression pinched her face.

'Is there something amiss?'

She shook her head vigorously and a furious blush stole over her cheeks. 'No, not at all. It's only that, well, there is a certain gentleman of your acquaintance whom I have found rather interesting in the last few years. I had hoped he would notice me after my come out, but three years have passed...' She toyed with the lace on her sleeve again. 'And he has not.'

Seth lifted his brow in a silent prompt for her to continue. 'Would this have to do with your rejection of so many suitors?'

She nodded and bit her lip. 'I wondered, if it was not too much bother…' She gave Seth a hopeful smile. 'If you would consider speaking to him. About me. To perhaps gauge his interest in me.'

'Who is the fortunate gentleman?'

'One of your university friends.' Caroline wriggled her shoulders, the way she did when she was a girl and couldn't contain her excitement. 'One you used to run about with before you joined the military.'

Seth's stomach went into a tight knot. Surely she was not referring to Kentworth. He'd just as soon offer his sister to the devil himself rather than allow Kentworth anywhere near her. Though truly, they were most likely one and the same.

'Who is it?' Seth repeated, his tone cold.

Caroline took in a deep, gulping breath. 'Lord Rawley.'

Seth stared at her, dumbstruck. 'Viscount… Rawley? With his perfectly combed hair and the pocket watch at his side?'

'Yes, isn't he just a dear?' Caroline bounced in the chair. 'He's more a gentleman than any other I've met. Will you please find a way to see if he has any interest in me whatsoever?'

'Yes, of course.' The answer came automatically and without any indication as to the thoughts jumbling in his mind.

Caroline popped out of her seat, ran to him to

deliver a kiss on his cheek, then dashed from the room with a distant squeal following her departure.

Lord Rawley?

Women never noticed him. If ever a man could be a wallflower, it would be the Viscount. Indeed, in the entire time Seth had known him, Lord Rawley had never once visited the light skirts in a brothel or made advances towards any woman. He'd looked, of course. What man did not? But any attempts at trying to court a woman had been disastrous.

Contrarily, Caroline was a lovely young woman who was accomplished and vivacious. Her dowry was substantial and her lineage could be traced back several hundred years. Any man would consider himself lucky to have the good fortune to catch her attention.

Seth leaned back in his chair and actually chuckled. Of all the challenges he faced upon his return to London, this would be by far the easiest.

The mirth died on his lips as he considered his own relationship. What had he done on the night of Violet's ball? He glanced out the window to where he could see the small garden at the back of Hollingston House. Violet was not out there.

Not that he had expected her to be when they both had only recently returned inside. However, he would remain vigilant. If she went out once more and he had the good fortune to catch her alone, he fully intended to ask her exactly what had happened the night of her debut.

He had to know, even though he suspected it would be excruciatingly terrible. Something that would require more than a single dance to make reparations.

Chapter Eight

Violet slipped out in the dead of night once more, this time with a different driver who Lottie had recommended. And this time with five questions that were carefully selected from a long list she'd composed earlier that afternoon. If she divided them between her lessons, she could glean everything she needed from Lottie for her exposé.

The list had taken the better part of her afternoon, pieced together in the shreds of time when Felicity was otherwise engaged. It would all be worth it.

When she arrived and the butler showed Violet into the drawing room, she did not hesitate as she removed her domino and mask. The gown beneath was blue silk with a tulle overlay on the skirt where whorls of silk ribbon had been stitched. It was perhaps too fine for the occasion, except the last visit had left Violet feeling shabby by comparison to Lottie's beauty.

While Violet could not change her body shape, much to her chagrin, she could at least choose a more flattering frock.

Lottie entered the room, carrying the glass of wine herself, which she handed to Violet with a sweet smile. 'It is so good to see you again.' Her gaze skimmed over Violet. 'You look positively radiant. That colour suits you.'

The compliment was genuinely given, but even with the exuberance of Lottie's words, Violet's attire was nothing compared to the plain green gown Lottie wore. Unadorned and simple, it served to only call attention to her perfect figure.

Just beyond her was a bouquet of hothouse flowers the likes of which Violet had never seen. It was the perfect deflection from compliments, physical appearances and painful failures. 'Goodness, those are lovely.' She indicated to the bunch of lilies and roses with bits of ivy woven between them.

Lottie glanced at them and a wounded expression flickered in her eyes. She recovered with a quick smile. 'Thank you. They're from an old friend.' She redirected her attention to Violet. 'Shall we begin?'

Violet nodded, fully prepared with her carefully selected questions lodged in her mind.

'I realise you may have concerns about me,' Lottie said by way of opening. 'I also realise you are taking a significant risk in coming here.'

Violet opened her mouth, but hesitated, unsure of how to respond to such a bald statement.

Lottie put a hand up. 'You needn't say anything. It's only that I want you to know, so you understand where I've been and why I am doing this now. You see, a lifetime ago, I was a vicar's daughter.'

Her claim took Violet aback. How did a vicar's daughter become a courtesan?

'It was foolish, I know.' Lottie's cheeks coloured prettily. 'But I fell in love and I gave too much.'

It was Violet's turn to feel her face grow hot. She was quite aware of what Lottie was speaking. Violet herself had once given too much.

'The man I loved promised he would come back,' Lottie continued. 'He did not. My father died shortly thereafter and I had no means of support. I tried as best I could to work in an opera house. Not the most esteemed of professions, I'm well aware, but then there are few options for women. I could not wed and found myself unable to support myself on the pittance of an opera dancer. I tried to resist the advances of men, but finally had to concede. For if I was to eat, I had to accept the new profession forced upon me.'

Violet ought to have been grateful for the candid story, for the words that would drip salacious details like the juices from tender cooked beef on to the column of the *Lady Observer*. Except Lottie's confession knotted like a ball of ice in Violet's stomach. How close had she herself been to such a fate as Lottie's?

'I'm so sorry.' The words slipped from Violet's mouth before she knew she meant to say them.

Lottie shook her head. 'I'm not looking for sympathy by any means. I only told you for two purposes. First, I want you to understand why I became what I did. Second, I want you to know something deeply personal about me.'

The former courtesan took Violet's hand in her delicate grip. 'What we discuss in these lessons will require an unquestionable trust between us. It is unfair to expect you to share, yet know nothing of me in return.' Her fingers squeezed against Violet's. 'Can you trust me?'

Guilt bit hard into Violet's awareness and did not let go. Lottie was giving far more of herself than anticipated. Before Lottie could sense any hesitation on her part, Violet forced a nod. 'You can trust me.'

And in that exact instant, Violet made the vow to never reveal Lottie's own personal story in any part of the exposé for the *Lady Observer*. Such secrets were meant to be kept between women.

Lottie pulled Violet into a companionable embrace. 'I'm delighted to hear it, my darling. Now, let us find you a husband. Is there a man you have your heart set upon?'

Lord Dalton's image flashed in Violet's mind

and seared something deep in her chest. The way he'd bent over the hedge to touch her, his hand firmly set against Violet's face, how his dark eyes had become pools of ink before he closed them in preparation for a kiss that never came.

'I'll take that as a yes.' Lottie's eyes sparkled. 'We ladies don't become that thoughtful over the idea of any man. We only do so at the idea of one man in particular.' She tilted her head and her glossy curls shifted over her shoulder. 'Am I wrong?'

It was so tempting to lie, but Lottie's request that they be honest with one another stilled Violet's tongue and she found herself shaking her head.

'And what do you think keeps him from noticing you?' Lottie queried. 'You're far too lovely to be ignored.'

'He does notice me,' Violet replied.

Lottie put a slender finger to the bottom of Violet's chin and tilted her head up to better meet her eyes. 'Then what is the problem, dearest?'

'I…' Violet faltered, her fears sticking fast in her throat.

Lottie's slender brows pinched together. 'Tell me so I can help you. What is keeping you from him?'

Because she was spoiled for any man, because she would never have a body like Lottie's, because he was a war hero and an earl and she… she was nobody.

Tears stung at Violet's eyes with a force that surprised her. 'Because I'm not worthy of a man such as him.' A sob burst from her, harsh and ugly and unexpected.

'Then I think I know what we need to work on.' Lottie had a handkerchief at the ready in a flash and extended it to Violet.

'Making me worthy?' Violet asked miserably.

Lottie smiled and shook her head. 'Making you understand that you already are and that you always have been.'

There were more tears as the night went on, when Violet peeled away the first layer of her heart as she explained her countless inadequacies and all the various ways she was entirely deficient.

Lottie listened carefully and with a patience that somehow managed to bring on more tears. What was it about the realisation of finally being listened to for the first time in a lifetime that rendered one a soggy pile of emotional mush?

Yet as the lesson drew to a close and as her tears dried, Violet discovered that even just discussing her past hurts made her feel exponentially better.

Her initial suspicion of what Lottie's instructions would entail had involved advice in flirting, kissing and seduction. What Violet had thus far received was something far beyond those things. It scored deep and penetrated the very heart.

And made her completely forget to ask even one of her prepared questions.

Seth did not see Violet in the garden again, though he had looked for her. Two days later, however, when the weather was far too fine to sequester oneself in a carriage, he happened upon her in Berkeley Square.

She was with her maid and little Lady Felicity, who was pointing excitedly to something in a shop window.

'Not now,' Violet said as he was walking up. 'You must be well behaved or you'll get none at all.'

'I want it now.' Felicity's face turned pink with outrage and she opened her mouth to wail.

'Lady Violet.' Seth tilted his hat to her. 'Lady Felicity.' He winked.

The little girl's petulant rage dwindled and her mouth closed before she could let loose a squall.

For her part, Lady Violet appeared quite flustered, her own cheeks red and her mouth pinched at the corners.

'Good day, Lord Dalton.' She attempted a smile. 'I trust you're well?'

'Even better now.' He grinned at her.

'You may not say that for long,' Violet warned under her breath. 'Felicity, please bid Lord Dalton welcome.'

The little girl narrowed her eyes. 'Good day, Lord Dalton.'

If everyone wished each other good day with the same vehemence, not a man under the sun would have a fine day ever again.

Except he was not irritated by her poor behaviour, not when her actions were ones with which he was so very familiar. Children did not misbehave without purpose. This particular child was afflicted by something Seth understood better than anything else: a distinct lack of attention.

It had been the same with him as a boy when his attempts at being the best at everything had slipped beyond his parents' notice. They had praised William constantly, commending his accomplishments, no matter how mundane or mediocre they might have been. It was then Seth had stopped trying. And it was then that his parents had actually paid attention to him.

Even displeasure was acknowledgement that he was alive, that he was an active member of the household. Better unhappiness than indifference.

He considered the little girl now and knelt down beside her. Eye to eye, giving her every ounce of his focus.

He tilted his hat to her as he'd done with Lady Violet. 'How are you today, Lady Felicity?'

She scuffed her toe on the ground. 'I'm well, thank you. And you?'

'Quite well, thank you.' He made a show of

looking about. 'Where is Hedgehog? I am quite eager to see what bonnet he's sporting today.'

A smile edged into her pout. 'He's in the carriage, wearing a yellow bonnet. There's a feather on it and it's driving him half-mad. He keeps rolling about in an effort to get at it.' She giggled.

It *was* rather a funny image. 'I imagine he'll have it removed by the time you return,' Seth said.

'I imagine so.' Felicity grinned at him so widely he noticed she'd recently lost a bottom front tooth.

'I was on my way to get an ice at Gunter's,' he fibbed. In truth, he'd been on the way to White's. 'Would you ladies care to join me?'

Lady Violet cast a longing glance towards the shop. 'I shouldn't…'

Felicity turned her face to her aunt. 'Mother says ices aren't for ladies who—'

'We should be on our way,' Lady Violet said in a rush. 'Thank you kindly for the offer.'

Whatever Felicity had meant to say had evidently rattled her.

'Nonsense,' Seth said. 'A man cannot eat an ice alone. Especially when he has the opportunity to do so with a lovely young lady and a well-behaved girl.'

'I'm not especially well behaved,' Felicity conceded.

'Truly?' Seth raised his brows. 'I'm sure that's not correct. Tell me something good you've done recently.'

Felicity scrunched her face in deep thought. 'Hedgehog was making a sound as though he was going to evacuate his stomach into Aunt Violet's slippers, but I moved him away before it happened.'

Lady Violet gave a squeak of surprise.

'That was very good of you,' Seth agreed. 'And quite deserving of an ice.'

Felicity beamed up at him.

'Shall we, ladies?' He rose, brushed off his trousers and escorted them both to Gunter's.

They ate their ices in the sunlit afternoon with laughter and good conversation. The unexpected detour left a warmth in his chest.

These were the simple moments in life, the ones he had missed during his time as a soldier. Moments where there wasn't danger lurking around him, where he didn't have to plan where he might hide in the event of an attack.

This was a slow reclaiming of pieces of a life he'd once lived, a life he had not truly appreciated. He only hoped he might gather enough to eventually be whole again.

When the ices were finished, he bid farewell to Lady Violet and her niece before making his way to White's. His pocket watch informed him he was nearly half an hour late for his meeting with Rawley, an offence he knew the Viscount would notice, but would forgive.

Seth entered White's and immediately found Rawley sitting beside a window with a fresh cup of tea in front of him and a steaming one in the empty seat across from him. He got to his feet when he saw Seth approach.

'Dalton.' He nodded in greeting. 'I see they still let you in.'

'Thanks to you, I'm sure.' Seth took a seat opposite his friend.

Rawley shrugged as if smoothing ruffled feathers so Seth wasn't blackballed was inconsequential. 'Is everything fine with Nash?' He settled back into his chair.

'Yes, of course,' Seth replied. 'I met with him and he is looking into the matter regarding the solicitor.'

Seth considered his friend objectively for the first time. Viscount Rawley was not an unattractive man. He had warm brown eyes, the same colour as his hair that was combed immaculately into a crisp side parting. His outfit complemented his colouring with varying shades of brown and green. While not the height of fashion by any stretch, it was finely made.

Seth was aware Rawley had been raised by his mother with not a single male influence in the home, leaving his demeanour, well, a bit gentler than most men of the *ton*.

No man in all the world was worthy of Seth's sister. But if he had to choose one who would be a good, kind husband to Caroline, it would be Rawley.

The Viscount smoothed his hair with the flat of his palm. 'Dare I ask why you're looking at me in such a manner?'

'You're not a bad man by far. Do you know that?'

'I should like to think so,' Rawley replied slowly. 'What is this in regard to?' He lifted the teacup to his lips.

Seth leaned forward in his seat. 'My sister.'

Rawley gulped at his tea, then sputtered out a cough. 'L-lady Caroline?'

'Yes.'

'What of her?' Rawley set the cup back into the saucer with a rattle of porcelain.

'What do you think of her?' Seth pressed.

'She's…kind. Friendly.' Rawley kept watching Seth as he spoke, as though closely gauging Seth's reactions to his stuttered words.

'Is that it?' Seth grimaced. 'Kind and friendly? Come, man, tell me what you truly think of her.'

'She's…' Rawley swallowed. 'She's very lovely.'

Seth nodded. That was better. 'What would you think about courting her?'

Rawley's eyes bulged.

'Come now, she isn't all that bad.' Seth held his hands out. 'She's actually rather a wonder with the household. She's always loved children and would probably make an agreeable viscountess.'

Rawley shook his head vehemently, and Seth's stomach dropped. He had thought the Viscount would have been elated to have claimed Caroline's attention. Rage flickered in the bowels of Seth's patience.

How dare Rawley think himself better than Caroline?

'It isn't her,' Rawley said with heavy insistence. 'It's me.'

Seth narrowed his eyes. 'You?'

Rawley leaned forward so he and Seth were bent together like school children mid-scheme. 'Look at Lady Caroline…and look at me.' The Viscount scoffed. 'I'd never be good enough for her. She's exquisite. Stunningly so. She's…'

Rawley exhaled. 'She's the most beautiful woman in the entire world.' He paused, reverent for moment, then leaned back and helplessly gestured to himself. 'And I'm me. I know nothing of romance or wooing or courtship.'

Seth shrugged. 'Regardless, she claims to have always been attracted to you.' He took a sip of tea and muttered into his cup, 'For whatever reason.'

Rawley bolted upright at that and pulled at his cravat, as though it had suddenly become too tight at his throat. 'I can learn all of those things,' he vowed.

Seth grinned and slapped his friend on the shoulder. 'Damn right you can. We'll be at Almack's tomorrow evening. I trust we will see you there?'

Rawley's face went pink, and he nodded. 'Yes. Yes, of course.'

Seth got to his feet. 'Wednesday it is, then.'

For all that Seth had failed at, he was finally setting his life to rights. First with the solicitor who had stolen his mother's jewellery, now with Caroline in taking the first steps to securing her preferred match. And soon with Lady Violet by making up for the dance he had missed so many years ago. Finally, after all this time, he would stop being such a damn disappointment.

Assuming it all went according to plan, that was. And it had to. He could not let everyone down. Not again.

Chapter Nine

As expected, the patronesses granted Seth a voucher into Almack's. He sat across from his mother and sister on the carriage ride, as dandified as he would allow Bennet to make him. The valet would have worked meticulously for hours if Seth had let him. Which Seth did not.

Caroline's fingers restlessly smoothed over her dress. Then fidgeted with her reticule. Then patted over her hair to ensure it was perfect. That done, she crossed her ankles, first one way, then the other.

'Heavens, Caroline,' their mother exclaimed. 'What vexes you, child?'

Seth's sister cast him a helpless expression.

He gave Lady Dalton his best bored look. 'Maybe it's another tedious assembly at Almack's.'

He'd said it in an attempt to pull their mother's attention from Caroline and, judging from the Countess's pinched lips, it had worked.

'Attending Almack's is what earls do,' she said firmly.

'I'm well aware of that, Mother.' He gave her a tight smile.

Caroline tilted her head in a silent plea, clearly not wanting them to fight. Seth swallowed down his next retort, for whatever good it might do him. Especially when his mother's mood was ostensibly peevish.

At that moment, the carriage drew to a hard stop. Lady Dalton spilled out of her seat with a shriek and crashed into the unoccupied space beside Seth.

Seth grasped her arm and helped haul her upright once more. 'Mother, are you injured?'

She popped up with a sniff and immediately brushed her hands over her coiffure. 'I am unhurt, despite your new coachman's efforts.' She jerked herself from Seth's grasp. 'You must hire another one. This armless friend of yours won't do.'

'He has one arm,' Seth retorted. 'He is learning to work around the injury and will be competent in time.'

'Competent in time?' Lady Dalton repeated, her tone snide. '"In time" isn't good enough.'

Seth frowned. 'He lost his arm for you, Mother.'

The Countess rolled her eyes. 'Don't be so theatrical, Dalton.'

Seth's heart thundered in his chest. 'It was for you and every other citizen of England. He made sure you could keep your fine home on Grosvenor Street, and your gowns with all their frippery and all the freedoms you take for granted every day of your life.'

Seth should stop. He knew he should, but the rage inside him went white hot and took control. 'While you were sipping tea and shopping on Bond Street, men were fighting. *Dying.*'

Caroline put a hand to his sleeve. 'Seth, please.'

He ignored her. 'Do you know that I almost died, too? There was a cannon aimed right at me, primed to snuff out an English officer. One of my men shoved me from its path and took the full impact of the cannon shot. Do you know what the blast of a cannonball does to a human body?'

'Don't be vulgar,' Lady Dalton snapped.

'It's not vulgar, it's reality.' Seth narrowed his eyes. 'Men explode when they're hit like that. In pieces, fragmented into nothing. It happened right in front of my eyes, even as I realised it should have been me.' The memory was too vivid in his mind. The horror too great.

Suddenly, he was on the wet ground of Mont-Saint-Jean with the cannonball moving in slow motion towards Brent, connecting with his body in a violent collision of gunpowder and gore.

'I could taste his blood in my mouth,' Seth whispered, more to himself.

'Seth.' Caroline's sharp cry snapped him from his trance.

He jerked his attention to the present.

Caroline gaped at him with large eyes, bright with tears. 'Please. Stop.' She blinked and one ran down her cheek.

He turned to his mother whose face was entirely leached of colour.

Too far. He'd gone too far. Damn it.

'Forgive me,' he muttered. 'I shouldn't…' He swallowed, unsure of what to say. He was spared having to come up with something when the door to the carriage slowly opened and Burton peered hesitantly at them.

'Eh, we've arrived.' The footman indicated over his shoulder where Almack's stood, its many windows lit with golden light against the inky darkness of night. 'If you're ready, that is. If you require a moment…'

Lady Dalton pushed towards the door. 'I assure you, I've had quite enough.'

Seth quickly alighted from the carriage to help his mother down. She ignored his proffered hand and swept past him. Caroline emerged next, putting her fingers lightly to his palm. She hesitated and shook her head, her mouth working without a single word emerging.

He nodded in the direction of the door. 'Go on.'

'I'm sorry,' she whimpered and slid out behind their mother.

Seth watched them go without moving to follow. Above them, figures in black jackets and resplendent gowns were visible behind the panes of glass, dancing to music that travelled out into the open night.

'Will you be joining them, my lord?' Burton asked.

Seth glowered at the building, opulent, decadent. Frivolous. Who cared who was important enough to warrant a voucher to Almack's? Who cared who wore aubergine or chartreuse or whatever ridiculous colour was in fashion now?

It was all a waste of damn time. It might be what earls did, but the existence earls lived was absent of any substance.

Seth whipped off his chapeau bras and tossed the hat on to the seat of the carriage. 'I can't do this, Burton.'

The footman looked to his left. 'There are carriages behind ours, m'lord.'

'Then park elsewhere while I figure out where I want to go.' Seth climbed back into the cabin.

Burton nodded and the door clicked closed. The carriage took off not even a second later. Only when Almack's rolled away from sight did Seth recollect the one reason why he had wanted to go there in the first place: Lady Violet. He'd promised her a dance.

Bloody hell.

He didn't want to dance. How could he when Brent's death was so fresh in his mind? So vivid?

It should have been him. Brent should be the

one at home with his family, with his boys and his wife. It should have been Seth who received that cannonball.

The carriage slammed to a hard stop. Seconds later, the door popped open and Burton slipped into the empty seat beside him.

Seth didn't bother to reprimand him.

The footman looked around the cabin with a slow nod. 'It's fine in here.'

Seth scowled. 'I'd trade it all to be back with my soldiers.'

'You are with your soldiers.' Burton leaned back and adjusted his injured leg in front of him. 'And besides, there are others here who are countin' on you.'

'I know,' Seth replied tersely. 'It's the only reason I bothered to return at all.'

'Harold'll take you wherever you want to go.' Burton screwed up his thin lips. 'He is trying, Captain.' He shook his head. 'I mean, m'lord.'

'I know,' Seth said gently. 'I don't intend to sack him, so you can put that from your mind. My mother can grouse all she wants, but I'm the Earl and what I say goes.'

The footman's shoulders relaxed. 'I suppose there are quite a few good bits about being an earl, then. Where do you want to go, m'lord?'

'Where do I want to go?' Seth repeated the question aloud. 'I *want* to go to a gaming hell and lose myself in a glass of strong spirits.'

Burton brightened at that.

'Where *will* I go?' Seth rephrased the question. 'Back to Almack's, as it is what earls do.'

'I'm certain Lady Dalton will be pleased with your decision.' Burton stroked a hand over the velvet cushion, grinned and slipped from the carriage.

But Seth wasn't going back because of his mother. He was going back for Violet. Though God knew her life would be better without him, he could not bring himself to hurt her again. Not when she was expecting him.

He was admitted to Almack's with his esteemed voucher three minutes before eleven o'clock and was led into the small, overcrowded room glowing gold with gilded pillars and small flames enhanced by gilt mirrors. The patronesses sat upon their dais at the upper end and regarded him with scrutiny before inclining their heads in a grudging welcome. He'd nearly been too late to enter, a point of fact they were all well aware of.

It was hot within the ballroom, oppressive with the heat of all those bodies. He eyed the refreshment tables in the supper rooms. Bowls of nearly clear lemonade and crustless bread with glistening smears of butter sat in an unappetising offering.

No wonder men drank before they arrived at Almack's. All this would be at least a modicum above abhorrent if only one were seasoned with a finger or ten of brandy.

A sweet, powdery scent caught his awareness and drew his attention from the insufficient fare.

'Lord Dalton.' The familiar feminine voice rose above the din of conversation and music around him.

He turned to find Lady Violet standing before him in a pink gown that made her cheeks and lips appear pleasantly rosy. It was the high-waisted sort of frock that hugged at her generous breasts and made his stare long to fall into them.

He kept his eyes on hers and tried to speak through the fumble of his mind. 'Forgive me for being late. I confess, I did not actually want to come.'

He winced inwardly. That was certainly *not* what he'd meant to say.

Violet couldn't help the crush of disappointment at Lord Dalton's statement.

'Oh.' It was a simple response. A stupid one that was really no reply at all.

Soon-to-be spinster forces war hero Earl to attend Almack's. He begrudgingly attends, to placate the poor, insipid fool.

Which might well lead to something rather like:

Soon-to-be spinster gorges self on stale bread and butter at Almack's, dying soon

*thereafter. Her last words were cited to be,
'I wish it had been cake.'*

'I mean, I want to be here.' Seth glanced around
them. 'Actually I don't. But I have been anticipating the opportunity to see you.' He grimaced.
'That was bad, wasn't it?'

She laughed, relieved they could both agree
it was indeed. 'It wasn't particularly good,' she
conceded.

Lord Dalton lowered his head. 'Shall I try
again?'

Violet held out her hand in invitation. 'By all
means.'

To her surprise, he turned around, then spun
about to face her once more and lifted a single
brow in a debonair manner that made her heartbeat skew. 'Oh, Lady Violet. Imagine seeing you
here.'

'Imagine.' She pressed her lips together to hold
back a laugh. 'And what a wonderful surprise to
find you in attendance as well, Lord Dalton.'

He cocked his chin at an arrogant angle. 'I believe you promised me a dance.'

Heat suffused her entire body. She had been anticipating this moment since their conversation in
the garden when he'd first asked. Then even more
so since having ices with him, when he'd been so
kind to Felicity.

Violet hadn't been the only one impressed with

him. Felicity had commented more than once on the Earl's kindness and might have mentioned a time or two how handsome he was.

Nervousness left Violet's stomach swirling. 'I believe I did promise you a dance.'

Dangerous. He was dangerous.

For her situation. For her heart.

'I have to ask.' He looked about as though ensuring no one could overhear their conversation.

She leaned closer. He smelled of shaving soap. No costly cologne or scented pomade, just clean male. And it was heavenly.

'What did you wish to ask?' she whispered.

His dark eyes fixed on hers, so fathomless she could fall into them and get lost. 'Did Hedgehog have his bonnet removed once you returned to the carriage?'

Violet couldn't help but smile at the silliness of the question. 'Yes, he did. The feather was torn to bits.'

'I don't blame the wretch.'

Violet laughed. 'I don't either, the poor creature. I am, however, quite impressed with you.'

'I don't know what I did, but I am glad to have done it.'

'Felicity,' Violet explained. 'I cannot seem to get the child to be well behaved. But you immediately curled her around your little finger in the space of a single afternoon. How did you do it?'

'I believe, based on what she's said of her parents, that she feels somewhat unwanted and abandoned by them. The best way to handle someone in her position is to make them feel wanted again. She just needs the right sort of attention paid to her.'

Violet had heard Felicity say the same things, but apparently had not listened to the same extent Dalton had. 'How do you know that?' she asked.

'If you recall, I had my own qualms with my parents, or rather they had theirs with me. As a result, I was quite rebellious as a youth.' He flashed her a devilish smile that made the air go thin.

'You were quite the rogue.' And, oh, he had been. Drinking, carousing and flirting so shamelessly with Violet that she lay awake many a night, imagining what it would feel like to have his mouth on hers, his hands on her body.

Dalton tilted his head. 'That's not too bad, then.' He slid a wink towards Violet. 'Rogues are charming, after all.'

'Oh, you certainly were.' Too charming.

He leaned closer. 'And now?'

The final notes of a country dance tinkled to a close.

She studied him, noting the crinkles at the corners of his eyes even when he wasn't smiling, the hard lines of his jaw that had been etched there by war. He'd been a flirt before he left, a wild, wicked second son with too much time at his disposal and an eagerness to fill it with salacious activities.

He'd come back weighted down with the burden of responsibility heaped on his square shoulders, claiming to be different; a better man. *But was he?*

'Confusing,' she answered honestly.

'Confusing,' he repeated.

Attendees took their places on the long dance floor.

'And dangerous.' She put a hand to her brow, wishing she could draw those words back. 'Shall we dance now?'

He hesitated before offering his hand. 'Dangerous?'

'Do you intend to repeat everything I say?' she asked. 'It will be quite a dull conversation if so.'

They stepped on to the dance floor, taking their place with three other couples. The opening notes of a quadrille began.

'I would never hurt you, Violet,' he said softly.

She sucked in a breath at his words, but it did not abate the ache yawning open in her chest. Because he had already hurt her. Terribly.

And because she was foolish enough that everything within her longed for him still.

The first pair of couples met in the middle and stepped in time with the music.

'I did hurt you, though, didn't I?' he said perceptively, almost inaudibly from her side. 'Tell me what happened during your debut.'

She suppressed a wince at his request, but it still sliced deep. 'Not here.'

'It was egregious.' His gaze followed the couples pairing up and gliding over the floor as he spoke.

She was glad etiquette dictated they keep their eyes on the dancers, lest he see the pain on her face. 'Do you really not remember?'

'I was in my cups.' He sighed. 'I was lost in my own world of selfish melancholy before departing for a life in the military. No one cared that I was leaving and I let it get the better of me. Or the worse of me, as it were.'

'I cared.' Violet broke propriety and looked up at him.

It was a brief moment, one broken by the quadrille that had them dancing forward to meet the couple opposite them. But it had been enough to see the raw emotion etched in his eyes. Regret.

The music brought them together long enough to take a turn, but nothing substantial enough to allow conversation. Violet's stomach clenched with anticipation when their part was done and they could once more return to the side while the other couples made their way into the centre to dance.

'Please, Lady Violet.' There was a pleading note in Lord Dalton's tone. 'I must know. Tell me what I did.'

'I…I can't.' It was hard to breathe suddenly, with the press of her raw heart against her lungs. 'Not here.'

'Where, then?' he asked. 'The garden?' His

suggestion came in a lowered voice, meant only for her. As it should. What he suggested was no chance encounter, but a request to meet alone. Unchaperoned.

Such things could ruin a lady's reputation and she'd worked too hard to keep hers intact regardless of whether it was deserved or not. She should say no.

But she didn't.

'Yes,' she whispered.

Her pulse quickened at her audacious agreement to his brazen invitation. She would be alone with him. Again.

Except this time, instead of a kiss, he was asking for her to bare her soul and put one of her deepest scars on full display. And she would do it. For him. Regardless of the nip of worry in the back of her mind. She'd been honest when she'd confessed to him that he was dangerous.

Even knowing this, she could not stay away.

Chapter Ten

Seth's heartbeat slammed with a tangle of eagerness and nerves and fear. Violet would be with him in the garden later, alone. To finally share what he had done the night of her debut. His energy ran high with anticipation, like when he charged on to the battlefield with his men behind him and the enemy in front.

Only this time, he was the enemy. Or rather, the man he used to be was. The egocentric wastrel who was content to throw his coin away and into dirty pint glasses, weighted game tables and painted women. That man was the one who had hurt Violet.

The current man was the one who walked the tenuous line between making it right and trying to keep his distance. All for her benefit.

And as he'd faced his enemy, he would now face what he'd done and endeavour to do what he could to make it right.

The remainder of his conversation with Violet through the dance had been lighter by comparison, comprised of Felicity's latest antics, Hedgehog's many dashes for freedom and rather agreeable shared recollections on their childhood antics. It was by far one of the most enjoyable conversations Seth had shared with anyone since his return to London.

The elevation to his mood remained after he returned Lady Violet to Lady Hollingston, who practically oozed with flattery upon his arrival. It was then he saw Rawley on the opposite side of the room from Caroline.

Seth had anticipated the two would be near one another constantly. If not dancing, then flirting. Why else would anyone attend Almack's if not to participate in one of those two activities?

He made his way through the crowd towards Rawley. The exertion of bodies dancing combined with the candles lit throughout the room left the air hot and thick. The ghosts of war whispered at him from the shadowed corners of his mind and sweat tingled at his brow.

He balled his hand into a fist.

Damn it. He was a soldier. A man who'd fought for his men's lives, for his country—and lived. Memories would not defeat him. For that was all they were: memories. Things of the past.

He breathed in slowly and concentrated on thoughts of Violet. The way she'd looked in her garden when he'd been about to kiss her, eyes closed with her long, dark lashes fanning across her cheeks, her supple pink mouth soft with expectation. How he'd wanted to pull her against him, to allow years' worth of desire to consume him. In his mind, he trailed his mouth down her throat while cupping a full breast in his hand, his thumb grazing a naked nipple.

His groin stirred and he brought his fantasy to an abrupt halt. Damn it. He'd almost gone too far. The last thing he needed was to lose his voucher to Almack's for offending the patronesses with an obvious erection.

His mother would certainly never let him live that one down.

Rawley stood only a few feet from Seth. A perfect distraction. He waved to his friend and approached. 'I'd have wagered you'd be spending most the evening with Caroline,' Seth said.

Rawley glanced away and brushed at the lapel of his jacket, as if it was not already perfect. 'Yes. I meant to approach her.'

'Meant to approach her?' Seth frowned. 'So you've not even bade her good evening yet?'

Rawley dipped a finger into his cravat and pulled it from his throat. 'I meant to,' he repeated.

'Why the devil have you not?'

Rawley seemed to shrink into himself. 'I'm afraid I…I won't know what to say. That I'll miss a dance step.'

'You've done these dances dozens of times.' Seth glanced at the open floor where a country dance was now in full tilt. 'Go to her now so you might speak at length before the next set begins.'

Rawley shook his head. 'I forgot my card.'

'What card?' Seth asked.

'The card he carries with dance steps upon them so he doesn't forget them.' Kentworth threw a hand over Rawley's shoulder.

Rawley, who usually tolerated Kentworth's obnoxious behaviour more than most, scowled at his friend and shrugged the Marquess away.

'Come now, Rawley, you needn't be so missish about the whole business of it.' Kentworth drank so deep from his lemonade, Seth was certain he had added a flask of flavouring to it. 'Why did you do this to him, Dalton?'

'Do what to him?' Seth demanded.

Kentworth rolled his eyes. 'Pulled him from the comfortable shell of his life. I've never seen the poor bastard in such a state. Look at him. He's gone all pink about the face.'

Seth turned his attention to Rawley, who indeed had become a bit discoloured.

Kentworth kept his hand wrapped around the glass of lemonade and removed his forefinger long enough to point at Seth without releasing the beverage. 'You should apologise.'

Was Kentworth truly the man Seth had once considered one of his closest friends? Had Seth really acted similarly in his youth? The answer tightened into a ball of self-disgust in his gut.

He glowered at Kentworth. 'Forgive me, Rawley. I apologise for hand-delivering you the knowledge that one of the most sought-after ladies of the *ton* is infatuated with you. I'm sorry to have placed the burden of an easy, agreeable match upon you.'

With that, Seth departed and made his way to the person who he truly did owe an apology to for how the evening had gone thus far. Caroline.

She stood in the supper room with a bit of dry cake.

'You must be forlorn to be eating that.' He indicated her plate.

She sighed and set it aside. 'Is it my gown?'

Her…gown? He looked down at the white frock adorned with red ribbons and silk twisted things he assumed were meant to be flowers. It wasn't unattractive.

'What's wrong with your gown?' he asked.

'That's what I'm asking you.' She sighed again.

He gave a helpless shrug. 'I…think… I mean…'

She watched him, her brows raised in expectation.

'It's a gown.' He spread his hands wide. 'It's… pretty.'

Her head fell back in exasperation. 'You're no help at all.'

Good God, what did she expect from him with this conversation?

'The flower things are a nice touch.' He waggled a finger at one of the silk ribbons. 'I dare say.'

She gave him an incredulous look and chuckled. 'Thank you for trying.' She shook her head and her dark curls swayed from side to side. 'What did I do to put him off?'

Him.

Rawley.

It was Seth's turn to sigh. 'The man is inept at handling himself around women, I'm afraid. I assure you, the fault is not with you.'

'You spoke with him?' Caroline gave Seth her clear and undivided attention. 'Did he say why he had not asked me to dance?'

Seth caught sight of Rawley across the room, hugging a wall as dearly as any wallflower. Perhaps Seth ought not to be so honest with Caroline. Except that his sister regarded him with wide, desperate eyes. If he didn't know her better, he'd swear she was on the verge of tears. Placating her with a lie would not do.

Forgive me, Rawley.

'He lost his card with the dance steps on it,' Seth conceded.

'He has a card with dance steps on it?'

'Well, he *had*.' Seth stressed the last word. 'Or he would be swirling you about the dance floor by now, I wager.'

Caroline pressed her hands to her chest and her

face took on a dreamy expression. 'Oh, he is just too precious.'

For the first time since his return to London society, Seth found himself wishing for a visit from Kentworth. He could use some of that lemonade.

'Seth, I have one more favour to ask of you.' Caroline folded her hands in front of her waist.

'Go on.' He nodded.

She glanced about to ensure no one was near enough to hear them. The supper room, however, was absent of anyone but them.

'I want to take lessons,' Caroline whispered.

What an odd thing to whisper about.

'What sort of lessons?' He matched her volume by way of teasing her more than in sincerity. 'Water colours? Bonnet making? I confess, I know of a cat who would benefit well from your handiwork.'

'No.' She giggled. 'Seduction.'

Seth straightened and looked through the crowd for Kentworth in earnest. He could truly use some of that bloody lemonade.

The house had gone silent the following day. Which is exactly what Violet had been waiting for. She had never set a time with Seth to meet him in the garden and they'd had to leave before she'd managed to arrange it. That had been an oversight on her part, a detail she'd been too rattled by nerves to adequately consider.

Lady Hollingston had taken Felicity to Gunter's for an ice. Violet had been invited to join them, but had declined. Not only because she wanted this opportunity to be alone to venture into the garden, but also because she tried to avoid eating any sweets when around her mother.

If she accepted a treat, she would be lectured on how she ought to avoid them. If she declined a treat, she would be lectured on how good it was to avoid them. Regardless, it always resulted in a lecture and the feeling of utter self-hatred for her plump, impossible body.

Violet leaned against the window to look out into the small formal garden behind their home, most of which was obstructed by the large elm tree. No one appeared to be outside. If memory served correctly, the gardener came on Tuesdays. Definitely not Thursdays.

Violet allowed Susan to secure a straw bonnet to her head with a perfect bow tied just by her right ear. She wouldn't be caught without a bonnet again. Once done, Violet quietly slipped from the house, making doubly sure no naughty feline followed. As she had assessed, the garden was empty. Unfortunately, so was Lord Dalton's.

In an effort to appear normal, she strolled along by the flowerbeds, mainly in areas she thought might be most visible from Dalton Place next door. She marvelled at the roses and the heady, sweet jasmine. She was just getting to the peonies when the click of a door opening pulled her attention to Dalton Place and the very handsome dark-haired gentleman entering the garden.

He grinned at her and approached the hedge, scanned quickly about and navigated the gap between their properties with considerable ease. Violet smoothed a hand down her white muslin day dress and belatedly realised she ought to have picked a more vibrant gown. At least something with a bit of colour to it.

'Lady Violet.' He bowed. 'Imagine finding you out here.'

'Imagine.' She sauntered to him and glanced up from beneath the brim of her bonnet.

He was immaculately turned out, as always, with his hair slightly mussed in a way that made her want to run her hands through the short strands. 'I enjoyed our dance,' he said in a low voice.

Her cheeks went hot. Heavens, was she blushing already? 'As did I,' she replied in a voice too shy for her own liking.

'I'm sorry it was six years late.' A muscle worked in his jaw.

She shook her head. 'Think nothing of it.'

'It's all I have been thinking of.'

'Truly?'

His eyes always were a perfect mirror of his soul, sharp with his emotions. Right now, his gaze reflected painful regret. 'Tell me,' he said. 'And spare me no details.'

'You did not come to the ball.' She shrugged as though it was a small matter to be easily pushed aside.

He took her elbow and gently led her to the shade of the elm tree, where no one would see them from any floor in either home. 'I want to know what happened that night.' His brows pinched together with sincerity. 'Please, Vi.'

Vi.

He hadn't called her that in years. First he'd used it when they were children, then when he got older, he used it as a form of flirtation, as though teasing her with her own name. And how it had made her heart flutter.

The same as it did now.

Her heart raced with such ferocity, it hardly left her lungs with the capacity to draw breath. Was she truly considering doing this?

Of course, not all the details could be shared. Not Lord Fordson. And especially not what had transpired with him.

No one would ever know that.

'You didn't come to the ball,' she said again, this time in an opening to the painful tale. She swallowed. 'I had expected you, it's true. You always had a way of talking to me that no one else did. It made me feel special. *You* made me feel special. And when you asked if you could have the first dance at my debut, I hoped—' She stopped short. She was saying far too much.

'You *are* special.' He watched her with a look of intense concentration. 'You always have been. Tell me, what did you hope?'

She shook her head, refusing to say what she'd meant to. How she'd imagined he might consider her for marriage. The idea was laughable now, but then it had been entirely plausible in her mind. Far too plausible. And foolish.

That was what she'd been—a foolish girl with a fragile heart, too eager to settle it into someone's palm.

A man like Seth, as the object of her affection, was guaranteed to bring her pain. One moment, he would rain compliments down upon her, the next he was out carousing with Kentworth.

She had been innocent then, but not ignorant. She'd heard the rumours of where they went. Of the women of ill repute. Better perhaps that he had broken her heart then in one swift blow rather than chipping off small shards and pieces over the course of a lifetime.

'You came to the house before the ball and told me that you would not be in attendance.'

'I was thoroughly intoxicated,' Seth said flatly.

'Yes.' Humiliation burned through her, as fresh and hot as it had been that fateful day. 'You came into the town house—I have no idea how you entered as none of the servants had admitted you. But you stopped when you saw me and you stared at me for some time. I could see you taking me in, my hair, my gown.' She bit her lip, hating the emotion tightening in her throat. 'You clearly didn't like what you saw, because it was then you announced you would not be attending my ball, or dancing with me.'

Her eyes stung with tears, but she swallowed them down. She'd spent far too long weeping over the mortifying incident.

'Did I say anything else?' he asked.

'No,' she replied. 'But you didn't have to. I knew exactly why you didn't want to come to my ball.'

'Because I was stupidly drinking myself into oblivion before joining the military and drowning myself in my own selfish loathing?'

She blinked. 'No, because of my gown.'

'Your gown?' He squinted his eyes in confusion. 'Why is it women always think it's the bloody gown?'

'Because it was hideous.' A sob rose in her throat at the admission.

'Why the deuce would you select a hideous gown for your debut?'

Ah, and there was the rub of it. Her shame. Not as bad as Lord Fordson, of course, but mortifying none the less.

'It wasn't the gown I had chosen,' she admitted. 'That one was far lovelier with silver tissue glittering over the skirt and sleeves with small silver beading stitched into the bodice. It was lovely.'

'Yet you didn't wear it.'

Violet looked down at the ground, stinging with fresh hurt. 'My mother had the gown made in a smaller size. I know I'm not a slender woman and it has always been to my mother's chagrin. She had hoped the desire to wear the gown would be great enough to make me lose the extra bit of weight I had gained the prior year. There was a second gown made, in case I failed. The hideous one.'

He stared at her blankly. 'Surely you jest.'

'I couldn't do it.' Violet blinked, but it was too late. Her tears had overcome her resolve and one fell from her eye like a dropped crystal. 'I tried so hard. I didn't eat for nearly a week. Then the first dinner party we attended, I ate so much, I made myself ill.' She'd been dizzy with hunger and the second something other than tea or water had hit her tongue, she'd lost all control. To this day, roasted pheasant tasted like failure. Rich with crisped skin, succulent meat that fell from the bone and a gown she would never be able to wear.

It had been disgusting how much she'd eaten and she'd paid the price for it after. Not only with the retching protest of her offended stomach, but also the scorn of her mother.

'I failed,' Violet whispered.

'And the other gown was your punishment?' he surmised.

Violet nodded miserably, alight with the blaze of her humiliation.

'Good God,' Lord Dalton said. 'That's…'

She winced, expecting his agreement at how pathetic she was and that even the promise of wearing that lovely gown hadn't been enough of an enticement to achieve her goal of slimming down.

After all, he'd always been well aware of her size. Certainly, he'd called attention to it on several instances when they were children, like telling her that she could climb trees because she was solid, or that she could survive any illness because she was so healthy.

She held her breath and waited for the words that would irrevocably cut her to the deepest part of her core.

Chapter Eleven

Seth stared incredulously at Lady Violet. His mind reeled with the story she'd told him. How could any mother be so cruel?

'That's dastardly,' he said finally, able to dislodge the words from his thoughts.

Violet blinked in surprise as though expecting a different response. God, he must have been truly awful for her to assume he'd agree with something so vile.

'You thought I would agree with her?' he asked in horror.

'You've always thought me plump.' She pressed her lips together and another tear ran down her cheek. 'You called me things like "healthy" and "substantial" and "solid". And I'll never forget how you looked at me before my ball when I wore that hideous gown.'

He shook his head. 'I meant those as good things,' he protested.

'Good?' She gaped at him. 'How could such phrases possibly be good?'

'Because you're—' He broke off before he said something crass.

'You made it clear how you felt about me the night of my debut.' Her eyes flashed with the depth of her wounds from that fateful moment.

'Tell me,' he said in a tone far steadier than he felt. 'Tell me what I told you that night, how truly awful your gown was. I want it all.'

She plucked a leaf from the elm tree and put all her attention on it as she twirled the stem between her fingers. 'It was pale lavender and made me look as though I was in half-mourning. The waist came too low and showed how round my hips were and the top was cut to reveal my shoulders.'

The description nudged at his memory. Perhaps gowns did truly have some impact. 'Did it have laces crisscrossing the bottom of your skirt?'

She startled. 'Yes. You do remember, then.'

'Only a bit.' He shook his head, detesting himself for the thickness of his intoxication back then that clouded his memory now. 'What did I say to you to let you know how much I hated it?'

'You stared at it for a long time and you didn't say anything.' She bit her lip. 'I hoped that meant maybe you liked it, perhaps it wasn't as bad as I had suspected. I asked what you thought of my gown.'

A memory formed in Seth's mind as Lady Violet spoke.

A memory of Lady Violet Lavell coming down the stairs to discover him standing in the entryway. She'd glowed with pleasure at his arrival, but his eyes had only lingered on her face for a moment before gliding down to her body.

God in heaven, that body.

Her frock had been a creation beyond anything he'd witnessed before. It had hugged her nipped waist and gone broad at the sensual curve of her hips. His fingers had itched to caress the feminine swell there.

He'd crept his gaze upwards slowly, savouring her. The drink had made him heedless of social propriety and time had left him ravenous for the voluptuous lady who lived next door. He'd wanted to take her in, one glorious inch at a time.

Her breasts… Firm with rounded cleavage, tempting as they rose above her neckline. Her shoulders had been bare and gleaming like pearls.

She'd fingered the silk of her skirt and watched him with an anxious stare. 'What do you think of my gown?'

What had he thought?

He'd wanted to kiss her until her lips were red, stroke his tongue against hers, give this sweet woman a taste of wickedness that would make her toes curl. He'd wanted to grasp her round bottom in his palms and grind the hardness of himself against the softness of her innocence. He'd wanted to shove her against the wall, tug down her neckline and take her nipples into his mouth to tease with his tongue and teeth until she cried out.

'You don't want to know what I'm thinking,' he'd muttered.

She had swallowed, her eyes wide and innocent. She had been innocent and he the epitome of sin. His body had swelled with a longing for her curves, with a need he could not sate. Not with her. She'd been meant for another—someone who would be a better fit for her. Not some useless second son who wasn't good for anything more than being cannon fodder for the enemy.

'Is it that bad?' she'd asked, a little laugh in her words.

He hadn't even wanted to make love to her in that moment. Not in the sweet, tender way men were supposed to do with their wives. He'd wanted to pin her to the wall and rub at her most intimate place until she was dripping with need for him. He'd wanted to ravish her. Hard. Deep. Thoroughly. So they were both glistening with sweat after.

'Oh, God, yes,' he'd ground out.

Then he'd turned away before she could make out the rigid outline of his manhood in his breeches.

He couldn't dance with her. Not like this. Not in that gown.

She was continuing the story now. 'I asked if it was so bad and you said…'

'Oh, God, yes,' he said for her.

She winced. 'You do remember.' She wiped a tear from her cheek. 'You were gone the next day. You never even said goodbye.'

Seth ran a hand through his hair. 'My meaning was wildly misconstrued that night. I didn't mean that I thought your frock was ugly. It was that you were…'

Luscious. Sensual. Titillating. Tempting.

God, he couldn't say that. Not to a wallflower who remained unwed at three and twenty. He'd mortify her.

'Beautiful.'

'Beautiful?' Scepticism laced her voice.

'I wanted to…'

Grab you to me. Stroke your tongue with mine. Make you cry out in passion. Taste you.

'To kiss you.'

Her lashes fluttered. 'The way you almost did recently?'

No. Deeper. More passionate. Greedier. Hungrier. Thoroughly and completely until you feared you might die without me inside you.

'Yes.'

She shivered. It was an almost imperceptible movement and told him in every wonderful way how much she had longed for that kiss as well.

Violet was a wonder of sensuality. A woman who would never have need of lessons from a courtesan like Caroline had mentioned the night before. The notion of seeking lessons in sexuality was truly preposterous and nothing Seth wanted to think of now. Not ever, really, except that he'd promised to consider the ridiculous notion and give Caroline an answer later.

He pushed the thoughts of the courtesan and his sister from his mind and instead focused on the lovely woman in front of him. The object of his desire for the last decade.

Violet.

He wiped at the bit of wetness on her cheek from a tear that never should have been shed and left his hand cradling the smoothness of her skin.

She gazed up at him with wide blue eyes. 'Are you going to kiss me now?'

He pulled her closer to him, putting her lush body fully against him.

Inappropriate. Vulgar. Sheer perfection.

'I am,' he said in a low tone.

Her breath caught. 'You aren't going to warn me off like last time?'

He should.

'God, no.' He grasped the blue silk ribbon of her hat and gently pulled the bow free. 'Last time I did, the offer was taken up by a cat.' The straw bonnet slipped off Violet's head and was caught by the ribbons Seth still held. 'This time there will be no one to intervene.' He paused. 'Unless, of course, you do not want this. If so, simply say no.'

He held his breath, waiting for her rejection.

It was what he deserved. God knew that. Violet knew that. Hell, even he knew that.

But she didn't say no. Instead, she stretched up on her toes, closed her eyes and whispered, 'Yes.'

Violet breathed in the delicious scent of shaving soap and warm male. Her skin practically hummed with heightened sensitivity, aware of the strength with which Seth held her to him. How very powerful his body was, a wall of muscle.

And the incredible hard, heavy bulk of his very obvious arousal.

That she had brought him to such a state made a steady pulse of need thrum between her legs. She wanted to arch her hips against him so that thick length of him pressed between her legs.

Sinful.

She was so sinful. This was wrong.

His mouth lowered to hers, a tender brush at first, then more firmly pressing to hers, his lips warm and surprisingly soft.

Even if this was wrong, it was also so wonderfully right.

A hungry whimper sounded from the back of her throat. Before she could even feel a flash of embarrassment at the sound, he gave a growl and he flexed against her. It was a wild, primitive display of lust that made her tingle in all the right places. She gave a breathy exhale, and his lips parted hers as his tongue brushed into her mouth.

There was a spiciness to him that encouraged her kisses, made her long to give more, take more. She could kiss him for a lifetime and still be unsated.

His hand shifted to the back of her head, cradling her in his palm while he tilted her head back and deepened the kiss. Her pulse escalated to something uncharted and erratic.

She had been kissed before by Lord Fordson. But it had never been like this.

Lord Dalton pulled her lower lip down with his thumb and sucked on it, teasing it slightly with the tip of his tongue. No, never like *this*.

She moaned, the sound quickly dissipating between their mouths as he kissed her once more. His free hand brushed over her neck, her collarbone, down to skim the sides of her breasts. Her nipples tingled at the nearness of his touch. Without thought, Violet arched her chest towards him. His hand hesitated next to her breast, then his thumb tentatively swept over the swell of it.

She let her head fall back with a moan. His mouth descended on her throat, kissing with hot panting breaths while his hand closed fully around her breast. He uttered a curse against her skin and swept a finger over her taut nipple. Though layers of cloth separated his digit from the little bud, pleasure danced up through her torso and spread through her entire body.

The pulse between her thighs had become an

insistent ache, demanding, needing satisfaction. The bulge of his arousal pressed against her stomach and only intensified her longing. She arched against him, flexing her hips upwards so their pelvises met.

He groaned, a low, deep sound that touched her at her core. She lifted her face and kissed him with all the lust thundering through her veins.

He broke off the kiss and rested his brow to hers, his chest rising and falling with his frantic breathing. 'We must stop.'

Violet's mind spun, dizzy with desire. She didn't want to stop. She wanted to kiss and touch until the hum of desire throbbing an insistent beat between her legs had been sated. It had been six years since the time with Lord Fordson. She had been ill prepared for that encounter.

But now her body knew. And it craved.

Oh, how it craved.

But hers was a secret that must be guarded no matter the cost. She pressed her lips together to savour the memory of his mouth and nodded.

Seth backed away and stared hard at her, his eyes deep pools of reckless emotion. 'I shouldn't have kissed you.'

His words plunged into her like a dagger. 'Please don't,' Violet said.

'Don't kiss you?' The corner of his mouth lifted.

Lust was so hot in her blood, it was difficult to breathe, to think. 'Please don't regret it.'

He closed the distance between them once more, but did not pull her back into his arms. 'Selfishly, I could never regret it. I only want to ensure your reputation remains intact.'

Her reputation was a sham hidden behind a veneer of reticence. She was a fraud. But she couldn't say as much aloud. How could she confess such shame?

He stroked his thumb down her cheek, tender and affectionate. It was all she could do not to close her eyes and lean into the caress.

'How is it you're not yet wed?' he murmured.

He had asked her that before. She shifted her weight, unsure of what to say. How did one explain the lack of interest in marriage when in her heart that was exactly what she had wanted? Once upon a time, long ago, before she'd met Lord Fordson. She'd longed for someone to love her wholly and completely and without condition, who truly thought she was beautiful and made her feel the way Lord Fordson had with his lies.

Seth's hand fell away and he backed away to give her more space. 'You've had suitors, though, surely.'

'I prefer the company of spinsters,' she replied staunchly. It was a prim response, one meant to discourage further conversation on the topic. But

Seth was a man unlike any other, especially since his return.

'What if a man did wish to court you?' he asked. 'Would you still prefer the company of your fellow wallflowers?'

Violet's breath caught. Did he mean to ask if he might court her? If so, how was she to answer such a request?

'I suppose it would depend on the man,' she stammered.

He tilted his head in concession. 'That's a prudent response.'

The sun had begun to sink into a bed of fluffy clouds overhead and cast the sky in myriad hues of purple, blue, pink and orange.

'I have a rather odd question to ask you,' he said suddenly.

Violet's heart nearly seized in her chest. If he meant to ask if he could court her, would she agree? One was not courted by a man without the intention of marriage if they were compatible.

And what if they were? What if he asked for her hand in marriage? He believed her to be pure.

It was too much. A tension gripped her chest and air was suddenly difficult to draw in.

'May I ask it?' he asked.

She nodded even as her pulse raced faster than Hedgehog fleeing a new fashion accessory.

Seth took a breath, paused in apparent contemplation, then opened his mouth and contin-

ued with what appeared to be a difficult question
to compose.

Violet's whole body went stiff as he finally
spoke. And it was not at all the question she had
expected. In fact, it was almost worse.

'What do you know of a courtesan who instructs young ladies?' Seth queried.

'A courtesan?' Violet squeaked.

'Yes, apparently there is a woman named Lottie who instructs the ladies of the *ton* on seduction
or something of the like.' Seth cleared his throat.
'It is rumoured the women who go to her marry
quickly as men are eager to wed those women
who have received such edification. Is this true?'

Violet nodded. 'So I hear.'

'What is your opinion on it?'

Violet gathered her thoughts and answered his
question with slow, careful words. 'I believe it to
be helpful to the women who require such assistance.'

'Interesting.' Seth nodded to himself. 'And you
don't find it at all appalling?'

She studied the rough striations of the elm's
bark and hoped he couldn't detect the guilt clenching in her stomach. 'She doesn't debauch young
ladies as I understand it. If such a thing does, in
fact, exist. I believe she helps ladies become more
attractive to men. They are still innocent. And
isn't that all that matters?'

She held her breath and waited for his response.

'Yes, of course,' he answered quickly. 'When you put it that way, I suppose it is not so bad.'

And there it was, his agreement to the importance of innocence. A purity she no longer possessed. That she'd been so stupid to have given away with the first set of compliments to breeze in her direction.

She was doing it again now—falling for a man's praises, giving in to clandestine kisses in a garden. Alone. Putting her reputation on the line after having just managed to salvage it after the first transgression.

Had she not learned her lesson already once before? Suddenly she felt foolish. A ridiculous girl who had endured a lifetime of inadequacy, willing to do anything to feel important. Wanted, needed, anything.

Violet turned to the town house. 'Forgive me, but I must be going.'

'Will you be at Lady Cotsworth's ball tonight?' he asked.

That night, Violet would be meeting with Lottie. It had been a hard decision to make. Lady Cotsworth was a known gossip and juicy titbits ran free as a stream through the ballroom of her home. But if Violet did not make time to meet with Lottie, she would never have enough information for her exposé.

Violet shook her head without offering an explanation, swiftly bid him good day and returned to the safe quiet of her home. Her heart slammed with deep resonating thumps that left her breastbone practically vibrating.

She should not meet with Seth again. She shouldn't have danced with him and certainly should not have kissed him. Except that even as she thought these things, she lifted the curtain to view the garden behind the town house and felt a pang of disappointment to find it empty. He was gone, but the memory remained. Of his touch, his kiss, the press of his arousal against her. How desperately she wanted him.

Violet's sigh fogged the glass. She would do well to stay away from Seth, for though he'd returned from war with stronger morals, he was far more dangerous now than he'd ever been before.

Chapter Twelve

Violet spent the remainder of the day alternating between a dreamy state of remembering Seth's kiss and crippled by self-castigation.

After all, what would a man like him want with her? He was wealthy, titled, a war hero and beyond handsome. He could have his pick of any woman he wanted in the *ton*. Surely he was not interested in her beyond that kiss and what he thought he might be able to encourage from her.

How could he be?

She'd excused herself to her bedchamber the moment Felicity and her mother had returned, citing a vexing headache. She'd laid down to rest, but had been unable to do so, even when the warm weight of a furry grey cat plopped down beside her. And while she did not sleep, the feline was a quiet comfort.

Hours later, when the house had gone still and amid a heaviness of her own doubt, Violet slipped on her domino and mask and made her way to the luxurious town house in Bloomsbury. Lottie had assured her last time she would help Violet realise her own self-worth.

If ever there was a time Violet required as much, it was now.

Once she'd finally arrived, was liberated of her disguise and Lottie breezed through the double doors, Violet was beside herself with anxiety.

Lottie paused and regarded her, brows pinched with concern. 'The gentleman who took notice of you?' she asked by way of enquiry as to what had Violet looking so bereft.

Violet nodded miserably, afraid her voice might shake if she spoke.

Lottie sat on a plush maroon sofa and patted the seat next to her. 'Come, dearest. Tell me what has you so upset.'

Violet sank next to her. 'He kissed me.'

Lottie's eyes snapped with a fire Violet never thought to see in such a kind face. 'Did he take advantage?'

Violet pulled at a loose thread on a seam of her pink silk gown. 'No, it was only a kiss.' A heart-stopping, head-swimming, stomach-flipping kiss that went on for ever and yet was over far too soon.

'Was it forced?' Lottie asked.

Violet abandoned the loose thread and shook her head. 'No. I…I welcomed it.'

The rage fled from Lottie's gaze and she gave

a relieved sigh. 'Then I am pleased to hear of the kiss. Especially of his restraint and respect.' Lottie's expression shifted to one of tenderness. 'Might I guess, then, as to what has you in such a state?'

Violet tensed for Lottie's assessment.

'You do not feel worthy,' Lottie said softly.

Hearing the words aloud made tears prickle anew in Violet's eyes.

Lottie put a hand to Violet's shoulder in comfort. 'Come now, you needn't worry over such things. You're a clever woman with a sharp wit and you're far too beautiful—'

'Please.' Violet gritted her teeth. 'Please don't placate me with such casual praises. If you genuinely wish for there to be honesty and trust between us, you cannot offer platitudes on my appearance.'

Lottie's dark blue gaze searched Violet's face. 'I think I see a different person than the one who stares back at you in the mirror.'

Violet shifted her focus to the interlacing vines woven into the carpet. 'I'm well aware of my deficiencies.'

'Deficiencies?' Lottie repeated as though she found the statement incredulous. 'Why do you feel this way?'

'It is evident in this body, is it not?' Violet hated the tears burning hot in her eyes and kept her gaze averted lest Lottie see them. She had already bared her soul once that day. What difference did a second make?

'I try not to eat, but even when I deprive myself of all sustenance, I never manage to slim down. And I do try to limit myself, but it's so hard.' Her voice choked off. 'What's worse is that I love food. I think of it. Far too often.'

'Of course you do when you're starving yourself.' Lottie put a hand to Violet's arm. 'Darling, you are lovely, truly. I would not say it if it wasn't so.' She pushed up to her feet and rang for a servant.

Violet squeezed her eyes shut, anticipating being escorted out at any moment.

Soon-to-be spinster remains in such a sorry state that a famous courtesan has rescinded her decision to offer instruction. And, yet again, soon-to-be spinster is an utter failure.

'Bring me a mirror,' Lottie demanded of the servant.

Violet lifted her head as the man returned moments later, carrying a large cheval-glass mirror. He set it soundly on the thick carpet, then promptly took his leave.

Lottie beckoned Violet with a wave of her hand. 'Please do come here.'

Violet grimaced at what she knew she would

be expected to do, then got to her feet and stood in front of the blasted thing.

'What do you see?' Lottie asked.

Violet's reflection regarded her with a mournful gaze. 'I see myself.'

'What do you like?'

Violet considered herself in the mirror thoughtfully. She had spent so much time loathing the frumpiness of her body, she hadn't taken the time to relish any positive attributes of herself. The turquoise gown she wore made her pale blue eyes stand out. She wore blue often because of her eye colour.

'My eyes,' she answered finally. 'I like the colour.'

'You have beautiful eyes,' Lottie agreed. 'And such thick, long lashes. I would give my eyeteeth for such lashes. Look again and tell me something else.'

Violet appraised her appearance and noted the smoothness of her skin. 'My skin is very clear.'

'It's lovely. And what of your hair?'

Violet shrugged. 'It's brown.'

'Oh, it's more than brown.' Lottie stretched a hand towards Violet's curls and traced a graceful finger over the pinned locks. 'There are gold tones and even red ones there, too. Did you know that?'

Violet tilted her head towards the mirror and caught the glint of the aforementioned colours in the glass.

Imagine that.

'Now tell me what you don't like,' Lottie said.

That took no thought whatsoever. 'My body, the thickness of my brows, my upturned nose, how I look in—'

'Your upturned nose?' Lottie shook her head and stood behind Violet. 'Your nose is perfect, your brows are wonderfully shaped and add expression to your face, and your body is not at all what you think.'

Violet slid her gaze from the mirror.

'It is *en mode* at present to be ridiculously thin, yes, but it is not worth starving yourself over,' Lottie continued. 'You have a lovely figure with a slender waist and a full bosom. I am candid in my lessons, you must understand. Believe me when I tell you that men love breasts.'

Violet's eyes went wide, and Lottie laughed. The sound was sweet and gentle, not at all mocking. 'I assure you, Lady Violet, you will captivate any man who takes the time to speak with you. You happen to have a particularly nice décolletage.'

Violet regarded her figure in the mirror once more. The tops of her breasts rose round and full over the neckline of her gown. She'd always hated it, thinking it as extra flesh squishing up from her clothing.

'Has the gentleman you fancy happened to glance down more than once?' Lottie asked. 'Even the good ones can't help themselves from taking a peek or two.'

Violet recalled how Seth's gaze had lingered on her bosom, how he'd cupped her breasts and groaned. Her cheeks burned at the realisation and Lottie laughed again.

'I knew it!' She spun Violet around and beamed at her. 'Darling, you must admit that you are far comelier than you've duped yourself into thinking all these years.'

'I suppose it isn't as bad as I had assumed,' Violet conceded.

'No,' Lottie said earnestly. 'It is far, far better. You are beautiful, Violet, and I do not mean that as a platitude. I mean it with the utmost sincerity. I have no doubt your gentleman did, too.'

A smile spread over Violet's lips. All at once the crinkles of anxiety smoothed from her mind. Seth had told her he thought her beautiful the night of her debut, that he'd wanted to kiss her.

'Thank you.' Violet beamed a smile at Lottie, grateful that the burden of humiliation and doubt had been plucked from her chest the way one might remove a stone from their shoe.

A vase of hothouse flowers stood behind Lottie. A new one, filled with pink and red tulips. 'From a friend?' Violet asked with a smile.

Lottie regarded the flowers with a sigh. 'A friend who is rather insistent, I'm afraid. One I wish I could welcome back into my life.'

'It's complicated,' Violet surmised.

Lottie gave a sad smile. 'Not all past hurts can be healed with time.'

Violet understood exactly. All the time in the world would not change what she'd done with Lord Fordson. It certainly would not undo her actions and make her pure once more.

Lady Cotsworth's ball had been as awful as Seth had anticipated. Worse. He hadn't lasted beyond the first set. As before, it had been too hot, too crowded, too bright. He'd had no distractions to take the tension from his mind.

Now, he paced his bedchamber and ran a hand through his hair. The footfalls of his shoes were silent on the thick carpet.

At least he was alone. Bennet had been fluttering around him like a nervous hen. But then, William's former valet was a little too attentive in his duties. Too eager to please.

Ghosts edged into Seth's thoughts—Brent's bright blue eyes, afraid in that fraction of a moment before his life had ended. Brave. Selfless. Death.

A knot of emotion lodged in Seth's throat.

It should have been him, damn it.

He lifted his glass of brandy and hurled it at the fireplace in a surge of rageful energy. The glass hit the hearth and shattered into pieces as the liquid flared in the flames.

It should have been him.

He sank on to a leather chair before the broad fireplace and cradled his head in his hands, squeezing, as if he could crush the images from his thoughts.

Think of Violet. Think of that kiss.

He brought it forefront in his mind and immediately the knots in his upper back melted. Her mouth, sweet and soft, that delicious moan that spoke of passion hidden beneath her reserved exterior. It had been torture to stop. But he knew if he kept going, he wouldn't be able to control where his hands went. How he'd longed to learn the body he'd dreamt of for so long, eliciting more of those breathless little whimpers of pleasure.

A knock came at the door. An unwelcome interruption. He'd told Bennet he didn't wish to be disturbed, but clearly the old valet wouldn't be so easily put off.

Startled from his fantasies, he shifted his focus to the ornamental carving on the corner of the fireplace. It was a medallion with a corner chipped off and repainted with the same white paint as the other. He'd never noticed it until now. The house was full of these old wounds that had been polished over with paint, with stucco. Even with the fresh covering, the old wounds were still there beneath, pocked and chipped and broken.

A knock came again.

He scrubbed a hand over his face. The urge to

roar at his intruder gripped him. He didn't want this disturbance to ruin the solace his aching head so sorely needed.

The knocking finally stopped. The reprieve, however, was short lived and followed by the soft click of the doorknob.

'Leave me,' he said from the cradle of his hands where he held his face.

'Seth.' The quiet, feminine voice was tender and painfully familiar.

He didn't want her to see him, not like this. 'Please, Caroline.'

The rustle of her skirts whispered across the room and carried with it the gentle scent of lilacs as she sank on to the floor in front of him.

'You left the ball early.' Her tone was absent of accusation. 'Bennet told us you were unwell.'

'I am and I'd very much like to be left alone.' He kept his hands over his face, desperate to be rid of her. To be rid of all people. He wanted nothing more than the press of solace, without questions, without concern or probing glances.

He'd left the ball almost as soon as he'd arrived. And even those few moments had been unbearable. The woman he'd been speaking with, a marquess's daughter who had just been introduced to him and whose name he couldn't recall, had prattled on, her shrill voice like sharp-edged pins in his ears, her cloying perfume suffocating. He had been rude, no doubt.

He didn't care.

He couldn't care.

There was so little of himself left to worry over it.

'Seth, what troubles you so?' She put her hands over his and carefully lowered them. 'You haven't been the same since you've returned. We used to talk.'

He kept his gaze fixed on the floor, not wanting to respond, not bothering to look up. Not when it took so much energy to do so.

He *used to* tell her everything long ago. When life was simple. When the worst weight on his conscience had been infuriating their mother or staying out until dawn. Long before he'd spent years fighting one battle after another, watching men die in front of him, facing down death with each new fight. Waterloo. His chest went tight.

'Seth.' Caroline raised his face to look at her. 'Do you remember how we used to talk late into the night?'

He nodded, unable to speak around the ache knotting at the back of his throat. What would it be like to tell her, to share the burden of memories slowly crushing beyond the armour of his ribs and squeezing his heart, his lungs?

Could he truly tell her how every time he closed his eyes, he saw that cannonball hit Brent? Could he tell her how social engagements with the crush of bodies and rise of a collective body heat was enough to put him back in the centre of that terrible battle on Mont-Saint-Jean?

Even thinking of saying these things aloud brought the stinging threat of tears to his eyes. He slid his gaze from hers lest she see his shame, his cowardice. He was a soldier, a man who led others into battle, not some weeping ninny.

'Is it because of the man you mentioned?' Caroline asked. 'Your soldier who...' Her words trailed off, as though she couldn't bring herself to repeat what he'd shared.

His mother had scarcely spoken to him since that incident, so appalled by the details he had so crassly thrown at her in spite. The reminder of what he'd said summoned him back to his senses.

He had not returned to London and assumed the earldom to be Caroline's confidant. No, he was here as man of the house to care for her and Lady Dalton. To be their pillar of strength. He could not let them know how terribly he crumbled beneath his polished exterior.

She didn't need to know that his skull was etched deep inside with horrors, or how he dreaded sleep and the awful terrors the night brought, or how simple memories could make his heart race, his breath pant.

He cleared his throat, breaking through the hurt.

Be a man, damn it.

'I have been in communication with Lottie,' he said finally.

Caroline frowned. 'We don't have to talk about that now.'

But they did. *He* did. 'She will see you tomorrow evening, just after midnight,' he continued. 'You'll need to wear a domino and mask, both of which have been provided.' He indicated the box tied with a black silk bow that had been delivered while they were at Lady Cotsworth's ball.

Caroline shook her head. 'Seth, we can discuss my lessons with Lottie tomorrow.'

'I meant to give it to you in the morning.' He proceeded on as if she had not spoken, in an effort to be well and done with the conversation. He lifted a shoulder in a casual shrug. 'Since you are here, it seems rather ridiculous to hold off on giving it to you.'

Caroline didn't move to take the box. She stood upright, the red silk of her fine evening gown crumpled and crinkled from where she'd knelt in front of him as she pleaded with him. Her gaze was fixed on him now, glistening with pain.

'I don't know why you won't talk to me,' she said with measured words. 'Something has been hollowing you out from the inside and it's breaking my heart to see it.'

The knot returned to Seth's throat, tighter and causing a deep ache.

Caroline gave a chagrined nod. 'I am always here if you change your mind.'

Seth kept his face impassive despite the storm of emotion raging inside of him. Caroline was the one person he had tried the hardest to never let down. Until, apparently, this moment.

She looked at the box with the black-silk ribbon and issued forth a quiet sigh. 'Thank you for allowing me to see Lottie. I know that was not an easy decision.'

'I want you to be happy.'

Caroline gave a wry smile. 'The same as I want for you, dear Brother.' She leaned forward, pressed a kiss to his cheek and departed the room, leaving the box from Lottie behind.

Seth pushed up from the chair and made his way to the window. The curtains were drawn, thick, heavy things that they were, but he had a mind for one last look at the elm tree before descending into the hell that passed for sleep these days. Perhaps visions of an angel would keep him from the devil's clutches this night.

He pushed aside the heavy green velvet and looked out to the garden below that adjoined to his. A hackney drove up to the back of the town house next door and a woman alighted from the carriage, the same woman he had seen before.

Except this time, he recognised that domino and mask. They were the very same ones sitting in the box with the black-silk ribbon that he'd received for Caroline. From Lottie.

The realisation struck him like a jolt of lightning. Lady Violet had been attending clandestine lessons with a courtesan.

Chapter Thirteen

Violet kept her head down as she navigated through the garden at the back of her home, intent on the rear door where she would be safe. Her heart galloped in her chest as her feet swished over the low-cut grass.

How did people sneak about without their hearts giving out?

She was only halfway to her destination when the worst sound cut through the silent night air: that of a door opening. And not the one she ran towards. She pulled the hood of her domino low and prayed that she might, by some miracle, blend in with the darkness and remain unseen.

That, however, was not to be the case.

'Lady Violet,' Seth's voice called quietly out to her.

If she were more adept at illicit activities, she might have been able to continue on as though she had heard nothing, then feign ignorance with an expert skill the following day. But Violet was an obedient girl. She always had been.

With the exception, of course, of that night of her debut. And she'd paid dearly for it and would continue to do so for the rest of her life.

She snapped bolt upright at the sound of her name being called and—horror of horrors—issued forth an anxious squeak.

'I didn't mean to frighten you.' He spoke in a hushed tone, clearly trying to keep from calling attention to them.

'Oh.' She waved a hand, the gesture stiff and awkward. 'You didn't. I was just…in the garden… um…admiring the flowers?' She turned a hopeful glance in his direction.

'You should see the peonies,' he offered drily. 'They're quite lovely this time of year if you can see them through your mask.'

'I thought violets were your favourite,' she said, unable to help herself.

'Oh, indeed they are. The loveliest by far.' He tilted his head at her. 'Even when adorned all in black with her beautiful face covered.'

Beautiful.

Lottie had called her beautiful. Indeed, when Violet stood before the mirror and opened her heart to what Lottie told her, Violet had even *felt* beautiful.

The very thought of it bolstered her confidence. She made her way over to the hedge separating their properties and gave him a coy smile. 'Is it not mysterious?'

He wasn't wearing a jacket or cravat and his shirt was untied at the neck, revealing his strong throat. Such an appearance was decidedly improper and intimate.

'Oh, very mysterious.' His gaze skimmed her face, flicked down to her bosom, visible through the parted cloak, then darted away.

Violet almost chuckled at that. Lottie had been right. Men could not help themselves. Even the good ones.

'Dare I ask what illicit activities you've been engaged in this evening?' He lifted his brow in a very earl-like manner.

Her face flamed hot and she was glad for the shadows cast over the darkened garden. She ought to make up a benign lie. Gambling would be an optimal choice.

It was not unheard of for ladies to don disguises such as the one Violet now wore and attend gaming hells. But if he probed her with questions or for answers, ones he well knew the answer to from his past experiences, she would certainly falter.

'May I guess?' he asked.

Violet swept her hand to him, palm up in invitation. 'By all means.'

'There is only one reason I can think that would have Lady Violet Lavell, notoriously missish wallflower, slinking through the night in a disguise.'

Violet lifted her chin, giving him her full attention.

He strode towards the gap in the hedge. 'You're burgling the homes along Grosvenor Street and you plan to abscond with your booty to a faraway island.' He made his way through the gap with two large, careful steps. 'Or you're attending private lessons from the very courtesan I asked you about.'

Violet wanted the ground to open up and swallow her. She regarded the firm soil underfoot and knew such a thing would be impossible. There was nothing for it but to tell the truth.

'You've caught me.' She put up her hands in surrender as he stepped closer. 'Do you think diamonds or rubies for my first day sailing in search of an island to inhabit?'

'Sapphires,' he answered without hesitation. 'With the blue of your eyes and the brilliant ocean at your back, you'll look utterly enchanting. Dare I ask if you need a second in command for this ship you intend to…commandeer? I do have considerable experience in battle.'

'Very well,' she replied breezily. 'I'd considered hiring a pirate, but I believe you'll do quite nicely.'

'I hope not to disappoint.' There was a note of sensuality hovering above his words.

Violet's skin flushed with desire and her heart doubled its beat.

He stepped closer, narrowing the distance between them and carrying with him that clean, wonderful scent of his soap and sensual tease of warm male. 'Why are you, of all women, seeking out Lottie?' he asked.

She parted her lips, uncertain what to say.

'If that is indeed where you've been.' His brows furrowed. 'Unless you have a lover…?' The question hung in the air with uncertainty.

'No,' Violet gasped. 'Of course not.'

Seth's mouth curled into an easy smile that made her recall the feel of his kiss.

'Yes, I've been seeing Lottie.' Violet glanced away with her admission, too embarrassed to watch his expression as she confessed.

'Because you can't get a husband?' Seth probed.

Violet sighed, hating how her whole body burned in what must be the greatest blush in all of London. She couldn't tell him of her plans with her gossip column, so she had no choice but to lie. 'Yes,' she breathed.

The skin around Seth's eyes tightened. 'The men of the *ton* are all fools.' He tenderly took her hand and lifted it to his lips. 'You don't need Lottie to help you win a husband, my darling Violet.'

A clash of emotions lurched through Violet. Excitement for the implication that there might be a man who was not a fool, one who was ready to claim her hand in marriage. Fear of having to be honest with him about her ruination.

Could she do it?

'What do you mean?' she asked through numb lips.

He took her hand and bent over it, delivering a tender kiss on her gloved knuckles. 'Good evening, Lady Violet.'

'What do you mean?' she asked again, her heart thudding so violently in her chest, she worried she might retch.

He straightened with a wink. 'Time will tell.'

He was impossibly handsome with his mussed hair and dark eyes, the way he watched her as though she were the only woman in all of existence. It would not be the way he would regard her if she was forced to reveal her greatest, darkest secret.

Her stomach slid down to her toes as he picked his way through the gap in the hedge and returned to his own home. She stayed beneath the elm tree for a long moment, letting her racing pulse still to a heavy, dread-filled beat.

What had she got herself into?

Seth hoped the odour of the public house wouldn't stick with him after his departure. Especially not with what he planned to do once his meeting with Nash had concluded. He couldn't possibly go reeking of old tallow smoke, sweat and ale.

Even in mid-afternoon, the interior of the public

house was awash with shadows despite the weak sunshine trying to eke its way through the dirty paned windows. The seats around them were full, mostly with men who appeared defeated and tired, some wearing the vivid red jackets of soldiers who had fought for the British Army at Waterloo.

Seth fixed his attention on Nash.

The former Runner hunched over his drink as though he could curl into himself and disappear. 'After Pattinson left London, he made his way to Bath. He was recognised and promptly left before the ball at the Upper Assembly Rooms that evening.'

'Where did he go afterwards?' Seth demanded. 'Did he attempt to sell the jewels?'

Nash's gaze slid about the room, taking note of every soul who entered, every person who rose or sat. He never once moved his head, keeping his actions discreet. 'No one has seen the jewels. I'll notify you if I locate them.'

'You'll find where he went next?' Seth lifted his glass of porter and took a sip of the heavy, dark brew.

Nash nodded. 'I hear the bastard is skittish, so I can't move as swiftly as I'd prefer. I'll report back to you once I have more information.'

Nash's eyes tightened.

'What is it?' Seth asked.

'Sometimes these men emerge after Parliament

recesses, when everyone departs for their country estates.'

Seth tapped his finger on the spotted glass of his porter. 'It doesn't matter how long it takes. I want him brought to justice.'

'Then it will be done.' Nash lifted his own glass and the two men drank their beer down.

Seth swallowed a second time to clear the grittiness of the dregs, thanked the man and took his leave out into the muddy streets where a hackney awaited him. He didn't have to sniff his jacket to know it held the fetid odour of stale tallow smoke.

It was indeed fortunate then that he lived directly next door to his destination: Hollingston House.

Bennet was beside himself with unmitigated elation as he helped Seth into his second outfit that day. The valet even insisted on another shave and proceeded to do so with such a skilled hand, Seth didn't feel a whisper of chafed skin afterward. The old valet might be a missish sort with a proclivity towards meticulous detail, but he did do a damn good job.

Seth looked in the mirror and nodded in approval. He looked far more respectable than he was. Even his unruly hair had been combed smooth. 'Good God, man, you are a wonder at what you do.'

Bennet puffed out his chest with pride. 'It's kind of you to say, my lord.'

'Well, it's the truth.' Seth clapped the man on the shoulder with gratitude. 'Thank you.'

With that, Seth made his way next door and requested a moment of Lord Hollingston's time. Nerves jittered through him as he wondered if he was doing the right thing. For him, yes. But for her…?

He was summoned almost immediately into the Earl's study, before he could allow himself the luxury of second-guessing his decision further.

There was a lot you could tell by the items a man surrounded himself with. Those who had paintings of every family member since the dawn of time had a tendency to look down their nose at anyone less aristocratic than they. Men who kept an array of liquors readily available, lined up in various shades of amber in cut-crystal decanters, had a penchant for alcohol.

Then there was Lord Hollingston who had simply books. A considerable number of books. The shelves covered the walls from the thickly padded carpet to the scrollwork on the ceiling above.

'Lord Dalton, forgive my delay in greeting you upon your return.' Hollingston rose from his seat behind the large desk. 'Thank you for requesting to see me.'

Seth crossed the room and shook Hollingston's hand. 'I confess I came with a purpose today.' He hadn't realised how hot his palms had become until they were encased in Hollingston's cool, dry hand.

An uncomfortable unease crept into Seth's awareness. He hadn't anticipated being so nervous.

'I assumed as much.' Hollingston's eyes crinkled with a smile. He went to a side table with one small decanter upon it, splashed a finger of liquid into a glass and handed it to Seth. 'I'm afraid all I have is brandy.'

Seth would take straight fire at this point. He accepted the glass with an appreciative nod. 'Brandy is fine, thank you.'

The Earl poured a second glass and sat in the large chair behind the desk. 'Please have a seat.'

Seth settled into proffered chair, which gave a wretched groan of ancient springs beneath his weight.

What the devil?

Seth cleared his throat to mask the creak of the springs still grumbling underneath him. 'I'm here to ask if you might consider allowing me to court your daughter.'

Hollingston furrowed his brows. 'You want to court Violet.'

'I do.' And it was true. Seth had wanted to court Violet for the better part of his life. Only, he had known she could do better. He still knew she could do better. But he would be damned if he let her attend lessons with a courtesan because she felt she wasn't good enough.

Hedgehog leapt on to the desk at that very moment in one deft move and splayed out on the polished surface. Hollingston untied the green bonnet from the cat's head, tossed it aside with disdain and rubbed at the fur between the feline's ears. 'Why?'

'I beg your pardon?' Seth asked.

Hedgehog's vibrating purr occupied the silence between them. Hollingston continued to stroke the little beast. 'Violet is my fifth daughter and her dowry is not as substantial as a first-born debutante who is seeking an eligible earl.' He lifted his gaze from the cat to Seth.

'Money is of little concern to me,' Seth replied.

Hollingston lifted his brows and frowned, tilting his head as though considering such a response. 'My daughter has been uninterested in marriage for years. Are you aware of this?'

'Perhaps she hadn't met the right eligible Earl.' Seth had said it in a bid to sound confident, but the words came out with an arrogant edge. He was certainly the furthest thing from the right eligible Earl. How the devil was he supposed to convince her father he was?

Hollingston speared him with a glare. 'You broke her heart the night of her debut. Do not think that has been forgotten.'

Seth shifted on the chair and it gave out a

squeal. He immediately stilled. 'I haven't forgotten either.' Seth considered his next words carefully. 'I have apologised for my shortcomings to Lady Violet and explained my flawed frame of mind then. I was a troubled youth.'

Hollingston snorted.

'A *very* troubled youth,' Seth amended. 'I'm not that man any more and have been trying to prove it since I returned.'

Only he was still flawed. With different demons. It would be best to put an end to this now, to simply walk out. But thoughts of Violet—her laugh, her smile, her kiss—stayed his concerns and left him rooted in the squeaky chair.

A door closed somewhere on the first floor. Hedgehog leapt from the desk and darted from the room.

Hollingston chuckled. 'We all come second to Felicity.'

'I believe Lady Violet's opinion of marriage might have altered,' Seth continued.

Hollingston leaned back into his large chair. 'Oh? Why do you say that?'

Why else would Lady Violet be attending lessons with Lottie if not to seek out a husband? Seth nearly asked the question aloud, but the questioning look on the older man's face stopped him.

Confound it. Lord Hollingston did not know his daughter was having lessons with the notorious former courtesan.

'People change,' Seth said simply.

Hollingston nodded slowly. 'If what you say is true and my Violet truly has had a change of heart, then I give you my permission to ask if she is willing to be courted by you. If she says yes—and that is a very heavy *if*—then you have my permission.'

'Thank you, Lord Hollingston.' Seth rose from the chair as it gave a rusty cry of indignation.

The Earl simply gave a little grunt. 'Don't thank me until she agrees.' He narrowed his eyes. 'And if she does, heaven help you if you break her heart again.'

Everything in Seth winced. He would not hurt her again. No matter what it cost him.

Seth smiled at the older man and waited for the servant to show him to the drawing room. The doors opened almost immediately, and Felicity skipped in with Hedgehog bounding behind her.

She stopped short and gave him a fine curtsy. 'Lord Dalton.'

Hedgehog stared blandly up at him, already adorned in a pink-silk hat with his little grey ears poking out of the top through two slits cut into it. Good God, how did Felicity have so many?

'I say, Hedgehog's bonnet is quite fetching today.' He approached them and patted the cat on the head. 'I'm waiting for your aunt Violet. I mean to speak with her.'

'Alone?' Felicity giggled.

He winked. 'I have something very important to ask her.'

Felicity grinned and nodded. She hefted Hedgehog into her arms, carrying the creature like a doll, and made her way back towards the open double doors.

'My mother says Violet is too fat to attract a fine husband,' Felicity said. 'But I don't think she's fat. I think she's pretty and perfect just how she is. And I think you would be a fine husband for her.'

'Felicity, who are you speaking to?' Violet's voice rose over Felicity's.

The little girl jumped in surprise. 'Good luck.' She plopped Hedgehog to the ground, and together they scampered off as Lady Violet rounded the corner.

She stopped abruptly and her mouth fell open in surprise. Her hands immediately went to her hair where the dark strands were carefully pinned into place.

He bowed to her. 'Lady Violet, I'd like to speak with you alone if we may.'

'Let us go to the drawing room, and I'll ring for tea.' Contrary to her words, her smile was brittle and her face pale. As if the surprise of him being there, of the obviousness of what their conversation would be, was entirely unwelcome.

Chapter Fourteen

Violet should have expected Seth's arrival at Hollingston House. In fact, she had expected it. It was just that she had not come up with a satisfactory response to what he ostensibly intended to ask.

She took her time leading him to the drawing room as her mind scrambled for purchase and a logical explanation.

'I trust you are well,' she said politely.

His smile was tinged with confusion. 'Yes, of course, and you?'

About to be ill.

'Perfectly well, thank you.' She opened the double doors to the drawing room with its decorative plaster white walls, yellow-silk curtains and lush carpet. Usually the room gave her a sense of happiness. Now it appeared more sallow than sunny. 'Here we are,' she said brightly.

Too brightly?

'I'll ring for a servant to bring tea.' She reached for the bell pull.

Seth shook his head. 'That isn't necessary, Violet.' He wore a fine, dark jacket and white cravat with a deep-red silk waistcoat. His wild hair had been tamed into place and there wasn't a hint of a whisker on his smooth jaw.

He had taken care with his appearance before arriving.

Her hands went once more to her own hair. She'd just removed her bonnet. Surely it was a mess. Surely *she* was a mess. After a stroll through Hyde Park to help work out some of Felicity's pent-up energy, Violet was entirely mussed and not properly prepared for company.

Or a proposal, for that matter.

She pressed her hand to her chest as if she could catch and still the anxious flutter of her heartbeat.

'I've enjoyed spending time with you in the garden,' Seth said.

Something cold and unyielding gripped her. *Please, no.*

'It's been quite pleasant,' she admitted. And indeed it had been. Why could it not remain as it was? Secret and hidden.

'I'd like to spend more time with you,' he said. 'Away from the garden, where we do not have to worry about prying eyes and whispers.'

'There will always be prying eyes and whispers.' She gave a weak smile.

'I have the utmost care for your reputation, Lady Violet, and will not see you besmirched.'

Besmirched.

It was such an ugly word. It sounded as if it had a big charcoal line crossed through it.

'I see,' she said softly.

He reached for her and, even as she hated the idea of marriage, of being forced to expose her secret, she craved his touch. It was for that reason she did not move away.

His hand curled around hers and he closed the distance between them, bringing the familiar smell of him that had followed her into her dreams the night before. That icy grip of fear loosened, softening with her affection for him.

His dark, fathomless gaze searched hers. 'Lady Violet, it would be a great honour if you would allow me to court you.'

She swallowed.

She wanted to say yes. She wanted to say no. Instead, silence pressed heavily between them as her pulse ticked with a frenzied beat at her temples.

'Your father said you had no mind for marriage.' Seth's warm timbre lightened the silence. 'I gather he is not aware of your visits with Lottie.'

Oh, bother.

Violet cringed. 'I…didn't tell him.'

'I presume your mother is not aware either.' He shook his head. 'I believe I may have got the wrong impression. Or perhaps I am unfavourable to you. I assumed you were interested in marriage since you were engaging in those lessons…'

Those lessons.

Violet's face burned.

'It isn't you,' Violet said quickly. 'It's…'

'You?' Seth suggested.

'Yes,' Violet said miserably. 'I…' She went through her mind, upending every idea she could imagine in search of a proper explanation. 'I am afraid of marriage. It's why I've been seeing Lottie, to help me get over my fear.'

There. And what was best, it wasn't even a lie.

'I see.' Seth's worried gaze did not appear any more relieved. 'If that is indeed the case, would you perhaps consider allowing me to court you? I don't need an answer immediately.'

Violet pressed her lips together. The simple action reminded her of how her mouth had tingled after their kiss, how her entire body had glowed from his attention, alight with desire and pleasure.

Dangerous. Dangerous. Dangerous.

'I'll think about it,' she whispered.

He smiled at her. 'I'm very pleased to hear it.'

'Will you be at Lady Norrick's soirée tonight?' Violet asked.

'I believe my mother has confirmed our attendance.'

'I will be there,' Violet said.

'Then I look forward to it.' He studied her, as

though memorising her face. A soft smile touched the corners of his lips. 'You are so very beautiful, Violet.'

His words were like honey pouring over her, golden and sweet and perfect. He lifted a hand to her face and hovered just before actually touching her jaw. She tilted her chin slightly higher, making it easier to touch his lips to hers.

But he did not. Instead, he stepped back to put a proper amount of space between them and bowed. 'I shall see you this evening, Lady Violet. Please do consider my request.'

'I will,' she said softly. 'Thank you for coming, Lord Dalton. And for your patience and understanding with my response.'

He paused as though he intended to say more, but instead offered well wishes for a good day and departed. She watched his proud, handsome figure disappear from the room and her knees went soft, barely strong enough to keep her upright.

As soon as the door clicked closed behind him, she sagged against the wall, nearly upsetting a small table with fragile notions. The door to the drawing room opened even as her head still spun. Lord and Lady Hollingston stood in the yawning doorway, their expressions keen.

'Well?' Violet's mother came closer. 'Will you allow him to court you?'

Violet's stomach tightened. 'I told him I would think about it.'

'That you would…?' Lady Hollingston gave an exasperated sigh. 'Violet, where are your senses? This is the best offer you will receive. Most likely the only one. You are too old to attract anyone else. And certainly age will not do your figure any favours—'

'Enough, Judith.' Lord Hollingston shot his wife a hard look. 'Is it any wonder she lost her confidence after her debut when you shamed her into wearing the dress you preferred?'

'Is it any wonder she detests the idea of marriage when you offer such an example of being a husband?' Lady Hollingston snapped back.

Violet pushed off the wall and waited for their bickering to stop. Their disagreements were a common occurrence. They used to hide their lack of affection for one another, but it had become more open as the years crept onwards and the house emptied of children.

Theirs was indeed an unhappy marriage, but that had never been the cause of Violet's trepidation. If anything, it had been the reason she'd wanted to wed, to escape.

'If you feel as though you can mother her better than me, then by all means.' Lady Hollingston held her hand out in invitation towards Violet and quit the room with her back ramrod straight and her skirt whipping around her ankles.

'Should I call you Mother now?' Violet asked with a little smile.

He scoffed. 'Insult me and see where it gets you.' He winked to soften his words. 'Lord Dalton seemed to think you had taken a liking to him. That perhaps you had changed your mind about marriage. Is that true?'

'I do like Lord Dalton,' she said cautiously.

'You do know not all marriages are like the one I have with your mother.' He cast a scowl over his shoulder. 'I didn't even much care for her when we first wed. Her family was ridiculously wealthy.' He sighed. 'And my title had little behind it but a name.'

Violet said nothing, afraid of interrupting this rare confession from her father. Generally his life, his past, was something he did not speak of.

As abruptly as it had started, it stopped. He smiled at her. 'If you enjoy Lord Dalton's company and you promised to think about the matter, I hope you truly take it into careful consideration. It would be a shame to lose out on a good match due to pride.'

He pressed a kiss to her forehead and left her in the capacious room with a war of indecision raging in her mind.

Was it worth the risk?

As soon as Seth entered the soirée, Rawley was at his side, asking after Caroline.

'Even if I told you she was here, which she isn't, you wouldn't do a thing about it.' Seth frowned at his friend, fighting back the temptation to tell Rawley what Caroline had been reduced to doing because of his crippling shyness.

'I keep meaning to approach her.' Rawley swiped a hand over his parted hair. 'I even walk towards her, but every time I get close, once I see her…' Rawley shook his head. 'She's so beautiful.' He pressed his lips together like an old man. 'I believe you may be mistaken about her feelings. Surely she doesn't mean *me*.'

'She does mean you and you're driving her mad with your inability to approach her.' Seth tried to keep his tone tolerant.

Rawley was a good man. A shy one, but a good one, none the less. It was on the edge of Seth's tongue to tell the Viscount the lengths he'd forced Caroline to go to in seeking lessons from Lottie.

In the end, Seth swallowed the words down and patted his friend on the shoulder. 'Out of consideration for my sanity and the number of times I must endure your name being brought to my attention, please speak to her when next you see her.'

Rawley grinned at Seth. 'Truly?'

'Truly.' Seth grimaced. 'I don't know how much more I can stomach hearing about Lord Rawley.' He put the back of his hand to his brow in mockery of a feminine swoon.

'Now you're just being rude,' Rawley accused despite the twinkle in his eyes.

'I wish that was indeed the way of it,' Seth muttered.

A woman with dark hair in a lovely white-silk gown with blue ribbons came into Seth's peripheral vision. *Violet.* His pulse tripped.

He'd been home scarcely a fortnight and already he couldn't take the tedium of so many balls and dinner parties and soirées. On and on they came in an endless stream. The time they took to prepare for, especially with a valet like Bennet, the polite facade Seth had to plaster on to his face, the idle conversations that required too little of his brain and too much of his patience.

But then there was Violet. The *only* reason he was in attendance at all.

Truly. He had a note prepared to beg off from the soirée, complaining of an ailment he presumed would serve as a valid excuse.

Lady Hollingston saw him and practically dragged Violet in his direction. The woman gave him a sharp-toothed smile. 'Lord Dalton, what a lovely surprise.'

But it wasn't the Countess who drew his attention, not when Violet stood before him with a smile on her full lips and amusement sparkling in her eyes.

'Would you mind if I took a turn about the room with your daughter?' he asked Lady Hollingston.

'Not at all,' she replied, her demeanour overly gracious.

Seth offered his arm to Violet, who slid her hand into the crook of his elbow, bringing with her that wonderful, sweet, powdery scent of violets. She didn't speak until they were out of earshot of her mother.

'I hope you're aware of how happy you've made my mother,' Violet said.

Seth recalled how Lady Dalton had ordered Violet's debut gown in a smaller size and suddenly found he didn't much care about what pleased the Countess.

'It isn't her happiness that concerns me.' He smiled down at Violet. 'You look beautiful this evening.'

Colour touched her cheeks and she thanked him.

The soirée was decidedly less crowded than the balls he had attended to date. And thank God for it. He might be able to actually make it through an evening. Especially with Violet at his side.

'I appreciate you taking the time from Lottie's to be here with me,' he teased suggestively in a low voice meant only for her.

'You must promise to keep my secret,' she whispered.

The lilting music grew louder as they approached the musicians and then softer as they passed around them.

'I assure you,' he said. 'I shall guard all of your

secrets to my dying breath. Might I ask a question, though?'

Violet's slender arm on his tensed slightly. 'Yes.'

In truth, Seth had a string of questions he had wanted to ask her, but settled on the one most pressing. 'Why are you afraid of marriage?'

She laughed, an unexpected sound tense with apparent nerves. 'It's a tedious story.'

He'd made her uncomfortable. While he hadn't intended to put her off, he didn't want to abandon the question. As an earl, his duty was to wed. He couldn't see himself marrying some insipid debutante. He wanted Violet, with life brimming over from her bright smiles and lovely blue eyes, with her sharp wit and confidence. The woman he didn't deserve.

There was something about her that settled him. All the anxiety usually roiling through him seemed to calm when she was around. He liked the relaxed ease he could enjoy while speaking with her. As though Waterloo had never happened, as if his mind wasn't terribly broken.

'I don't mind tedious stories,' he replied patiently.

'My parents.' Her fingers curled around his arm, gripping him more firmly. 'Their marriage is—'

A bang exploded from behind Seth. Quicker than gunshot he shoved Violet behind him even as the images descended upon him.

Brent standing straight and tall, his blue stare meeting Seth's for one brief, determined moment before the cannonball slammed into the young soldier.

Blood everywhere. On Seth's uniform. In his mouth. Hot pieces of the man who had been in front of him.

Oh, God.

Bullets whizzing by him, slow and thick, as if in water, like fat bees buzzing past. Until one tore into the head of the man beside him. The collision of metal with flesh sending the soldier careening backwards…

Blue eyes entered his line of sight, watching him carefully, mouth moving slowly.

'It was a tray,' a gentle voice said as the woman's lips moved. 'A dropped tray just behind you. Come, let us go outside.'

A hand curled around his and he found himself being led through a room that was threatening to close in on him out into the cool embrace of darkness.

'Breathe.' That same voice spoke in his ear.

He sucked in a mouthful of air. It carried with it the sweetness of flowers, a damp chill of night on the edge of a rainstorm. There was no gunpowder in his nostrils. No blood in his mouth. He blinked and found he stood on the veranda with his hands braced on a stone railing.

A comforting heat pressed against his fingers.

He glanced to his left hand and found a woman's lace glove resting atop it. He followed her arm to a pair of perfect breasts, then a beautiful face. A familiar face.

Violet.

Mortification fired through him. 'Forgive me.' He cleared his throat and straightened. 'I…'

I what? I'm a coward? I'm broken? I can never leave this hell in my head? Or maybe, *You should forget me before I draw you into these depths with me?*

She gave him a gentle smile, one absent of pity, thank God. 'You needn't explain if you'd rather not.' Her hand continued to rest on his and he had no plans to move it.

In truth, he didn't care to explain it. He never wanted to speak of it again.

However, he had an obligation to. He had asked to court her because he hoped to eventually wed her. If he were to do either of those things, she should know him. Truly know him.

And that started with telling her the truth.

Chapter Fifteen

Seth drew in a deep, calming breath in anticipation of what he needed to say, what he'd been dreading to confess. 'I am not the same man I was when I left for the military.'

'I'm quite aware of that,' Violet said it sweetly and he knew she misunderstood.

'Yes, outside of all that.' Seth looked out to the garden with the small lamps burning like golden globes in the distance. Half the moon's face was hidden, obscuring the natural brilliance of its light. It looked like a night for wooing angels, not sharing demons.

The veranda behind them was empty, lit by the glow from the town-house windows. The muted sounds of laughter and music wafted from the closed double doors.

He and Violet were alone on the balcony, but for how long?

This was the ideal opportunity to tell her. Why,

then, did it feel like ripping off a bandage that had become stuck to the wound?

'I spent a lot of my time away fighting in battles,' Seth said. 'But none was as bad as Waterloo.'

Violet kept her attention fixed on him, her face illuminated by the half-moon, making her smooth skin appear creamy. 'I imagine no battles are easy,' she said softly.

He gave a mirthless chuckle. 'They are not. I remember the first time I fought when I—' His mother and Caroline had reacted poorly to the details of Brent's death and he immediately staunched his words lest he cause offence.

'When you…?' Violet asked.

Seth shook his head. 'Such things are not fit for a lady's ears.'

Violet's fingers curled around his hand and it was as if she had wrapped all of him in an embrace. She was comfort and peace and acceptance.

'You needn't worry about me,' she said. 'I am not prone to sensitivity. And I think speaking of it will do you good.'

He nodded. 'My first battle—it was the first time I took a life.' He swallowed around a ball of tension. 'He was an older man with dark hair that had gone grey at the temples and wide brown eyes. I remember thinking of him afterwards, about his family. His sons and daughters, his wife. Maybe he didn't have them, but I imagined he did and he would never come home to them because of me.

It was a horrific realisation, but when you are in the thick of it, when it's you or them…'

Violet's free hand rested on his forearm. 'I am glad it was not you.'

'Sometimes I wonder about how I feel about that,' Seth responded in truth.

Violet's smooth brow crinkled and she opened her mouth to speak, but the doors to the ballroom opened. Quickly, she pulled her hands back.

The warmth she left behind cooled, but a subtle hum of her touch lingered. Through the layers of his gloves and his sleeves, he continued to detect that pleasant presence.

A gentleman passed them with a nod and slipped off into the garden where a woman's soft laugh rose up from the distance.

The veranda went silent once more and Violet regarded Seth anew. 'If you hadn't come back, your mother would have been beside herself.'

He scoffed. 'I doubt that.'

'*I* would have been disappointed,' Violet said.

A smile lifted the corner of his lip at that. 'Would you?'

'Well, you did owe me a dance.' She lifted her chin in a coquettish tilt that made him want to catch her face in his hands and kiss her soundly.

If all worked to his advantage, if the cards fell in his favour, he would have a lifetime to kiss her. Again and again and again. And so much more.

'I'm grateful for having the opportunity to finally make amends for my foolish, youthful mistake.' He cast a surreptitious glance around the empty terrace and slid his hand towards hers, desperate for her touch. 'I only wish I could have returned to you a better man than I am.'

She settled her fingers over his with a shy glance. 'What happened?'

He knew exactly what she meant. 'I didn't think anything could be worse than killing another man. Until my own men died through the years. Ones who I knew had wives and families waiting for them. I was an officer, a captain—those men were my responsibility and I took it seriously.'

Many of his soldiers did come back alive, far more than other regiments, and he was damn proud of that. He cared for his men more than he cared for himself.

'But Waterloo…' Seth gathered his strength against the tightness blazing in his chest. 'It was unlike any battle I'd fought before. It had rained the night before and I'd been with the fellow officers in attendance at the Duchess of Richmond's ball when we learned that Napoleon's army was advancing on Quatre Bras. We were told to go to our regiments. We had no idea what the battle would become. Many of us were still in our dancing slippers.' He tried to give a wry laugh, but it choked off.

'How awful.' Violet shifted closer and cast a look at the door to the ballroom. Their proximity to one another skirted the edge of propriety, but he could not bring himself to ask her to step back. Even for her own good. Not when her nearness brought such comfort.

'We fought there before moving on to Waterloo two days later. It was that battle...' He clenched his jaw. 'It didn't matter what I did to help my men, we were decimated.' He closed his eyes to stave off the visions pressing at his brain. 'The cannons tore through my soldiers. At one point...'

His throat went tight, cutting off his words. He looked out at the garden to gather his wits.

Violet's hand rested on his shoulder. But he shook his head. For the life of him, he could not summon those terrible words.

'What I saw...' He swallowed at the ache, but it did not abate. 'It stays with me.' His voice caught and he had to pause a moment before resuming. 'The battle was so crowded, we were bumping into one another, and it was hot as a furnace with the blasts of the guns and cannons. It was hell: all fire and smoke and death.'

He rubbed his free hand over his face. His palm had been made cold by the stone he'd gripped and was a blissful reprieve against his cheeks.

'Seth.' The way she whispered his name pulled at his heart in the most exquisitely painful way. As if she understood his pain and accepted him despite it.

'It's not just at night in my dreams.' He stared

hard out into the garden so she would not see the pain of his confession. 'It happens during the day as well. The smallest instances will take my thoughts back to Mont-Saint-Jean. When the hearths are lit and there's the chalky odour of flint and fire, when I'm at a ball and someone bumps against me, when the heat of a room blazes from all directions, or drums are added into an orchestra. Who puts drums into an orchestra?'

'The drums were an awful addition,' Violet agreed. 'Or when a serving tray is dropped?'

'Yes.' His head sagged forward. 'This is my worst self, a part of me I don't know that can ever change. I am uncertain if I will always loathe attending social functions because of what emerges from my mind. I may be haunted for ever by memories of men who died too soon, too violently. Especially the man who died for me.'

This was the part of his confession he'd dreaded the most. He'd had it in his mind earlier that night to try to convince her to allow him to court her, not discourage her.

'I wanted you to know this in your consideration.' He looked away as that damn ache returned to his throat. 'I'm a broken man, Violet. I do not know that I can ever be made whole. I think it only fair you ought to be aware of this as you make your decision. I'll never deserve a woman like you.'

She didn't say anything for a long moment. Finally, he turned to study her face in the moonlight and found silent tears running down her cheeks. She blinked at them and swiped her cheeks with the back of her fingers.

The double doors opened and Lady Hollingston stood in the doorway, a foreboding shadow backlit by the soirée. A reminder they had lingered too long outside.

The Countess cleared her throat noisily, calling attention to how close they were standing together.

Violet drew back and cast a regretful look towards her mother. 'The garden. Tonight. I'll give you my answer then.' She swept her hands over her face, clearing away the remnants of her tears.

He inclined his head, knowing the answer he deserved and selfishly hoping against it. 'I'll watch for you.'

She offered him a quick curtsy and swiftly made her way back into the soirée, pausing once to glance at him over her shoulder.

He had not expected his words to sway her towards a swift yes, yet her lack of an answer had struck him deeper than anticipated. It would be better when they were alone, without having to be concerned with potential interruption.

Now came the worst part: the waiting.

Violet was not outside in her garden more than a moment when the rear door to Dalton Place opened. Her heart leapt into her throat and she spun towards the sound.

Seth.

He strode towards her, wearing only his shirt-sleeves and breeches, no hat upon his head or gloves on his hands. His gait was sure and confident, not at all the man who had been cracking at the seams only hours ago.

He made his way to the gap in the hedges and stepped on to her property.

He offered a small bow. 'Good evening, my lady.' His voice was silky smooth in a way she found she rather liked.

'Lord Dalton.' She stepped forward in the dark and took his hands in hers, pulling him towards the shadows where they wouldn't be seen.

He followed her, looming over her, so masculine and powerful. But she knew how vulnerable he could be and it endeared him to her all the more.

'You left after I went inside,' she accused. 'I didn't see you again.'

'I don't relish social events.' He stroked her cheek with the back of his hand. 'I only attended to see you.'

After what he'd told her, she understood why he didn't enjoy social events, yet he had still gone. For her.

'I have your answer.' Had her voice trembled as she spoke? She hoped not, but was nearly certain it had. Her nerves tangled on themselves and left her practically rattling.

This was dangerous. Impulsive. No, she'd thought far too much about it for her decision to be considered impulsive.

It was, however, a great risk.

Courting more often than not led to marriage. Perhaps this time together would show her that Seth had not changed from the reckless youth after all. Perhaps she would realise she'd been a fool to lose her heart to him.

But maybe she would realise he was exactly the man she feared he had become, one who could sweep her off her feet and make her fall in love.

Definitely dangerous.

He was gazing down at her with expectation.

She had wanted to say no. It would have been safer, a guarantee that her secret would remain safe. But learning how imperfect he was had swayed her.

He had shown her his best self when he came to ask her if she would allow him to court her, with his hair immaculately tamed and wearing his finest clothes. But it was his worst self, as he'd called it, that had drawn her.

Because he was not the only one to have a worst self.

'Yes,' she whispered.

'Yes?' He repeated her answer with a modicum of uncertainty. 'You'll allow me to court you? Even…even with what you know of me?'

She nodded, pushing aside her fear for once.

After all, it need not even be considered as yet. It was only courting, not marriage.

'Violet.' He cupped her face in his hands.

Their eyes locked and the connection they'd shared before immediately snapped together again. His mouth lowered to hers as she closed her eyes in expectation.

His lips were as soft as she remembered, brushing ever so tenderly before fitting against hers. Kissing him again was like the satisfied sigh at the end of a good book, or like a meal when one was starving—it was everything right exactly when it was needed most.

He tilted her head back at a deeper angle and her mouth parted. His tongue swept against hers and prickles of pleasure bloomed over her skin. She touched the tip of her tongue to his.

It was brazen to do so and perhaps spoke of experience she shouldn't possess for her to exhibit such audacious behaviour. But she could not hold herself back. Not when she wanted to taste him and his sensual, masculine spiciness. Not when she wanted her hands on his body and his on hers. Not when she had spent the rest of the evening after they met consumed with thoughts of *this*.

Shared breath panted between them as the stroke of her tongue grew bolder and his more aggressive. As if they were both ravenous for the other.

His hands shifted over her back, sliding lower

as their kiss deepened until his palms cupped her bottom and pushed her against that wonderful hardness of his arousal. She gasped in pleasure, her knees so weak with longing they nearly gave out.

He nuzzled her chin with his mouth, then her neck, followed by the sensitive place behind her ear. Delicious chills teased down her skin, thrilling her in the most wonderful ways.

'Violet,' he moaned into her ear.

Her nipples tingled where they pressed into her stays. That didn't stop Seth's hand from curving a path up her body and brushing the nub with his thumb as he'd done the night before.

She whimpered with delight and ran her hands over him, unable to stop. Unwilling to stop. And hoping he'd do likewise.

Her greedy fingers trailed over his chest and the solid muscle beneath his thin shirt. Their kisses had gone beyond passion to something out of their control.

It wasn't until a clattering carriage drew to a stop behind Seth's town house that they pulled apart, gasping for breath, eyes wild with lust. A carriage door clicked open and a woman dressed in a black-silk domino and mask stepped out as Seth drew Violet deeper into the shadows.

He pressed a finger to his lips to show she ought to remain quiet as the woman raced quickly

through the garden and in through the rear doorway of Dalton Place. Violet turned sharply to Seth.

He had claimed to be different and yet a woman
was joining him at his home in disguise.

'Who was that?' she demanded.

He shook his head.

Violet smoothed her dress and took a calming
breath to still her thoughts. They still spun after
going from being kissed senseless to suspecting
Seth had a lover attending him at his town house.
'You don't know who she is?'

He held out his hands in a helpless gesture and
shrugged.

'Don't you dare presume I'll believe she was
your mother.' Violet stiffened as an excuse silently
worked over his lips.

'She wasn't my mother.' A muscle ticked at
his jaw and Violet sensed the truth was near. He
heaved an aggravated sigh. 'She was my sister.'

'Lady Caroline?' Violet blinked in surprise.
The dark-haired beauty had remained unwed despite many suitors. And many offers of marriage,
if the rumours were to be believed.

Perhaps she had vices that ran too deep for marriage. Gambling. Drink. A darker, more salacious
sin?

'Did you not recognise the attire?' Seth asked,
incredulous.

Violet shook her head and glanced back towards the door Lady Caroline had slipped through

as if doing so might recall the image of her more clearly.

'It's the same one you wore the other night when returning home at a late hour,' Seth prompted.

Violet hadn't purchased those items. They had been given to her by—

She gasped.

Seth groaned. 'Tell no one. She insisted and wouldn't be put off. I had no choice but to agree.'

'But why?' It was Violet's turn to be incredulous. Lady Caroline had the perfect figure—slender, willowy, graceful. She was well accomplished and possessed a genuine warmth that made her instantly likeable.

Why would someone like Lady Caroline possibly need Lottie's assistance in obtaining a husband?

'Lord Rawley,' Seth said drily. 'The man is far too shy for his own good, so my sister is trying to see what she can do to encourage him to demonstrate his affections. It's ridiculous, really.'

Violet thought of Lord Rawley with his impeccable appearance. Every hair was in place and smoothed regularly to ensure it remained so. His clothes were neatly pressed and without as much as a stray thread or hint of lint. While polite and respectful, he was hardly a sought-after gentleman.

'She must be quite enamoured of him,' Violet said wonderingly.

Seth scoffed. 'You don't know the half of it.' He

met her eyes and his expression softened. 'Though I feel the interruption came at just the right moment.'

Heat scalded Violet's face. She had wanted it to go further, the way it had gone the other evening. It was wrong, she knew. And sinful. And so indescribably tempting.

He stroked a hand down her face. 'You're so innocent, Violet. Beautiful and pure. I would never forgive myself for marring your pristine reputation.'

Her stomach clenched.

Innocent. Pure. Pristine.

Fraud.

She offered a tight smile.

'May I call upon you tomorrow?' he said. 'We can go for a walk, perhaps through Hyde Park.'

Hyde Park, where the *ton* paraded themselves, on display for everyone to see. He wanted *her* to be with *him* for all to see.

Her smile relaxed into something more genuine and everything within her melted. 'Yes,' she replied. 'I would like that very much.'

'As would I.' He lifted her hand and bestowed a gentle, affectionate kiss. 'Goodnight, my Violet.'

She swallowed. 'Goodnight, Seth.'

He remained where he was as she made her way into the town house where she pressed her back to the garden door once it was closed behind her and gasped for breath. What was she doing allowing him to court her? To take her to Hyde Park? To steal kisses in the darkness and abscond with her heart?

She should never have agreed to allow him to court her, but she had given him her answer and now it was too late. There was no way this would not end badly.

Soon-to-be spinster dared place herself in the arms of war hero Earl, a gentleman far too handsome ever to be with the likes of her.

All was well and good between this mismatched couple until he asked her to wed him.

It was then, Dear Readers, that the lady confessed to having placed herself on the shelf—not because she was shy or uninterested in marriage, but because she was spoiled goods. A social pariah.

Violet exhaled a pained sigh.
What had she done?

Chapter Sixteen

Seth skimmed over the *Lady Observer* column the following morning while sipping a piping-hot cup of tea. Sunlight poured into the window and lit the blue and white room with such brilliance, it nearly hurt his eyes.

Details of Lady Norrick's soirée were described in great detail: what was worn, down to the ostrich feathers in a certain lady's turban that had accidentally jabbed her husband in the eye. Allusions as to who danced with whom, people Seth didn't know well enough to care about. Apparently, the baked custard was worthy of the saints themselves and was described in such gratuitous detail, Seth regretted leaving before having had the opportunity to sample it.

Strange that his abrupt departure was not mentioned, nor was Caroline's absence or even the amount of time he was on the veranda with Violet. Surely at least one of those occurrences would fall under the scent of a social-function gossip hound.

Come to think of it, he hadn't seen himself or Violet's interactions mentioned at all in the gossip column. At least nothing outside of a brief mention of his return to London. It was for the best, of course. But still, it was quite odd.

'Do you actually read that?' Caroline sank gracefully into her seat across the small table from him.

A beam of sunlight streaked over the table and made the curl of steam rising from Seth's teacup glow smoky grey.

'I wanted to see what all the hullabaloo was about.' He lifted his shoulders.

'And?' Caroline reached for it.

Seth scowled. 'There's considerable detail about gowns.'

She laughed. 'Oh, but did you see Lord D.— that's Lord Devonington—danced with Lady S. in her sparkling gown—that's Lord Norrick's eldest daughter?'

'No,' he said slowly.

'She's barely come out.' Caroline gave a shocked gasp. 'He's beastly old to consider such a young thing for a wife. Last year, he set his sights on Lady Eleanor, now the Duchess of Somersville.'

'Ah, yes. Lady Violet's cousin, correct?' He vaguely recalled the red-haired young woman. He did, however, know Somersville quite well. They had gone to university together with Rawley and Kentworth. He was a good chap with an eye set on adventure like his father.

'Yes. The new Duchess was the first one to hire Lottie to help her find a husband and she landed a duke!' Caroline tapped her spoon at the top of her egg, gently breaking its shell.

'And you've set your cap at a viscount,' Seth drawled. 'I feel as though I ought to be charged less.'

'Oh, stop—you.' Caroline cast him a chastising glance as she peeled back a sliver of delicate eggshell to reveal the quivering white beneath.

'While we're on the topic, how did your first lesson go?' he asked.

'Capitally.' Caroline dashed a few grains of salt over the egg and buttered a toast point. 'I'm quite sure I'll know exactly what to do when I next see him.'

'Thank God.' He rolled his eyes with exaggeration.

She glared at him with mock outrage and he laughed.

'I only wish to see your happiness,' he said with sincerity.

A smile replaced her false hostility. 'I'm well aware. It appears you've taken quite an interest in a certain lady yourself.' She dipped her toast in the egg so the tip dripped with golden yolk. 'Lady Violet. Cousin to the Duchess of Somersville.'

Seth felt his mouth curl up at the corners. 'She has agreed to allow me to court her. God knows I don't deserve a woman the likes of her.'

Caroline swallowed the bite of toast in her mouth and clapped her hands. 'Of course you do,' she protested. 'I'm so pleased to hear it. She would be a wonderful sister to have. It appears everything is going well for us.'

Indeed, it certainly did seem to be the way of it. How he'd become so fortunate to have Violet to see past his demons, he would never know. He settled his fingertips on the folded note beside his plate, received from Nash only an hour before describing a ruby bracelet in perfect detail that had been discovered just outside Bath. There was no question about it, the bracelet was the exact one that had belonged to Seth's grandmother and was one of the missing gems.

Seth had previously ordered Nash to purchase any of the jewels located and had funds at the ready to procure the valuable family heirloom. Once Seth had the bracelet, he would show his mother and tell her what it was he'd sought to do. After all, caring for one's family and easing their troubles was what an earl did.

Lady Dalton appeared in the room, blending into the shadows with her black mourning clothes. Her cold gaze fell to Seth. 'I hear you had quite an eventful evening last night.'

'Oh?' he asked in a bored tone.

'I'm referring to the inordinate and highly inappropriate amount of time you spent on the veranda with Lady Violet.' Lady Dalton waited by a hard-backed chair for a servant to pull it out for her. Only then did she sink into the seat with a regal air most reserved for supper parties. 'Really, Dalton. You should have remained in the ballroom with her. It would have been far more respectful and earls are always respectful. It's what they do.'

Seth bit the inside of his cheek to keep from rolling his eyes. After all, refraining from rolling one's eyes is also what earls did.

'Lady Violet has agreed to allow Seth to court her.' Caroline waggled her brows at Seth while their mother's gaze was averted from her.

'Is that so?' Lady Dalton lifted her teacup to her lips and took a dainty sip.

'It is.' Seth didn't bother to stifle the indulgent puff of pride from his chest. 'She has agreed to let me escort her to Hyde Park this afternoon.'

'Indeed.' His mother replaced the teacup on the saucer with such grace, it did not so much as clink.

He awaited her praise like an overeager hunting dog. After all, finding a wife was also what an earl did. Courting her and bringing their relationship to the public notice in a very socially acceptable way was also what earls did.

'Mind you're careful,' Lady Dalton said slowly. 'Not all ladies are as they seem.'

Caroline cleared her throat and popped up

from the table before Seth could question what his mother meant.

'I must be off,' Caroline said quickly. 'I've promised to help roll bandages with some of the ladies to send to Brussels to aid the wounded soldiers who are still recovering.' She came around the table and pressed a kiss to Seth's cheek. 'We are terribly grateful to have you returned home safely to us.'

Her tone was pointed and sharp and appeared to be aimed directly at Lady Dalton.

'Is there something I ought to be aware of regarding Lady Violet?' Seth asked once Caroline had departed.

Lady Dalton didn't bother to look up from the scandal sheet she was skimming. Not the *Society Journal*, he noted. One she'd carried in with her. One which clearly had more detail in it than the *Lady Observer* had detailed in its column if she already knew about his time on the veranda with Violet.

'Of course not.' Lady Dalton's reply was brusque and cool.

Which meant that there was indeed something he ought to be aware of and Seth *would* get to the bottom of it.

For all the contents of her wardrobe, Violet had absolutely nothing to wear. Poor Susan was red-cheeked and glistening with a sheen of sweat from her efforts of pulling gown after gown from the wardrobe.

The one with the pink roses was too large, the lavender one was too small, the muslin gown's bows weren't quite right and another had stitching across the sleeves that was far too silly.

'What are you doing, Aunt Violet?' an all-too-familiar voice enquired.

Violet nearly cringed. The last thing she had time for was Felicity's antics.

'I thought my door was closed,' Violet said.

'Oh, it was.' Felicity flopped on to the edge of Violet's white-lace canopy bed and patted the empty space next to her. Hedgehog leapt up to her side like an obedient dog. Though how the cat could see where he was leaping with his large, be-ribboned blue hat was beyond Violet.

'Are you dressing for your first public outing with Lord Dalton?' Felicity kicked the back of her heels against the bed frame.

Clack-clack, clack-clack, clack-clack. 'You're going to marry him,' she said in a sing-song voice.

'Not necessarily,' Violet protested. 'We're simply deciding if we're compatible.'

Clack-clack, clack-clack, clack-clack.

Felicity gave a knowing smile that revealed a missing tooth. 'You'll be wed before the end of the Season.'

Her certainty knocked at Violet's heart. It was

a ridiculous reaction to the claim of a little girl. What did a child know of love or marriage?

'Do stop that.' Violet indicated Felicity's feet. 'Why would you possibly say something so bold?'

Felicity hopped from the bed and approached the pile of gowns. 'Because I've seen how you look at Lord Dalton.'

'And how do I look at him?' Violet demanded, responding to Felicity's taunts despite herself.

When would she ever learn?

'It's how Father used to look at our governess.' Felicity said it so matter-of-factly that Violet was shocked into silence.

The girl continued. 'She was the one we had before all the others. She was plump, like you. We liked her. Father loved her. That's what Mother said once.'

Susan gave a sound somewhere between a grunt and a squeak.

Felicity did not acknowledge it or, hopefully, had not heard and continued. 'Mother doesn't know I overheard that conversation, but I'm sure it's why she's always off visiting with friends and why Father is as well. And they definitely don't look at each other like you and Lord Dalton do.' She pulled a blue frock from the pile. 'This one, I think.'

Violet took the gown with a note of thanks. The poor child, to have seen such a scandalous dissolution of her parents' marriage. 'I'm terribly sorry that happened,' she said.

'I miss Lady Emily.' Felicity lifted a shoulder, as if she didn't care, but it was evident from her lowered gaze she truly did.

It did not escape Violet's notice how Felicity claimed to miss her governess, but not either of her parents. The more time Violet spent with Felicity, the more she realised Seth was right about the girl. She felt abandoned and unwanted.

'Yes, definitely this one.' Felicity fingered the silky fabric of the blue gown.

Violet cast her niece a sceptical look. 'Are you suggesting that because it matches Hedgehog's bonnet?'

'It brings out your eyes,' Felicity said innocently. Then she giggled. 'And it does rather become his bonnet nicely.'

He glared at the three sets of eyes that turned to him and Violet couldn't help but laugh. 'The blue one it is, then.'

Felicity beamed with pride at having her opinion taken and Susan appeared glad to finally have a gown selected. And Violet…well, Violet was simply anxious no matter what she wore.

It would be the first time, the *only* time, she'd ever let a man escort her. Never before had she thrown herself so recklessly to chance. But then, never before had it been so tempting.

With little time to spare, Susan worked a miracle in not only getting Violet into the gown, but managing a fetching style of curls and twists for her hair as well.

Because of her contribution towards the overall ensemble, Felicity was invited to join them, as long as she remained with Susan. Felicity readily agreed. As long as she could bring Hedgehog.

Violet allowed the bartering, seeing no harm in it. That is, until the little girl pulled out a collar and long lead and attached them to Hedgehog so that he could be trotted about like dog.

It would be almost laughable if it wasn't so embarrassing. After all, they were going to be entering Hyde Park at the fashionable hour. Violet nearly reprimanded her, but when she found herself nearly prefacing the rebuke with what 'ladies didn't do', she quashed the protest.

She'd listened to a lifetime of what 'ladies didn't do'. If it made the girl happy to walk her cat, then she could walk her cat. Especially when Hedgehog lived up to the expectation of being highly fashionable.

As they had a gate on their street leading directly to Hyde Park, it seemed ostentatious to take a carriage and meet Seth there. Instead, they had agreed to meet in front of Violet's town house at exactly five o'clock.

'What luck to stumble upon such lovely ladies.'

Violet sucked in a breath at the masculine, sensual voice. It took only a small statement, but immediately her skin tingled with awareness and incredible sensitivity.

Seth.

She straightened from where she'd been standing over Hedgehog and smiled at him.

'You told her to meet you in front of our town house,' Felicity said. 'That isn't luck. It's good planning.'

'That it is.' Seth laughed.

His gaze skimmed respectfully over her and his smile widened. 'That's a lovely gown, Lady Violet.'

She curtsied. 'Thank you. Felicity selected it for me.'

'That is quite an eye for fashion you have, my lady.' He knelt in front of Felicity, heedless of his trousers. 'I trust you and Hedgehog are quite well.'

She grinned at him and nodded emphatically. 'I hope you marry Aunt Violet so you can be my uncle,' she whispered.

Violet's mouth fell open with horror.

Seth, however, simply laughed. 'I'll do my best not to ruin my chances.' He got to his feet, dusted off his knee and offered Violet his arm. 'Shall we?'

'There are only two and a half hours left of the fashionable hour.' She slipped her hand into the crook of his elbow.

'Then we shall have to make the most of them, shan't we?' Seth smiled into her heart.

The wonderful clean scent of him surrounded

her, the same as it had the previous night. She'd fallen asleep with that scent clinging to her skin.

'Do you think the ribbons might be too much?' Seth asked discreetly.

Violet startled and glanced at her gown where a narrow line of ribbon ran along the seam.

'I don't mean you,' he whispered and looked pointedly at Hedgehog, who skulked forward on his lead with several ribbons trailing after him from his hat.

Violet smothered a laugh behind her hand. 'It may be a bit much,' she conceded quietly.

Scth winked at her. 'You know I have to ask something of a personal nature.'

'A personal nature?' Violet glanced behind her to ensure Susan and Felicity were out of earshot. As the maid had promised, they were. In fact, it would be easy to imagine Violet and Seth were alone were it not for the cat on a lead trotting a foot in front of them.

'Yes.' Seth regarded her and the skin around his eyes tightened somewhat. 'I want to know a little more about the *Lady Observer*.'

Violet's blood chilled. All this time she had been worried he would discover she was no longer a virgin. Never once had she suspected he might realise she was the *Lady Observer*. It hit her like a hammer and left her reeling.

Chapter Seventeen

Seth had hoped he appeared more nonchalant than he felt. Her agreement to allow his courtship had left him elated. And anxious. She made him want to be better—to be the courageous war hero society expected of him, to be stronger than the tidal wave of memories on the battlefield.

The combination of it all left him far more nervous around her than he'd ever been before. As it was, his question about the *Lady Observer* was most likely ridiculous. After all, what man actually bothered to read such drivel?

'The Lady Observer?' Violet said in a strangely choked voice. 'Do you mean the…scandal column in the *Society Journal*?'

Dear Lord, was she laughing at him?

He inwardly winced. He was as bad as Rawley at this moment.

'I do.' He tried to catch a glance of her face beneath the brim of her straw bonnet. Without success.

He did, however, immediately recognise the bonnet.

It was the same one she'd worn that day in the garden when they'd first kissed. When he'd pulled free the silk ribbon and let it slide from her hair. When he'd sampled the sweetness of her lips.

The garden had been his favourite place when he'd been a boy, a reprieve from the stuffy doldrums of the house where the rules were heavy and freedom was practically non-existent. As an adult, it was swiftly becoming a favourite place yet again, for a series of very different, very tantalising reasons.

They followed the trail of people walking into Hyde Park from Grosvenor Gate. Shade from the large walnut trees blotted out the late afternoon sun momentarily as they strode on.

'What about the *Lady Observer*?' Violet asked.

'It is your preferred gossip column, is it not?' He knew it was, of course, but hoped his aloofness might come off more masculine than his bumbling start to the topic.

Why the devil had he brought it up in the first place?

He knew why. It had been an attempt to find some ground for conversation between them. Between his nerves about finally courting Violet and the intense vulnerability he'd displayed with her the night before, he'd been afraid his mind would go blank.

'Do you feel the scandals reported within are… well…somewhat deficient?' God, he was sounding like a ninny now. The idea to bring up the topic had seemed like such a good one earlier when he'd tried to think of ways to impress her. Speaking about it aloud now made him realise how foolish a topic it truly was.

'Why would you possibly say such a thing?' There was a sharp note to her tone, as if he'd offended her.

He was botching this into a proper mess.

'Do you not think it's odd that she has not reported a thing about our interactions?' He tilted his head. 'It appears my mother reads *Ladies and Notions* and they wrote quite the article on the amount of time we were missing from the soirée when we were on the veranda last night.'

'Surely the author of every gossip column cannot see everything,' Violet offered.

'Then perhaps it is a good thing she could not see us in your garden,' he whispered.

She laughed and surreptitiously glanced about as if she was worried someone might have overheard. A flush covered her fair cheeks and her eyes sparkled.

The memory was clearly a pleasant one for her as well. Good. He'd certainly spent a considerable amount of time savouring their moments in the garden together.

Her kisses had been as hungry as his own, her body so lush and alluring under his hands.

Whatever layer of ice he'd let frost over his confidence finally cracked with her sweet laughter and the conversation resumed between them with a more natural flow. Without the subject of the *Lady Observer* coming up again. Thank God.

What was more, the walk accomplished exactly what he had wanted. As they strolled through Hyde Park, led by an odd little feline and trailed by a precocious girl and doe-eyed maid, every man and woman took notice.

Violet seemed oblivious as she reminisced over hilarious moments from their youth together. But Seth was quite aware of every eye that swept over them. And he especially noted the ones that lingered. He squared his shoulders with pride. Lady Violet Lavell was his to court, his to wed. And he wanted everyone to know.

Prior to the moment he saw Violet with her scandal sheet, he'd never considered reading one on his own. He'd done so only to see what it was she found so fascinating. Aside from making him hungry with the detail in which the food had been described, he'd found them tedious and bordering on intrusive.

Seeing how gossip swarmed around them right now, however, left him craving the need to purchase every one printed about this day. *Ladies and Notions*, the *Society Journal* and anything else he could get his hands on. He wanted to be well aware how many people had acknowledged his courtship of Violet.

When the fashionable hour drew to an unfortunate close, Seth saw Violet, as well as her entourage, home. He could only imagine what the scandal sheets might say about Hedgehog. The idea of it nearly made him laugh.

Seth let the smile of his restrained mirth linger on his lips. 'I've enjoyed myself immensely.' In truth, if he'd known what a pleasurable experience it was to court Violet, he would have done it six years ago. If he hadn't been such a cad then.

Violet slanted her eyes coyly at him. 'As have I.'

Her maid and Felicity stood off to the side as they awaited Violet.

He lingered despite needing to let her go. 'I want to see you again.'

'I'm going to see Lottie tonight.' Though she said the words softly, they plunged into his chest like a dagger.

Why would she need to continue to see Lottie if she was already being courted?

She licked her lips, nervous in a way that suddenly set him on edge. 'I need to speak with her,' Violet said. 'At least one final time.'

Seth nodded slowly.

'Will you meet me in the garden after I return home?' Violet asked with a breathlessness that piqued his arousal.

'I shall be watching for your return.' He offered her a cordial bow, then tipped his hat to her maid, Felicity and finally Hedgehog before departing to his town house next door.

Gibbons welcomed Seth home and advised him that a parcel and note had arrived from a Mr Nash. The quirk of his eyebrow as he said Nash's name implied how the stodgy butler felt about the man.

Excitement shot through Seth. The parcel was no doubt the ruby bracelet. He grinned at Gibbons and patted his shoulder. 'I've paid someone to seek out the solicitor who stole the jewellery from us,' he confided in the older man.

Gibbons opened his mouth, then closed it. 'I'm glad to hear it, my lord.'

Seth narrowed his gaze. 'But…?'

'But nothing, my lord.' The man snapped his lips shut and lifted his head, hands stubbornly tucked behind his back as though he could physically hide the words he clearly wasn't saying.

What the deuce was amiss with the household at Dalton Place?

Seth suppressed a sigh. No doubt the servant was doing what he thought best. Seth couldn't fault him for that. Instead, he left instructions with

Gibbons to notify Lady Dalton that Seth wished to speak with her upon her arrival home, then went to his study.

As the butler had said, a small box and note were left on the centre of the desk.

Seth lifted the box to reveal a bracelet of fat rubies arranged like the petals of a summer rose, its centre winking with diamonds. The piece was set in a dainty gold bangle. There was no mistaking the item. Not when he'd seen it so many times in his childhood on his grandmother's wrist and had even seen it on many occasions on Lady Dalton's. It had been one of her favourites as it always reminded her of her mother when she wore it.

She would be pleased to see it returned.

Seth unfolded the note and the elation in his chest dimmed at the words.

My contacts indicate that Mr Pattinson suspects he is being followed. This will cause further delays.

Seth ran a hand through his hair in frustration. If the solicitor had become even more suspicious than he already was previously, he would be even more difficult to follow. Seth only hoped it wouldn't slow progress too much. Not when he was so eager to have the man apprehended before the Season came to an end.

* * *

Violet floated up the stairs to her bedroom. She shouldn't allow Seth to affect her so. She ought to steel her heart against his charm, cast aside the trove of shared memories and lock away her dreams.

For that was what so much of it came down to: her dreams. The ones when she thought Seth only flirted with her to tease her and couldn't help but desire him regardless. The ones she'd thought she'd cast off after what happened with Lord Fordson.

Her stomach curdled at Fordson's name and soured the happiness of her mood with the reality of the situation she must face. Seth's question earlier about the *Lady Observer* reminded Violet she had more than one secret that left her vulnerable.

Did he suspect anything?

His question had been so abrupt, Violet had nearly choked on it. It had been a dangerous oversight to leave herself out of her own scandal sheet. Then again, she'd done nothing to warrant space in any scandal sheet for years. Until now.

Heat flushed through her at what she had done to deserve to be the opening line of the *Lady Observer*.

Soon-to-be spinster meets war hero Earl for a lovers' tryst in the garden behind a

*town house, where the wallflower found her-
self blooming with kisses that rendered her
senseless...*

Goodness how that would set the tongues of
the *ton* wagging.

Fortunately for her, that was not the story that
would be told. Still, something needed to be put
out there.

She flopped herself on her bed, stared at the
ceiling and let her thoughts drift.

The door to her room was flung open and the
clatter of little feet raced across the floor before
going suspiciously silent. Felicity flew over the
top of Violet suddenly and landed on the mattress
with a plop and a raucous laugh.

Violet shrieked in mock surprise. 'I'm being attacked.' She lifted a pillow and carefully pushed
at Felicity with it.

The little girl wrinkled her nose and giggled,
taking up her own pillow. They battered each other
with the soft weapons for a spell, until they were
both out of breath with laughter and collapsed to
the large mattress once more.

Through it all, Hedgehog had sat at the foot of
the bed, one leg stretched out while he cleaned
himself in a most vulgar fashion. No doubt his
behaviour was the result of vengeance for the collar and lead on their public outing. Violet couldn't
blame him.

'Why don't you want to marry Lord Dalton?' Felicity asked.

'I... It isn't that I don't wish to marry Lord Dalton, it's that...well, it's a very large step.' Violet pulled herself to sitting.

Felicity did the same and nodded solemnly. The girl had a habit of appearing far older than her seven years. Most likely that came from being the eldest of her siblings.

'Lord Dalton cares for you and I know you care for him.' Felicity pursed her lips. 'Perhaps you can think more about the idea of marriage? You'd be a wonderful mother.' She gave Violet a gap-toothed smile.

'That's kind of you to say.' Violet ruffled Felicity's silky fair hair. The girl had been extraordinarily well behaved of late. All directions were followed without argument and there hadn't been a single tantrum.

'It's true.' Her niece looked down at the white cotton coverlet and gave a little sniff.

'Are you well, Felicity?' Violet asked. 'Shall I have an infusion made for you?'

Felicity shook her head. 'It doesn't matter.'

Violet drew up short, startled by the hard edge to the little girl's tone. 'Hedgehog needs a new bonnet. The blue one looks ridiculous.'

'Felicity?' Violet said.

The cat's green gaze flicked towards the little

girl as she slid towards him, scooped him up and ran from the room.

Violet called after her once more, uncertain if she ought to go after her niece or not. As it was, Violet knew she preferred solitude when she was upset. Perhaps it was best to leave her for a while. By the time Violet was finished writing the latest edition of her gossip column, Felicity would surely be more amenable to conversation.

Violet eased off the bed and glanced down the hallway, finding it absent of a little girl or even a beleaguered cat. With one final worried look at the empty hallway, Violet returned to her room and shut the door, leaving it unlocked should Felicity decide to return. Violet went to her desk and withdrew a sheet of paper and picked up her quill. She tapped it against her lip as she always did when she considered what to write.

It was how she'd got started in the business of scandal sheets. She hadn't always been able to find her voice, but she had been able to find a pen. Writing what she witnessed, who scorned who, what victories some shared and defeats others endured.

Most especially, she preferred to write about women who had gone through a rough time of it to come out gleaming on the other side. Like her cousin, Eleanor. A lady cast off so late in the Season for another. It was shameful what Lord Ledsey had done to her, though he'd certainly got his just deserts. After being stripped of his title for attempting to murder the Duke and Duchess, his hand had become infected and he'd perished from his wounds.

Writing about the Duchess's success in attracting the attention of the Duke of Somersville the prior year had brought a note of vindication for Violet.

It was that idea she now focused on for herself. Except she could not mention Lord Fordson, of course. Or that she was indeed the author of the *Lady Observer.*

She drew in a satisfying inhale then let it slowly exhale out between her lips as she closed her eyes and envisioned herself as she would one of the subjects of her gossip column. It took only that brief moment to capture herself in her mind's eye. She held it there, dipped her quill in a pot of ink and began to write.

Happily-ever-afters can come to the most mundane of wallflowers. A certain lady once deemed too plump for marriage and all but set firmly upon the shelf has finally found a man to draw her from the background she'd spent a lifetime fading into.

Since the certain gentleman's return from his brave efforts on the Continent, he has been seen with the perhaps-not spinster. And, while their meetings have always had an air

*of the clandestine, they have now been seen
for the first time truly together in public.*

*Led by an odd-looking creature in a
bonnet...*

She smiled as she wrote that bit.

*...the perhaps-not spinster strode through
Hyde Park at the peak of the fashionable
hour on the proud arm of the newly minted
Earl...*

She paused and read what she wrote, noting she
had unintentionally written *perhaps-not spinster*
rather than *soon-to-be spinster*. This time, however, even the part about Hedgehog did not keep
the smile on her face.

Oh, heavens. That didn't sound at all flattering.

She scratched a large X over the piece and tried
again.

*Love is not only for the conventional
beauty, but also for the perhaps-not spinsters who have blended into the background
of society—*

Violet set her quill down with a puff of frustration.

No matter how she put it, describing her cir-
cumstances was far from complimentary. How
had she put it for others?

She slid open a drawer, removed several stacks of texts on etiquette and revealed a bundle of the *Society Journal* beneath. She flipped to her column one by and one and skimmed over the articles. Her heart slowly stopped.

What she had intended as capturing a lady's victory, especially one where a man was at fault for having led to her unhappiness in the first place, she had instead succeeded in revealing their greatest weaknesses. Her fingers came to her lips to stifle a gasp.

There had been the debutante who had fallen at her own ball, only to wed Lord Bastionbury, the Marquess every woman had fawned over. Except in describing the lady, Violet had used the words 'calamitous' and—she winced—'lacking grace'.

Heart pounding, Violet flicked through the previous instalments of the *Lady Observer* to the *on-dits* she'd written about her own cousin, the Duchess of Somersville. Violet had been proud of that piece and felt as though Lord Ledsey had truly been proclaimed the cad he was.

And truly he did appear perfidious. But then, Violet got to the part she'd written about her cousin.

> *Regardless of where the blame lies, the tale has not ended happily for a lady who masks it so well she's earned the unfortunate moniker of Ice Queen.*

*She has watched the entire heartbreaking
scene unfold before her dry eyes with a composure tightly reined, as if she were bored.*

*While this only perpetuates rumours of
her cold nature, one cannot help but wonder at her ability to maintain such stoicism
after everything she's been through in recent years.*

*If her heart is truly ice, as some claim,
it stands to reason that it will shatter more
easily when broken...*

Tears stung Violet's eyes. In her attempt to put
Lord Ledsey to shame, she had trumped up Eleanor's deficiencies to elicit more sympathy for her.
And while perhaps it had done that, it had also
made her appear, well, pathetic.

Violet gave a soft cry and the paper crumpled
under her hands. All this time, how had she never
realised what she was doing?

And she now intended to do the same to Lottie? The woman who had helped her, who had
championed Violet's success and encouraged her
to be kind to herself when most others fed words
of deprecation.

Violet tried to drag in air through the burning
pain in her chest. She had never meant to write
hurtful things about all those ladies. She'd only
meant to help them. Oh, how miserably she'd
failed.

She realised now she couldn't do the same to Lottie. Which meant her lessons and the exposé—all of it—would have to come to an end. And that meant Violet had only two options remaining: the first was to become an unpaid governess to Sophie's children. If the other three were like Felicity, it might not be so bad.

She shook her head at herself, unable to believe she was actually considering being responsible for all those children as a viable option.

And perhaps that was because the second option was even more frightening: telling Seth the truth about Lord Fordson. Because it wasn't just that she was no longer a virgin. It was that she had been so swiftly won over, that she'd capitulated to his fake charm with such ease.

Unlike the ladies whom she had written about in such poor light, Violet truly was pathetic. And now she understood just how much.

Chapter Eighteen

Seth opened the double doors of the sitting room to find Lady Dalton perched rigidly at the edge of the blue velvet sofa.

His mother turned to him. 'I was told you wished to see me.' She smoothed her black skirts. 'I've already rung for tea. It should arrive momentarily.'

Seth sat down beside her and offered her the small box.

She regarded the parcel, but didn't take it. 'What is this?'

'A gift.' He grinned in anticipation.

For the first time in his life, she would be pleased with him. He passed the box to her and anxiously bounced his knee.

A hesitant smile touched her lips. 'A gift?' Her fingers hovered over the seam of the box in preparation to pull it apart.

Seth leaned closer, eager to see the surprise on her face. 'I put a considerable amount of effort into obtaining this. I believe you'll be quite surprised.'

She drew the top away, revealing the ruby bracelet nestled in a bed of white silk. The colour drained from her face as she stared down at the lost piece of jewellery. Stark tendons stood out against her slender throat from the high black collar of her mourning gown.

Seth's elation melted into confusion. 'It's your mother's bracelet.'

She turned slowly to him, her eyes aflame with emotion. 'How could you?'

'How could I?' Seth stammered. 'I went to great expense and effort to procure your mother's bracelet. I intend to have all your gems tracked down and repurchased. I thought...' He shook his head, baffled and angry. Yet again he'd managed to make a mess of things.

She crushed the lid back on the top of the box. 'Do you have any idea what you've done?'

'No.' The final thread of his patience pulled taut and broke beneath the immense pressure. 'I don't know what I've done. I haven't a clue what I've possibly done to displease you after a lifetime of always causing you so much unhappiness. I've never been perfect like William. I'll never be perfect like him.'

'Don't even speak of him,' his mother snapped. 'You have dredged up the past to lay yet more scandal at our feet. I had become reconciled to these items being lost. A worthy sacrifice to salvage our good name.'

Seth got to his feet. 'What the devil are you talking about?'

He had gone too far. As he always had. Only this time he didn't care.

His mother rose from the sofa, tears bright in her eyes. 'William was always the one who caused unrest.'

Seth startled at her words. 'I beg your pardon?'

'He needed constant praise or he became a beast of a child.' Colour rose in his mother's cheeks. 'He was in line to be the next Earl. We couldn't have him react in such a manner in public. Not an earl's heir.'

Seth stared at her incredulously. Was he hearing correctly?

'You never required the constant reassurance he did,' Lady Dalton said. 'You were such a good child. Well mannered, intelligent. Until you got older and discovered drink and ladies.' She gave a cry of displeasure and put a hand to her chest as though merely thinking of it caused a sharp pain. 'At that point, I didn't know what to do with you and was too embroiled with your brother's scandals.'

'William had scandals?' Seth pressed.

His mother exhaled a heavy sigh. 'Mr Pattinson was well aware of those scandals. He threatened to let word of them drip out one at a time if we did not comply with his wishes.'

'And what were those?'

'Mr Pattinson wished to have the jewels and be left in peace.' His mother's eyes filled with tears. 'I hadn't meant to alert anyone, truly. But when I went to collect all the jewellery...'

'It was noticed,' Seth surmised.

She offered a stiff nod. 'He was greatly displeased and fled town so quickly, he left before the final few pieces could be given to him.' She fingered the delicate emerald earbobs she wore. 'It didn't matter. News of how easily I'd been duped made its way through the *ton* like wildfire. I'm sure I looked like the greatest of fools. Only no one understood why I'd been so readily hoodwinked.' She turned away and touched the crook of her forefinger to the corner of her eye.

It was that one subtle move, evidence of his mother crying over what he had left her to face alone, that pushed him over the edge. Guilt burned a hole straight through him.

'If you don't stop him, what's to keep him from demanding more money from us in the future?' Seth asked. 'What did William possibly do that was so bad?'

'Please do not make me speak of it,' she said on a shuddering exhale.

'I must know.' Seth approached his mother and put his hands on her shoulders.

He hadn't noticed how slender she had become. The mourning gown covered almost all of her in voluminous dark skirts. Beneath the black bombazine, her arms were little more than twigs that felt thin enough to snap. Up close, he could see how the worry of the last few years had etched lines on to her regal face.

All this time, he'd assumed the weight beneath his mother's burden had been all his doing. Now he understood it had been William's. However, it was Seth who had left his mother vulnerable for a man like Pattinson to rob.

'I must know.' Seth spoke more softly as he guided her back to the plush sofa.

A servant came in as she was lowering herself to the blue velvet. Seth sat beside her and poured his mother a cup of tea, adding in the lump of sugar he knew she preferred and stirring until it was thoroughly dissolved.

Lady Dalton accepted the tea with a grateful smile, though tears still shone bright in her eyes.

'Will you tell me?' Seth asked. 'I will do everything in my power to ensure we are protected.'

'Oh, Seth.' His mother's gaze searched the surrounding air as if she could find an answer there. 'He debauched ladies.'

Seth winced. It was scandalous, of course, but nothing that might cause familial ruin.

'Unfortunately, there are many rakes in the *ton*. I'm sure such gossip can be ridden out—'

'He died from syphilis.' Lady Dalton's face hardened. 'He had been diagnosed by a physician three years prior to his death.' She sucked in a deep breath. 'Yet he continued to try to debauch ladies of the *ton*. I…' She swallowed. 'I had him committed and made excuses of him being too ill for company. I couldn't think of anything else to keep him from hurting others. And he was truly ill. He needed care I couldn't provide.'

Seth's mother stared down at the floor, the perpetual rigidity of her back bowing under the burden of such awful secrets. 'Mr Pattinson found the receipts and called them to my attention. No matter what excuse I gave, he saw through it. I don't know how he knew, but he did. All of it. He threatened me with that knowledge. We would have been totally ruined if I hadn't done what he asked.'

Seth stared at her in horror. It was a good thing he was sitting rather than standing when faced with such news. William. The brother he had always assumed to be so perfect had actively sought pleasure at the possible harm of others.

Syphilis.

'I gave up on him.' A sob erupted from his mother. 'He died in there. Alone.' She put her hands over her face and wept with a force that crushed Seth's heart.

He opened his arms and his mother, his fragile, broken mother, fell into them and cried until her tears ran dry. He patted her back, painfully aware of how the cage of her ribs jutted against the fine black fabric of her gown.

He understood then that the black attire was not mourning for the son she had lost, but for what it had cost her to do what was right.

Seth would face that now. Not only would he bring Mr Pattinson to justice, but he would ensure the scandal never emerged.

Violet was nearly in tears with resolve by the time Lottie entered the double doors of the drawing room. The woman rushed to Violet in a rustle of grey silk.

'Darling, what is it?' Lottie asked.

Violet kept her attention fixed on the interwoven vines on the rug beneath her slippers. Before she had begun her lessons with Lottie, she had thought this would be an easy thing to do: learn a bit about seduction, write about the courtesan and her wanton ways and publish an exposé that would get the *Society Journal* into every household.

She had not expected Lottie to be so considerate, so forthright and kind. Nor had Violet anticipated she would learn so much about her own heart or finally begin to truly accept herself. Certainly she had not expected Lottie to become a friend.

But there it was. Violet was in agony over what she had almost done and Lottie stood there, oblivious to the ugly truth as she sought only to console.

'I have not been honest with you.' Violet's

words trembled as she spoke. 'I have lied to you about my purpose from the first.'

'Have you?' Lottie said in a gentle voice.

'I am...' Violet swallowed hard and set some steel to her spine. She had to do this. It was only right. Violet squeezed her eyes shut. 'I am the author of the *Lady Observer*.'

Her admission was met with silence. She blinked her eyes open.

Lottie stared at her, brow furrowed. 'I see,' she answered slowly.

'I am being forced to choose between marriage or retiring to the country to look after my sister's children. They seemed like little beasts until I met the eldest.' Violet couldn't help her affectionate smile as Felicity came to her mind. 'She's actually rather pleasant, but I imagine the others are still quite...well, feral. Is it terrible to say that about one's family?'

Lottie tilted her head.

Violet clamped her teeth down to prevent herself from speaking further lest her nerves make her ramble on and on for all of eternity.

'I don't believe it's terrible if it's true.' Lottie said with a patient smile.

'It very well may be,' Violet admitted. 'I thought to avoid it all by earning money from... well...'

'Exposing the truth behind Lottie's Ladies,' Lottie offered.

Lottie's Ladies. Well now, that *did* have a nice ring to it.

Not that Violet would be using it.

The truth of what Lottie said squeezed at Violet's chest and she nodded sheepishly.

'It's not a bad idea.' Lottie touched a finger to her chin. 'I'm surprised no one has attempted as much before considering the amount of speculation as to what my lessons entail.'

'But it was a bad idea,' Violet countered. 'I deceived you. I pretended I required your assistance.'

'Did you not require it?' Lottie lifted a single dark, perfectly sculpted brow.

Violet fell quiet at once as she recalled how Lottie had brought in the cheval-glass mirror. How Violet had been forced to confront what she actually liked about herself and what it had meant to her to finally concede she was not as hideous as she had presumed all those years.

'I don't teach seduction,' Lottie said softly. 'I will not help a lady learn to kiss better, or take off her clothing in a sensual manner, or whatever lurid details the *ton* likes to say of me. My purpose is to enable women to realise their true potential, to push beyond the box society shoves them into. To know it's empowering for a woman to be confident, to like herself.'

Lottie gave a little pout. 'Sadly, I do not think that makes for a very interesting article.' Her pout blossomed into a coy smile that expressed an absence of any remorse as she made her way to a fine cherrywood table with a crystal decanter of rich red wine atop it beside the bosom of a sculptured naked woman. Lottie poured two glasses and handed the first to Violet, keeping the second for herself.

Violet cradled the heavy crystal glass in her palm. 'But you do help women find husbands.'

Lottie chuckled and shook her head. Her thick, glossy locks caught the candlelight and shone purple-blue like a raven's wing. 'I help women find themselves.' She drank from her wine glass, the action lovely and dainty. Even the flex of her slender throat as she swallowed the wine held allure.

'Women generally lack confidence in themselves.' She curled her fingers around the glass as she casually held it. 'Something men have in abundance for a reason unknown to me. It's quite an imbalance.' She sighed. 'I merely seek to right the scales of that injustice and set a woman's assuredness in herself to the same level a man possesses. Or as close as can be obtained.'

'So, you weren't trying to help me find a husband?' Violet concluded.

'I was trying to make you appreciate yourself for the woman you are.' Lottie ran her hand over the top of the maroon sofa, the movement graceful. 'Though it appears you have found a man who would make a fine husband.'

The pain returned to Violet's chest, vice-like and terrible. 'I'm going to make a mess of it all.'

Lottie's hand fell away. 'Whatever do you mean?'

'I'm ruined.' Violet set her wine glass to the marble-surfaced table and her knees gave out. She plopped on to the firm sofa.

'Did he take advantage of you?' Lottie asked, her voice hard.

'*He* didn't.' Violet folded her arms over her chest and bent over. As if she could cradle her own hurt within.

Lottie lifted her head in understanding. 'That's why you faded into the background in the first place.'

Her assessment was so accurate, it brought tears to Violet's eyes anew. 'I couldn't let anyone know.'

Lottie sank on to the sofa beside Violet and brought with her a sweet, delicate scent of gardenia. 'Please don't let your past transgressions interfere with your chance for happiness now.'

Violet shifted her gaze from her instructor and let it settle on a harp placed at the side of the room near a shuttered window. 'What are you saying?'

Lottie's warm hand folded over Violet's. 'Tell him the truth.'

Violet gasped and snapped her attention back towards Lottie.

The former courtesan's eyes softened. 'If he loves you, he'll understand.'

Violet slid her gaze to the flowers on the solid

marble surface of the table. Peonies this time, so fresh, the water in the vase was probably stained green with the juice dripping from the base of their thick stalks.

'Like a certain friend you know?' Violet ventured.

This time Lottie did not bother to mask the hurt puckering at her brow. 'Yes.' She reached out and ran the tip of a manicured nail over a fragile pink petal. 'Some relationships are sadly beyond repair.' She smiled, a despondent, tired smile that shadowed the smooth area beneath her eyes. 'Do not allow yours to become irreparable. You have a chance at happiness.' She shook her head and her face brightened. As if melancholy could be so easily released. 'Take it.'

Violet sucked in a hard breath to gather in her strength.

'It won't be easy,' Lottie said. 'But it will be better than having a secret hanging over your life.' She lowered her head, pointedly watching Violet. 'If you truly love him, of course.'

If you truly love him.

The words hit Violet like a slap.

Did she love him?

She floundered with a response and finally gave an insipid nod.

Lottie got to her feet and smoothed her skirts. 'I suppose this will be the last time I shall see you, Lady Violet.'

Violet rose as well and was surprised by a clench of sorrow in her chest. As if she were bidding farewell to a good friend for a final time.

Much to her surprise, Lottie wrapped her slender arms around Violet and pulled her into a warm embrace. The way a mother might do with a child.

'Take care of yourself, Lady Violet.' Lottie pulled away and met Violet's eye. 'Know that I am always here.' A devilish glint flashed in her eye. 'And I'll never tell your family you were here. Now or later, should you need to see me again.'

Violet's mouth fell open in preparation to ask how Lottie knew.

The courtesan simply winked and strode towards the door. 'Most of my clients do not pay in actual coin when they get my bill,' she called over her shoulder.

Violet had guarded the incoming correspondence like a hawk. A job not easily done with their butler eyeing her with suspicion. When Lottie's bill came in, Violet had sent Susan with the payment post-haste in coin. Violet hadn't paid like a peer. She should have known better.

Her thoughts shifted to Seth and apprehension curled into a tight ball in the pit of her stomach. Lottie was right. He needed to know.

Chapter Nineteen

For the second time that night, Violet waited with anticipation knotting her stomach. She wanted the hackney ride home to last a lifetime, so she could delay having to tell Seth that she was no longer a virgin.

Would he be horrified? Disappointed? Disgusted?

She clenched her eyes shut, unable to bear the anticipation of such a reaction from him. He was the only man to ever make her feel beautiful. Aside from Lord Fordson, though considering how quickly his compliments had fled once he had what he'd wanted, he no longer counted.

She clenched her hands in her lap as the carriage drew to a stop at the rear of Hollingston House. The duration of the trip had gone far too quickly. Her heart was beating like a frantic drum, her breath came too short and fast. Her thoughts spun in her mind, dancing headily.

The door snapped open and, just like that, she was out of time.

She stepped from the carriage. All too soon, the path underfoot went from firm brick to soft grass.

She walked slowly into the small garden behind her home and looked up at Dalton Place. A man's shadow appeared in a second-floor window, back-lit by the golden glow of candlelight.

Seth.

He was gone as soon as he appeared, no doubt making his way down the stairs and to the back door. Violet settled a hand over her chest as if she could physically stop its frantic pounding.

She should never have put herself in this position. She should never have allowed him to court her. She should never have allowed herself to kiss him. She should never have allowed him to ease his way into her heart.

The rear door to Dalton Place clicked and his voice filled the night air, quietly calling to her.

She stepped from the shadows, and he traversed the gap between their gardens.

A smile lit his face. 'Violet.' The way he said her Christian name was so tender, so intimate, it made her insides flutter.

'Seth,' she breathed.

He rushed to her and drew her into his arms. His hand immediately found her jaw, stroking her skin and tilted her face towards his to gently bestow a kiss. His lips were warm and he tasted rich and smoky, like brandy.

It was a tantalising combination when mingled with his clean, naturally masculine scent. She could breathe him all day. Kiss him all day. All night.

No.

She pulled her head back from him. 'I have to speak with you.'

His gaze skimmed her face and lingered on her bosom before sliding back up once more. 'You look beautiful.'

'You mean my breasts do?' she accused in a chastising tone.

'You look beautiful and I also have a fine appreciation for your breasts.' He grinned.

'You're wicked.'

He drew her more tightly against him. 'My love, you don't know the half of it.' It was said with a growl, almost like a threat.

My love.

Chills danced over her skin and desire pumped through her body in hot, dizzying bursts that left her breathless.

Which was, of course, why telling the truth was so hard. It would be easy to fall into banter and kissing with Seth rather than do what she needed to do and confess.

'I'm so grateful you've allowed me to court you.' Seth's tone turned tender. He ran the back of his hand down her cheek and his dark eyes shone with affection. Solely for her.

'You're witty, intelligent, and beautiful.' He lifted his mouth in a boyish half-smile that knocked her senses askew. 'You're so innocent, my sweet flower.'

Her pulse caught at his last words.

Fraud. She was a fraud.

He lowered his head and nuzzled his nose against hers as though he intended to kiss her again. 'What did you wish to tell me?'

She wanted to tip her head back and allow him to kiss the confession from her mouth. But she couldn't. She didn't deserve him. He was the best thing in her life and she would have to give him up.

'I have a confession to make.' She leaned back from him once more.

His brows pinched together and he released her, opting to hold her hands instead of her body. 'Of course. What is it?'

'I…' Her frantic mind summoned an imaginary picture of Seth's lip curling up in disgust. What if that became reality? What if he cast her off and she lost him for ever?

Her heartbeat slammed with such force, she could scarcely think straight.

'Nothing you've done could possibly be that bad.' Seth's tone was patient and kind.

Oh, but it could be. Violet drew in a long inhale, though it did nothing to quell the raw hurt in her chest.

Of course, she could wait. Until he proposed. *If* he proposed. Why subject herself to the humiliation now if it was all for naught?

In an instant, without any additional time spent dwelling on the thought, the words were out of her mouth before she could stop them. 'I'm the author of the *Lady Observer*.'

He blinked once and his smile dimmed slightly. 'Are you serious?'

She nodded and tensed for his reaction. This was not the secret she had tried to prepare herself to tell. But now it was out and she couldn't draw it back in.

'I was going to do an exposé on Lottie,' she admitted. 'It's the true reason I went to see her.'

Shame burned her face.

Seth's wary smile pulled into a slight frown. 'You didn't intend to share the identities of her other students, did you?'

Violet should never have brought this truth up for discussion. She never should have even mentioned a confession at all. In a single moment, she had ruined everything.

She swallowed around the tension building in her throat. 'I meant to initially, but then I got to know Lottie and now that I know Lady Caroline...' Violet shook her head. 'I looked back on what I had written previously and realised how hurtful those words could be to others.' Her voice broke. 'I couldn't do the exposé. I don't even want to write the *column* ever again. Of all people, I know how deeply words can cut.' A hot tear slid down her face. 'I never meant to hurt anyone.'

Seth brushed the moisture from her cheek. 'You've never been malicious. I know you didn't mean to cause harm.'

'It's terrible.' Violet looked away, too ashamed to even face the man who meant more to her than she cared to admit. Even to herself.

'You stopped before anyone could get truly hurt.' He closed the distance between them. 'Violet, you are a good person. Better than someone like me deserves.'

She was going to protest, but he pulled her against him, wrapping the strength of his arms around her. Her eyes closed at the embrace as all her senses gave in to him, savouring him. His clean scent, the heat of their bodies together, the undercurrent of desire humming in her blood.

Slowly, tenderly, he tilted her face upwards and closed his mouth over hers.

Seth would keep things chaste between them this time. Especially when they'd been nearly caught before. The garden in the rear of their homes was hardly a place for a tryst.

But when his mouth touched hers, when the sparks of attraction flickered to life, it was far too easy to linger. An extra caress of his lips against hers, a sampling just a beat too long of her sweet, delicate scent.

The powdery perfume of violets scented the air around him, immersing him in her. In Violet.

All of her consumed him, overwhelming his memories and ghosts with the most exquisite euphoria until Mont-Saint-Jean wasn't even a whisper in his mind. He wanted to lose himself in the sensations of Violet—her softness, the sweetness, her lovely perfection. There wasn't another place in all the world he'd rather be at that moment.

She gave a little hum of enjoyment and leaned into him, opening her mouth. Seth caught her face in his hand and kissed her once more, intending to keep things between them innocent.

But then Violet teased at his mouth with the tip of her tongue. The act was brazen and far more enticing than Seth wanted to admit. In that moment, he ought to have released her, backed away and bid her goodnight.

He ought to.

But he did not.

Not when the draw of losing himself in her was so damn alluring. Not when he had wanted this for so many years.

His hand slid into the back of her coiffure to gently angle her head to better access her mouth. The glossy strands were cool silk against his fingers. All of her was that way: smooth, lovely, perfect. His lips parted and he took control of the kiss once more, stroking his tongue against hers.

She whimpered and put her hand to his chest. The touch was simple, but the feelings it wrought were entirely far too complex. Longing, of course, but also affection, respect.

He shouldn't—

She rose on her toes to further deepen their kisses and arched her body against him. He tried to resist the temptation. For her sake. For her reputation…

He shouldn't be doing this, but damn him, he couldn't walk away.

His hands skimmed down her body, brushing aside the fine fabric of her domino and whispering over the sides of her breasts as they descended down her curves. He recalled how she'd felt in his palm, her heavy breast, the hard nub of her nipple. He had fantasised about that moment often, replaying it in his mind, imagining taking it further.

Her hands smoothed over his chest, sampling the feel of him with the barrier of linen between them.

Seth kissed his way down her chin, to the length of her graceful neck where the delicate violet perfume grew headier, spiced with the natural feminine fragrance of this woman's beautiful scent. It went straight to his head, the same as drink on an empty stomach, and left his thoughts swimming.

His lips found the sensitive place between her neck and her shoulder. She leaned her head back with a moan, yielding herself to him completely. He ran his hands back up her waist to her breasts. He cupped the weight of them in his palms and pushed them up slightly so the rounded tops of her bosom nearly spilled out.

He stared down at them, unable to stop himself from imagining how they might bounce with each thrust of his body into her. With a groan, he leaned over her, tracing the neckline of her muted grey dress with his tongue.

She held tighter to him and whispered a single word into the night.

'Yes.'

Before he could stop himself, he tugged at her bodice with trembling hands. Her full breasts spilled out into the moonlight for him to admire, smooth, creamy skin and topped with rosy nipples. He bent and ran his lips over the right nipple, an intentional tease that had her writhing with anticipation before he suckled the first bud into his mouth.

She gasped and practically fell against him. He easily caught her with one hand while cradling the silkiness of a breast in the palm of another and kissed her full lips again. His manhood throbbed with desire, rock hard and straining at his fall.

She curled her right leg around his left one, drawing their pelvises close, so close, until his arousal nudged her lower stomach. The pressure from even that brief contact was nearly his undoing. He groaned and suddenly they were lowering to the ground together. His mouth found her breasts again, nuzzling, kissing, licking, sucking.

Her gasps and whimpers in response to his attentions quickly disposed of the last shreds of his morality. Suddenly, he was reminded of that rake again, the man he'd been before he left. The one with skilled fingers and a wicked tongue who knew well how to pleasure women.

But he wasn't that man any more. And it wasn't women he wanted. It was just one. Violet.

He lay over the top of her in the soft, summer grass. The dewy freshness of it rose around them and the shadows obscured them in a shelter of privacy.

'Touch me,' she whispered.

Touch me.

Dear God. He hesitated, plagued with thoughts of William who had debauched ladies. Except he'd had no intention of marrying them. Not like Seth had with Violet.

'Please.' Her tone was pleading now, desperate.

He shifted his hands between them, skimming down her skirts to run his fingers over the cleft between her legs. She cried out.

He kissed her swiftly to muffle the sound and froze. When it was apparent no one had heard, or bothered to investigate the sound, he curled his middle finger into the folds of her gown where it nudged between her legs, rubbing her sex beneath.

The heat of her yearning was evident and he knew, if it were not for the layers of fabric separating them, she would be slick with need. Her hips ground against his touch, the quickening of her breath indicative of how close she was to climax.

The mere thought of hearing her cries of release were almost more than he could bear. In fact, he *needed* to hear them. A sweet memory to cling to that evening as he drifted to sleep, enveloped in recollections of Violet.

He prudently lifted the neckline of her gown to cover her breasts once more.

She clung more tightly to him. 'Please, don't stop.'

'I won't, but nor will I ruin you.' Even as he spoke, he lifted the hem of her gown. He paused to stroke her stocking, marvelling at her neat ankle and shapely calf. His touch skimmed over the white cotton to the bare skin inside of her knees.

'I think you don't know what *ruin* means,' she gasped.

'But I do,' he murmured. Up her inner thighs he went, the skin there impossibly soft. He didn't stop the agonisingly slow trail of his fingers up her legs until he brushed the slit of her sex.

Her hips jerked and she sucked in a hard breath.

He lay on his side as he leaned over her, propped

on his elbow, intending to kiss her, to swallow up every moan and whimper she would issue.

'There?' he teased.

She nodded.

He found the bud of her sex with his thumb where it was swollen and hot with the need to release. 'And there?'

She leaned her head back. 'Oh, God, yes.'

With his free hand, he carefully held the back of her neck, drawing her face higher once more to kiss her as his fingers moved over her with an expertise he had not used in many, many years.

Chapter Twenty

Violet should not have been lying on the grass in her garden with Seth next to her. Certainly she should not have allowed him to put his hands under her skirts or touch her so intimately.

But she did not have a single regret on the matter. Not with the way her body seemed to soar above that garden, above London, above any amount of morality that had been scolded into her throughout her life.

Seth's mouth moved over hers while his hand… Heavens, she didn't know what he did with his hand, but it was exquisite. Heat prickled at her palms and feet and every muscle in her body went taut with anticipation.

Her breath came faster and her heart slammed against her ribs so frantically, it was a wonder they didn't crack.

'Yes,' Seth growled between their kisses. 'Come for me, love. Come for me, my beautiful Violet.'

Love.

My beautiful Violet.

Even if he had pulled his hand from her at that very moment, his words alone were enough to tip her over the edge where she recklessly fell into utter bliss. Her body clenched in delicious spasms that spiralled her senses beyond a place they'd ever been before.

Seth kissed her again and again, muffling the sounds of her pleasure until she had control of herself once more. Spent and languid, her head fell back on to the soft, damp grass as she gazed up at Seth and the starlit dark sky above him.

Lord Fordson had never touched her like that. He'd never made her body react in such a way.

'That was the most sensual, lovely thing I've ever seen,' Seth said quietly.

Heat singed her cheeks. 'You watched me.'

He groaned. 'The pleasure on your face, those little breathy cries.' Despite the gruff, blatant lust in his voice, he eased his hand from her and carefully smoothed her skirt into place.

A glance down at his groin confirmed he was still fully aroused. A thick column of hard male flesh strained against his breeches.

Violet bit her lip, eager to show her own attraction to him as he had so generously done to her. She pulled him closer and kissed him again, this time letting her hands roam further than she'd been daring enough to do before.

Her fingertips grazed the tip of the large bulge, but he caught her hand. 'No.' He shook his head. 'I won't take your innocence.'

She opened her mouth, ready to confess it all. To tell him about how she was already ruined, how she burned for him, how if she didn't have all of him at that exact moment, she might go truly and completely mad.

Except it was at that exact second that the rear door to Hollingston House was flung open and her mother's voice cut through the air. 'What is the meaning of this?'

Violet jerked her hand away from Seth, hoping they were shielded enough by the shadows that her mother hadn't seen... Her insides clenched with mortification and shame.

Oh, God, what *had* her mother seen?

'I fell,' Violet said quickly. 'And Seth was—'

'Seth?' Lady Hollingston snapped.

Violet winced.

Seth jumped to his feet and helped Violet to hers. Thank goodness, he'd pulled the top of her gown up earlier. Or at least as well as he could with her lying down. If she faced her mother with her breasts draped over her neckline, she might truly perish from mortification.

'Forgive me, Lady Hollingston,' Seth said. 'The fault is entirely mine.'

'Come in at once, both of you.' The Countess pulled the door open wider. 'This instant.'

Violet closed her eyes and wished to be anywhere other than where she was.

Seth offered her his arm, as if they were in a ballroom preparing for a dance rather than having just enjoyed a moonlit tryst in a place where anyone could have seen them.

Where, of all people, *her mother* had seen them.

God, this could not be any worse.

'I'll do what's right,' Seth said under his breath.

Her eyes widened. *What's right.* That meant he would marry her.

Apparently it could be worse.

Shamefaced, Violet allowed herself to be led into the kitchen where a candle lit the room in a brilliant glow.

'I fell,' Violet protested. 'Lord Dalton was simply helping me to my feet.'

Her mother frowned. 'You must have fallen several times to appear in such a state.' Her gaze slid to Seth, skimming down his body. She stopped at his midsection, then darted her eyes away as if the corner of the ceiling had suddenly become the most fascinating thing she'd ever seen. 'You are hardly properly attired. Your dishabille is not only unacceptable, but paired with your lack of a chaperon could ruin a lady.'

Violet cringed at her mother's delicate dance around Seth's very obvious arousal.

Seth shifted uncomfortably from one foot to the other. 'I believe I have forgotten my jacket.

And my cravat.' He cleared his throat. 'As well as my waistcoat.'

'Yes,' Lady Hollingston agreed. 'I can see that.' She turned to him and looked somewhere over his head. 'Did you seek to debauch my daughter on the grass like some field hand?'

'I'll marry her,' Seth said firmly.

Lady Hollingston met his eyes. 'I trust you will.'

'I beg your pardon?' Violet said, finally finding her voice. 'Do I not have a say in the matter?'

Lady Hollingston spun on her. 'You lost that opportunity when you allowed him such liberties with your person. Truly, for a woman nearly on the shelf you should know better.'

Violet opened her mouth, but before she could get another word out, her mother continued in a voice that could only be described as shrill. 'You should be grateful for this happenstance, Violet. Truly, I thought no man would ever want you. Perhaps if you'd been able to keep your fingers from the dessert tray, or could try a little harder to eat less, you would not be in this situation.'

Violet stung as if she'd been slapped.

'You're a fool,' Seth said sharply.

Lady Hollingston put her hands on her hips. 'I beg your pardon?'

'I said you're a fool,' Seth repeated. 'Violet is a beautiful woman who is admirable and intelligent and everything you have never been. How such an incredible lady managed to blossom beneath such sharp words is a testament to her strength. I would caution you to have a care in how you speak to your daughter as she is soon to be my Countess.'

Lady Hollingston's mouth fell open and her cheeks coloured. She pulled open the door, stepping back to allow him to exit. 'I suggest you call upon Lord Hollingston first thing in the morning to discuss the marriage contract. You may leave, Lord Dalton.'

He cast a glance back at Violet, clearly seeking confirmation she would be all right. She nodded, though in truth she dreaded being alone with her mother after his departure. Not out of fear for her safety, but for the stinging rebuke she would no doubt receive.

Seth frowned, clearly not eager to leave. Lady Hollingston cleared her throat and he slipped out into the night.

The Countess methodically closed the door, engaged the lock and turned to Violet, arms crossing over her chest. 'It appears we will be having a wedding after all.' She paused and studied her daughter. 'Should I even ask about the domino?'

Violet shrank inside of herself and shook her head.

Lady Hollingston sighed. It was a long, exhausted sound that implied she would rather not know, that she was past the point of continuing to care, that she knew Violet would soon be someone else's problem. 'To bed with you, child.'

Grateful to have avoided coming up with an excuse to explain the domino, Violet quickly slipped from the room. It wasn't until she was alone in her bedchamber that the enormity of her situation crashed down upon her shoulders.

She would be marrying Seth. She would be Lady Dalton. And she had an enormous secret she hadn't yet shared with him because she had been too much of a coward.

Seth had woken early the following day. While he had not been plagued by nightmares of his time at Waterloo, he had not slept well. He had nearly ruined Violet.

After having been so disgusted with his brother's antics, Seth was little better himself. No, he hadn't tupped her, but they had been intimate. Very intimate.

In truth, if Lady Hollingston had not emerged when she had, would Seth have been able to resist taking Violet? She'd been ready enough, her body slick and hot and swollen. For him.

His thighs twitched at the memory, but he shoved the thoughts from his mind. Now was not the time for thinking of titillating transgressions. It was for making them right.

He waited with barely tethered patience in the drawing room for his mother and sister to join him. They came in some time after ten. He'd already penned a missive to Lord Hollingston asking for an urgent meeting first thing that morning.

His mother and sister came down within minutes of one another. They exchanged pleasantries and he allowed them a moment to take a sip of tea before speaking up. 'I shall be speaking with Lord Hollingston this morning.'

A smile spread over Caroline's face. 'Oh? About what?' She sat forward, her brows raised in expectation.

'About marrying Lady Violet.' He had thought of what he would say to his mother and sister, of course, but he hadn't considered how proud it would make him to say those words.

His mother gave a brittle smile. 'That's fine news, Seth.'

'We could have a wedding at Dalton Manor.' Caroline sat upright in her seat, her eyes shining with eagerness. 'We can use the summer roses for decoration. And there's the small parish church just in town. Oh, it will be lovely.'

Seth chuckled at her enthusiasm. 'The Season is very nearly over. I should think we will want to wed prior to then and in one of our homes here.'

'By special licence, then.' Though his mother gave an approving nod, a small line showed between her brows.

'Before either of you anticipate planning her wedding, I shall speak more with Lady Violet and inform you of my lady's desires.' Seth lifted his teacup.

'Seth,' Lady Dalton said softly.

Seth? She hadn't called him Seth in an age.

He regarded his mother and disliked the concern creasing her brow.

'Regarding Lady Violet…' She drew in a long, slow breath. 'You should know that William—'

The door opened and Gibbons entered.

They all turned to him. He offered a bow and held out his silver tray with a note upon it. 'Lord Hollingston asks that you read this post-haste.'

Seth took the missive with thanks and unfolded it.

I would see you immediately.

Seth had been anxious about his discussion with Lord Hollingston, but the single line sent tension tightening through his body. This would not be as easily done as the conversation with Lady Dalton and Caroline.

He offered an easy smile to them now, as though nothing were amiss. 'If you'll excuse me.'

Seth had it in mind to stop off with Bennet so the valet might freshen up his appearance. However, knowing the man's penchant for perfection, Seth might never leave Dalton Place and Lord Hollingston's note encouraged expediency.

After a brief pause in front of a mirror, Seth made his way next door and was promptly shown into the study where a dour-faced Lord Hollingston glowered at him from behind a large desk. He indicated the chair on the other side of the desk. 'Sit,' he commanded. 'If you please.' The latter was added in an apparent effort to be civil when his demeanour was anything but.

Seth sank on to the seat, remembering too late how loud the damn thing was. He suppressed a cringe as it squawked in protest beneath his backside.

'You've taken liberties with my daughter,' Lord Hollingston accused.

Seth sat with such stillness, the chair didn't make a sound. He kept his shoulders squared and his gaze level as he replied. 'Yes. And I intend to wed her, as I told Lady Hollingston. I wished to speak with you first thing this morning to ask for her hand in marriage.'

'That is the right thing to do, isn't it?' The anger drained from the older Earl's face. 'Do you love her?'

Love?

The chair groaned from beneath him. Seth had never loved a woman enough to know what love was.

'I care greatly for her,' he replied.

'That's luckier than most,' Hollingston grumbled. 'What did she say?'

'"She", my lord?'

Hollingston's bushy brows drew together. 'Violet. I'm assuming you've already asked her.'

Seth opened his mouth, ready to say she'd agreed, but then recalled the night before. When Lady Dalton and Seth had done most of the speaking as Violet's life was planned out for her.

Hollingston scoffed. 'I'll give you the same answer I gave you when you asked permission to court her: if she says yes, then that is my answer as well.'

'Is she available that I might speak with her?' Seth rose from the damnable seat.

'I'll see to it that she is.' Hollingston rang for a servant. 'You can wait for her in the drawing room.'

Silence fell over them as they waited on the servant to arrive. In that time, Hollingston openly appraised Seth. 'My wife informed me what you said to her before you left last night.'

Seth's mouth tightened, a hint of his rage returning anew at what the Countess had said to Violet. Seth's mother might have been indifferent to him for the better part of his life, but Violet's mother was downright cruel to her. He'd hated leaving Violet at her mercy the night before. Had it been up to him, he would have wed Violet on the spot and brought her home with him to Dalton Place.

Seth set his jaw. 'I won't apologise for it. I don't condone what she said to Violet, nor do her words hold any truth.'

The lines around Lord Hollingston's eyes crinkled deeper. 'You've grown into a man of conviction, Lord Dalton.' His mouth lifted in a half-smile. 'I find myself hoping my daughter says yes to you.'

'As do I.' Seth inclined his head graciously towards the Earl as a servant entered.

Seth followed the servant to the yellow drawing room. The lingering scents of breakfast hovered in the room, steeped tea with a sweet note of jam and a briny hint of ham.

He was directed to a matching sunny-coloured sofa, which he sat on for a moment before his nerves overcame him.

He rose to his feet, prepared to pace when the double doors opened and Lady Violet entered.

She wore a white-muslin day dress, virginal and lovely. Her hair was bound back in a knot that was less intricate than the styles he'd seen her wear. There was a quiet intimacy to it and he couldn't help but wonder if she wore her hair in such a manner at breakfast with the family where things were less formal—before house calls and social functions required a more put-together appearance.

He liked seeing her thus. It made him think of informal breakfasts with her and a quiet, happy life together, one where he could trade nightmares of the past for dreams of the future.

But first, she had to agree to marry him.

Chapter Twenty-One

Violet knew precisely why she'd been summoned to the drawing room. That suspicion was confirmed when she walked in to find Seth waiting for her.

Apprehension gripped her and the exhaustion of a night without sleep left her thoughts spinning. No doubt he was there to speak to her about what had happened, to confirm their marriage.

He came to her in two strides. 'Violet, forgive me for what transpired last night. I… I should have refrained from kissing you.'

They'd done more than kiss, of course, and his words brought back a hot tingling sensation throughout her body. His fingers had moved against her most intimate place, stroking her to a state of such exquisite pleasure.

'I enjoyed our kisses,' she replied. 'I am as much at fault.'

He reached up and gently caressed her face.

'You are always so gracious.' The corners of his mouth ticked downward. 'I should have been more in control of myself.'

Violet's stomach clenched. Would he still feel the same way once he knew the truth?

She had to tell him. Now. She drew in a breath to speak, but he rushed on. 'I realised this morning that the decision to wed was made not between you and me, but your mother and me.' He reached for Violet's hand, cradling it in his large one, and gazed deeply into her eyes so she felt as though she'd tipped headlong into the depths of his soul. 'Lady Violet, will you do me the immense honour of agreeing to marry me?'

She hesitated, unprepared to be given a choice at all in the matter. Nor was she prepared for how the question would make her emotions soar.

How wonderful it would be to say yes, to agree without caveat. Without having to confess such an awful truth.

'Seth.' She opened her mouth to speak and fear shuddered through her. She could lose him. She probably would lose him.

But he had to know.

He shook his head. 'Please don't say no just yet, Violet. Please take a moment to consider my proposal.' He folded his other hand over hers. 'I'm not asking because we were caught in a compromising position. I'm asking because I want to marry you. Because I care greatly for you. I have no desire to wed anyone but you. You're unlike any other woman of the *ton* in all the best ways.'

He cared greatly for her? He might as well have plunged a dagger into her chest. Her throat went tight with the ache inside her ribs.

She pulled her hand from his and bit her lip. 'Not all the best ways. I'm not...'

The words stuck fast in her throat and welled there, practically choking her.

'If you're not ready, we can have a long engagement.' He offered her a small smile, one that flicked up at the corners in a brief show of nerves. 'I'd thought to procure a special licence if you wished to wed before the Season ends, but if you'd prefer to wait, we can.'

She shook her head and swallowed. 'Seth, I... I'm not a virgin.'

His brow furrowed. 'I beg your pardon.'

'It was the night of my debut.' Her words caught. 'I was in that hideous dress my mother made me wear due to my failure and...' She slid her gaze away, hating to admit Seth's part in that night. 'You had just left. I assumed you thought me ugly and, well, my heart was shattered to bits. There was a gentleman who comforted me and asked if he might dance with me that evening.'

Seth watched her silently as she spoke, his face absent of any expression she could use to gauge his emotions.

'He was charming.' She sighed at her own foolish younger self. 'He said all the right things. He...'

'He what?' There was a sharpness to Seth's tone.

'He made me feel beautiful.' A warm tear trickled down Violet's cheek at the admission. 'All my life, I had been made to feel as though I was unattractive—too fat. My mother, my sisters...'

'Me,' Seth said quietly.

Violet kept her head lowered, unable to look at him as she nodded silently. 'He was the only person who ever said things that made me feel as though I was something more than a frumpy woman. I thought him in love with me, I assumed he was of a mind to marry me, but I was too afraid to ask. As though I might break a spell somehow woven over this man who was far too attractive to be drawn to someone like me. I was desperate to do anything to keep his attention.'

She sat on the sofa. 'When it was done, he left immediately. He didn't call upon me the following day or the one after that. When next we saw one another, he treated me with a cool, cordial politeness that indicated what I had been suspecting, what I'd been fearing the most.'

She swallowed in an attempt to clear the hurt from her throat, but it did little good. 'He had used me.' She fingered the edge of a ribbon on her gown. 'I knew myself to be ruined and so I allowed myself to melt into the background. If no one paid me any notice, I would never have to share my secret. I could remain quietly ruined and no one would be any the wiser.'

It was the first time she'd spoken the truth aloud. Hearing it in her own ears made her realise how absolutely pathetic it truly was. She covered her face with her hands, not wanting to see Seth, or the obnoxiously sunny yellow room. She didn't want to face any of it. Least of all herself.

The cushion shifted beside her and the familiar scent of warm male and shaving soap told her Seth was at her side.

'Violet.' He said her name softly.

She scrunched her eyes and kept her face down towards the carpet. Every part of her was scraped raw by finally exposing the truth. Her eyes were gritty from lack of sleep and barely contained tears. She wanted nothing more than to be left alone, to throw herself upon her bed and weep until her eyes ran dry.

His fingers brushed her cheek, turning her face towards him. She kept her eyes closed, as though somehow that might prepare her for his rejection.

'Open your eyes,' he said.

She did as he asked and held her breath, fearful of what would follow.

Seth's heartbeat slammed in his chest and his thoughts reeled. Of all the reasons he'd suspected

Violet had let herself fade away, being ruined was not one of them.

Violet watched him, her wide blue eyes fixed on him with a cautious trust, hesitant hope. Tears left her lashes spiked and cheeks wet.

She looked so vulnerable that he wanted to curl her into his arms to protect her for ever.

He had done that to her. By not dancing with her that night. He'd made her feel as though he thought she was so unappealing that he'd rather leave than spend a single moment with her. He had pushed her into that man's arms. Whoever it might be.

Ice chilled his blood.

He knew exactly who it might be. His mother's words prior to Seth receiving the missive summoning him to Hollingston House flew back in his mind. Something regarding William and Violet.

'Who did this to you?' he demanded. 'Who took your innocence?'

She shook her head. 'It doesn't matter,' she whispered.

But it did. To Seth. If William had lain with her and now Seth was to marry her… His stomach churned. William had been diagnosed with syphilis. Seth was no physician—he didn't know how long someone might have the disease before a diagnosis could be ascertained.

'Who was it?' Seth asked again.

Violet's eyes filled with tears. 'Please, I don't wish to say.'

'I want to know,' Seth replied. 'I *need* to know.'

'It doesn't matter,' she repeated. 'He's dead now anyway. He was killed in a duel with a jealous husband.'

Ice formed into sharp-edged knots in his gut.

He's dead now anyway.

Dear God, it *was* William.

An image flashed in his mind of his brother drawing Violet into the dark shadows of the garden as Seth had done, kissing her as Seth had, sliding up her skirts…touching her.

Anger lashed at Seth. If his brother was still alive, it would only be long enough to meet over pistols at dawn. Energy swelled like a savage beast inside Seth's chest. It flared through his muscles and left them tense in preparation for battle. His senses heightened as they did before a fight, hearing everything, seeing everything, *feeling* everything.

And there was much to feel.

Betrayal. Fear. Disgust.

'Tell me his name,' Seth said in a low voice.

Violet stiffened at the ugliness of his tone. 'Please. It's too…' Her eyes welled with tears and she wiped them away. 'It's too mortifying. I've already humiliated myself enough.'

Seth frowned. She was insistent on keeping her secret.

But did she know about William? About his illness? Could it remain dormant in the body and affect the victim years later?

'Have you had any symptoms of syphilis?' he asked.

She blinked at him and her mouth fell open in outrage. 'I beg your pardon?'

Seth drew from his memory to recall soldiers who had suffered from the disease. 'Sores on your person, a rash. Sometimes a sore throat or—'

She leapt up from the seat and backed away from him. 'How dare you?'

'Violet, I—'

'I confessed to you the secret I've been carrying inside of me for six years, the secret that ended any dreams of marriage or children or love.' A sob escaped her lips and she covered her mouth with her hand as if she could catch it and pull it back in. 'And you are concerned I might have syphilis?'

'I don't think you do,' Seth said hastily. 'I don't understand why you just won't tell me who did this to you.'

Her face coloured a vivid shade of red. 'Because it's utterly mortifying, Seth. Because I've been a fraud for six years and the one person I thought might actually accept me has made me feel worse than the man who ruined me.'

Good God. When she put it that way, it was terrible of him. What had he done?

'Violet.' He got to his feet and reached for her, but she snatched her hand away from him.

She stiffened her back. 'Good day, Lord Dalton.' Her words frosted over the sunny room, then she spun on her heel and departed the room despite his calling after her.

He pursued her to the double doors of the drawing room and paused. Should he chase her through the house? It seemed rather uncouth, but it was better than letting her get away.

Her footsteps pounded up the stairs over his head. He turned down the hall towards the staircase and met their butler, Wilson.

The older man remained stoically in Seth's path. 'May I help you, my lord?'

A door closed upstairs with considerable force and disappointment crushed Seth. Violet would not be accessible today.

Emotions swirled through him like a chaotic blizzard, pieces so powerful, so thick as they congealed together in a massive blob that they were indistinguishable together. Indiscernible and overwhelming.

Seth's shoulders sagged. 'I'd like to be shown out if you please, Wilson.'

'As you wish.' Wilson indicated with a white-gloved hand. 'This way.'

Seth was shown out of Hollingston House, but didn't bother to take the short path home. Instead, he made his way to the mews and asked Harold to bring the carriage round. He could use some time at White's, in the company of gentlemen, without all the drama of marriages and debauching brothers and ladies who had fornicated with one's brother.

Even as he climbed into the carriage, another image flashed in his head of his brother drawing up Violet's skirts, touching her creamy inner thighs. Did she make the same breathy cries of pleasure for him? Did she look up at him with that same dreamy expression?

He put his head in his hands as he did so often when plagued by memories of war and wished he could expunge the thoughts from his mind with sheer willpower alone. The carriage came to a hard stop that nearly sent him flying from his seat.

He burst from the carriage before Burton could get the door for him and leapt down without using the dainty little step. 'Have a care with those stops, Harold,' he called sharply over his shoulder.

'Sorry, m'lord.' Harold's jovial voice met Seth's back.

If Seth hadn't been so drunk the night of Violet's debut, he would not have leered at her in that dress. He would not have had to hide his lustful thoughts behind an unapologetic absence. She would not have been left at the mercy of other men with her pride bruised and her confidence crumbled.

'Dalton.' Rawley joined Seth. 'Are you well?'

Seth requested a glass with two fingers of brandy. 'I've been better.'

'I spoke with Caroline last night.' Rawley gave

him a shy smile. 'Do you think she minded that I spoke of my adverse reaction to shrimp?'

Did William tug down Violet's dress? Did he fondle her full breasts? Kiss them as Seth had?

'I worried after the fact that it might have been ill mannered.' Rawley brushed his fingers inside his pocket where his watch sat. 'I've been plagued with worry over it all night.'

Did William's teeth tease over her rosy nipples? Did she cry out for him?

Rawley cleared his throat. 'I say, Dalton, you really don't seem well at all.'

Seth pinched the bridge of his nose. 'There is a courtesan—'

Rawley began vigorously shaking his head. 'I'll have none of that.'

The servant delivered the brandy to Seth and he took a deep, burning sip. Could fire cleanse hell?

He was about to find out.

'There is a courtesan who instructs ladies of the *ton* in the art of flirtation,' Seth finished his original statement. 'Her name is Lottie. You ought to see her. Not for pleasure, but for instruction in how to talk to a woman. For God's sake, man, it could not be easier. My sister is infatuated with you. Yet at every turn, you make her think you are lacking in interest. Do yourself, and her, and me for that matter, a favour and make an appointment for instruction.'

Rawley's nose twitched. 'She instructs men?'

'I imagine she does.' Seth took another swallow.

Rawley nodded in quiet consideration. 'Thank you for your counsel.'

Seth grunted, not certain if he was pleased to be done with the vexing conversation or annoyed that he would be left at the mercilessness of his tortured thoughts. Perhaps it was a little of both.

If he had been at the ball that night to dance with Violet, William would never have had to fill in for him.

A sudden realisation slammed into him that left the brandy in his empty stomach swirling.

Even if William had taken advantage of Violet, Seth's sin was far worse than hers, for he had turned his back on her.

He was right when he said she was better than he deserved and not just because he was a broken man. He was an idiot.

It was time to show her that he had truly changed from the foolish youth who had walked away all those years ago into a man who cared about her above all else. A man who might some day be deserving of her.

Chapter Twenty-Two

∞

Violet could cry no more. Or so she thought. Every time she considered she might truly be emptied of all tears, a single thought of how Seth had looked at her reduced her to a watering pot once more.

Syphilis.

The gall of that man! To presume she might be diseased.

Clearly he didn't believe it to be only one man who had ruined her. Might as well be all of London for how he perceived her. She wanted to laugh at the ridiculousness of it, except that the question had made her feel vile. She'd said enough terrible things to herself throughout the years she'd chastised herself for her transgressions. But never, *never*, had she felt as low as she had when he asked if she'd exhibited signs of syphilis.

A knock came from Violet's bedroom door. She cringed deeper into a vast mountain of pillows.

The rap sounded again.

'Please go away,' she muffled into a pillow.

'It isn't your mother, if that makes a difference,' Lord Hollingston said.

Violet dragged herself into a sitting position. 'It does.'

'So I may enter?'

'Yes,' she replied in a small voice.

Lord Hollingston entered the room with tentative steps, his gaze slowly descending on his surroundings. He hadn't been in her bedchamber since she was a girl just out of the nursery.

'Your mother took Felicity to the park to take some air. The girl has been melancholy.' His stare lingered on the silver-tissue gown on the dressmaker's form. 'Why the devil do you keep that?'

She didn't bother to glance in the direction of the gown. Doing so only reminded her of Seth, of the night of her debut, and caused far too great an ache in her chest. 'To remind myself I can do better.'

'Rubbish.' He stalked his way to the gown. 'I've half a mind to burn the wretched thing.'

'Please don't.'

He hissed out a breath and glared at the gown. 'Very well.' He tucked his hands behind his back. 'Tell me why you're so upset, sweet girl.'

She shook her head. 'It doesn't matter. All you need to know is that my schedule has cleared and

I am now available to Sophie to be at the beck and call of her children.'

'Do you wonder if they all have cats?' her father mused with an affectionate smile.

A tentative smile spread over Violet's lips. 'Is it wrong that I rather hope they do?'

'The girl has turned out rather well.' Her father stepped closer to where Violet sat up in bed. 'Spirited as ever, of course, but she's a good child. I have no doubt you would tame the others as well. But it isn't necessary.'

'Not necessary?' Violet studied her father curiously.

He heaved a heavy sigh. 'I had thought to have you find a man you could love. Not all marriages are happy ones, I understand that.' He rolled his eyes. 'Be assured, I understand better than most,' he muttered. 'But many are. Your cousin, Eleanor, has a fortunate marriage. I'd hoped you'd find a match like that, a man to make you light up the way you used to.'

'The way I used to?' she asked.

'Before your debut. Before your mother harangued that joy out of you.' Her father indicated the pink-silk chair near the table by Violet's bed. 'May I?'

Violet nodded and sat on the edge of the bed.

'She wasn't always so difficult.' Her father sank into the dainty seat. 'Before any of your siblings were born, we had a child—a little girl. She did not live past the age of three. Your mother blamed herself. Once your eldest sister was born, your mother became obsessed with ensuring everything was perfect when it came to her children.'

Violet pressed her lips together. She hadn't known about a sister who had died, nor her mother's reaction to it. The anger in her heart softened with sympathy.

'Everyone gave way to her,' her father continued. 'Until you. You've always been a free spirit, my Violet.' His eyes crinkled with affection. 'I dare say you nearly gave her an apoplexy on more than one occasion. The more you defied her as a child, the more she tried to control you.' Lines showed on his face as he frowned. 'I should have spoken up before, prevented her from…' He spread his hands. 'From taking your light. I thought love might bring it back. I see now that is not the case. Forgive me, Violet.'

She shook her head. 'You've nothing to apologise for.'

'Your tear-stained face would suggest otherwise.' Her father pushed up from his chair. 'I'm afraid I've made quite the mess of things. But if you do not wish to marry, then I will not force you. Nor will I force you into the country. You may choose what it is you wish to do.' He hesitated. 'Do you know what that might be?'

The thought of going to the country for ever did not hold appeal, but neither did regressing to a muted life once more. Nor would she continue her efforts in writing the *Lady Observer*. Not after realising the hurt she'd most likely caused.

Marriage. To Seth. For a whisper of a moment, that had held considerable appeal. Until she recalled how terribly he'd rejected her.

What would Lottie say in this moment?

But even the woman's wise words fell silent in Violet's mind.

Violet shook her head miserably. 'No. I don't know what I would like to do.'

'You have some time.' Lord Hollingston went to her and pressed a kiss on the top of her head as he'd done when she was a girl. 'But a decision will need to be made.'

Yes, it would. And not a single one promised to make her happy.

Her father cleared his throat. 'If I may make a suggestion…'

She looked up at him.

'Lord Dalton appears to a man of conviction.' Lord Hollingston puffed his chest out as he presented his endorsement. 'And he seems to care for you a great deal.'

Violet choked down a sob. Even if Seth truly did care for her a great deal, it clearly wasn't enough.

Hollingston House's butler was rather cross with Seth. Wilson wouldn't outwardly say it, of course, but then, he didn't need to. It was evident in the flush about his face that made the wisps of snow-white hair stand out like tufts of cotton.

'My lord, I'm afraid Lady Violet is not accepting callers.' Wilson's tone had lost its sympathy.

'Go to her again,' Seth replied. 'Tell her I refuse to leave Hollingston House until I've spoken with her.

'My lord, I've gone to her three times already—'

'A fourth time, then,' Seth countered. 'And a fifth and a sixth. However many it bloody well takes.'

Wilson bowed, most likely to cover a grimace. 'As you wish, my lord.'

This time the butler did not come down for a longer stretch of time and Seth dared to hope. Perhaps that meant Violet had changed her mind, that she would indeed come down.

His realisation at White's, and even his irritated conversation with Rawley, had sparked an understanding in him. Seth had lowered Violet's confidence that night of her debut—he'd left her at the mercy of William as surely as he'd abandoned his own family in their greatest time of need after William's death. Hell, even in handling him when he became so ill.

As he was making reparations to his own family, so, too, did he need to make them to Violet. And that included putting William from his mind to be with her.

If it wasn't too late, that is.

He stared at the closed double doors of the drawing room. Would she give him the chance?

He didn't deserve it. Even Seth knew that. But it didn't mean he couldn't hope.

After an interminable stretch of what felt like an eternity, the double doors opened. But it was not Wilson who walked through—it was Violet.

She wore a different muslin gown, this one with yellow ribbons that were as sun-coloured as the room he was in. Her hair had been neatly styled from the knot it'd been in earlier that day. She lifted her head, appearing entirely put together and nonplussed.

'You insist on seeing me.' She put her hands to her hips. 'I'm here to inform you that I wish for you to leave.'

Seth widened his stance. 'I won't go.'

'I don't want you to stay.'

Seth shook his head. 'Please give me a chance.'

'Seth.' Her voice cracked.

'Violet,' he said her name with all the regret roiling inside him.

Her face crumpled. 'Leave me be.'

He rushed to her side. There was a pink tinge to her nose and a red-rimmed, bloodshot appearance to her eyes told him what her stoic demeanour tried to mask: she had been crying.

And he'd been the cause.

'I will not leave you.' Seth reached for her.

'I trusted you.' She pushed him away. 'Leave me to pick up the pieces you left when you shattered me.'

'No.' He didn't reach for her again, not if she didn't wish him to. But he wouldn't leave, damn it. Not until they had this conversation.

She shot a hurtful glare at him. 'So you can break me again? And again? And again?'

He winced. She was right. He had spent a lifetime hurting her when all he'd ever wanted to do was be there for her, with her.

'I want to help you pick up the pieces.' He stepped closer and the ache in his chest was nearly more than he could bear. 'I want to ensure you will never be anything but whole again.'

Even if he was not.

She drew in a shuddering breath and strode towards the chair nearest the tea tray that had been laid out by a servant some time earlier.

He followed her. 'I'm an idiot.'

She lifted her head and regarded him. 'I believe we've had this conversation before.'

'And I told you I'd changed.' He gave a mirthless chuckle. 'Clearly, I have not.'

She did not contradict him. Instead, she poured them both tea with hands that trembled so badly, the delicate china rattled.

Seth sank on to the chair beside her. 'You accepted me as I am. I have not afforded you the same courtesy.'

She lowered her head, appearing to be rather taken with her teacup, and gave a little sniff.

'Violet,' he said softly. 'Forgive me.'

'Even if I forgive you, it does not change what I've done.' She set the teacup down untouched and wrapped her arms around herself.

He shook his head. 'I don't care what you've done. It was never the act in any event. I certainly cannot judge you with my tarnished past. I confess…' He grimaced. 'I confess, it was a shock to discover you had…'

'Lost my innocence?' she supplied with a bitter note.

'No.'

Damn. This was harder than he'd anticipated. He got to his feet and paced. 'I mean, yes. It's only that, well, the idea that William had taken such liberties with you, it was hard to accept.'

She furrowed her brows. 'William?'

'Yes, William. My brother.' The weight in his soul lightened with a thread of hope. 'Was the man not William?' he asked slowly.

'No,' she said softly. 'He was…' She scrunched her eyes shut. 'Lord Fordson.'

Fordson.

Seth knew something of the man. He was a year younger than himself, a foppish profligate who was far too pretty for his own good with a silver tongue that'd eased his passage under many skirts. It did not strike Seth as uncharacteristic that Fordson would stoop to debauch an earl's daughter.

'Why would you not say?' Seth asked.

'I told you why,' Violet cried. 'It was hard enough to be honest with you about the one moment I ruined my entire life. To give you details—it felt so sordid. It made me feel too exposed. Too vulnerable.'

'I'm apparently a complete fool.' He leaned his head back in frustration at himself. 'I assumed it was William since he would have been in such close proximity to you and with his penchant for debauching ladies...'

Violet cast him an incredulous stare. 'Your brother? Truly?'

'He had syphilis,' Seth explained. He didn't stop there, he detailed the whole of it. William being placed in an institution to protect women and even what happened with Mr Pattinson and the jewels. 'It is why I asked you questions about it,' he concluded. 'Please do forgive me.'

Violet nodded slowly. 'I had no idea.'

'My mother...' Seth sighed. 'She tried to tell me something about William and you. I thought...' He ran his hand through his hair with irritation at himself.

'William tried to flirt with me on several occasions,' Violet confessed. 'But he was not the brother I wanted.'

'Wanted.' Seth lifted his brows. 'Still want?'

Violet looked down, not with anger, but with a shy demur. His heart skipped a beat. Seth took her hand in his and loosened her arm from its tight grip around her torso. 'I am not perfect. I have not led a perfect life. And clearly I have a penchant for speaking before I think. I don't deserve you, Violet, but I hope to God you are willing to take me anyway.'

She bit her lip. 'Are you…?'

'Proposing? Yes.' He sank to his knees before her. 'I love you, Violet. I was too daft to realise it before I very nearly lost you. But, looking back, I've always felt this way. The reason I never said goodbye to you before joining the army, the reason I never danced with you the night of your debut, was because I was a coward. I loved you and it scared me witless.' He took her hand in his. 'The only thing that frightens me now is the possibility of losing you.'

Tears swam in her eyes.

'Marry me, Violet.' He kissed the back of her hand. 'Please.'

She put her free hand to her mouth and gave a little sob. He hoped it was one of joy.

'You do deserve me,' she whispered. 'You see imperfection in yourself and find so much wanting. But I see you as you are, Seth. You are brave and you are strong, far more so than I think you'll ever realise.'

Seth swallowed hard. She wouldn't say these

things to him if she didn't believe him. She'd never been a woman for idle talk. If she saw these things in him, he would not contradict her. But he would spend a lifetime proving her right.

'Do you mean…?' He lifted his brows, wanting her to say it.

She nodded. 'Yes. Yes, I will marry you.'

Yes.

Had ever so small a word held such visceral impact?

He leapt up and swept her into his arms. Lady Violet Lavell, soon-to-be Violet Dalton, his wife.

Even as he held her to him, even as he longed for nothing more than to kiss her and touch her, he swore to himself he would not be alone with her until they were wed. He had abused her trust and would do anything to get it back, for it was not lost on him that she had not returned his sentiments of love.

The hollowness inside his chest filled that moment with a promise—to himself and to her: to spend every day being the man she thought him to be. To be fully and completely worthy of her love.

Chapter Twenty-Three

A special licence was procured to minimise the wait for marrying and to allow them to wed in Violet's home. The morning of their wedding had arrived in the blink of an eye only days later.

Violet sat before her dressing mirror as Susan curled the last of Violet's dark locks with heating tongs in preparation for the simple coif she'd chosen for the wedding.

Violet glanced at the blank corner of her room where the silver gown used to stand in reminder of her failure. Like her father, Seth had declared his desire to burn the thing, but Violet had insisted it be set up in her new suite.

This request had been made during a walk in Hyde Park together as Seth had refused to see Violet alone until their wedding. Though he knew she was not a virgin, he would not bring himself to take her until they were wed.

A knock sounded at the door.

Susan carefully set the tongs down and gave a little squeal of delight. Violet gave her maid a curious look as Susan rushed to the door, opened it and returned with a wide box in her arms. 'For you, Lady Violet.'

Violet got up from her seat and went to the bed where Susan had laid the box.

A note was on top with careful writing.

For you to wear or keep or burn as you so desire.

   I want only your happiness, now and for ever.
All my love,
Seth

All his love. He had proclaimed that love with a vehemence that had stunned her when he'd proposed to her. And despite the considerable affection she held for him, she had been too much of a coward to tell him how much she loved him.

She had been hopeful about marriage and love too many times over. First with Seth when they were younger, then Lord Fordson, then again with Seth. It had been a miscommunication, yes, but his initial reaction to her past had cut her to the quick and left her with the pathetic need to secure a guard around her heart.

Experience had taught her it was far too fragile. Violet lifted the lid off the box and sucked in a breath. The silver gown was nestled in a cloud of tissue paper. Seth had not only given her the hope for happiness in the future, he had given her the silver gown back. The gesture was marvellously considerate.

She cast a look to Susan, who just kept grinning.

'Do you want to wear it, my lady?' Susan asked.

'Yes, I do,' Violet said softly.

The maid set to work, fastening Violet into the silver gown. The panelling at the sides to make it a size larger had been expertly inserted and was nearly imperceptible. Violet made her way to the cheval mirror by her wardrobe. The skirts rustled as she walked, whispering of the dreams she'd once had when she'd put it on order at the modiste six years ago.

Those dreams were now being realised. Finally.

She stared into the mirror and ran her hands over the fitted bodice. It was every bit as beautiful as she'd imagined it would be. She'd never had the opportunity to put it on, always being slightly too large to fasten it regardless of how much she'd starved herself.

She turned to the side, marvelling at the delicate pleating in the skirts, how the waist nipped in at the middle and the way the top hugged her breasts in an elegant but enticing manner. Seth would approve most enthusiastically of that last bit.

Seth. He had been her friend when she'd been

a lonely child in London, a flirtation when she'd been on the cusp of womanhood and nothing more than a dream when her world had shattered. He'd come back into her broken life and helped her make it whole again.

'Oh, my lady,' Susan breathed. 'It's lovely.'

'It is,' Violet agreed. 'Please take it off now.'

Susan's elation faded. 'I beg your pardon?'

'This gown has represented failure for far too long.' Violet put her back to her maid. 'I prefer to begin my married life in a gown ready for new memories rather than one stained with old ones.'

'I rather like that.' Susan set to work unfastening the back of Violet's gown.

Violet looked to the dressmaker's form, now adorned in an elegant frock of pale blue silk with small puffed sleeves and a skirt that swept the floor behind her as she walked. It was simple and complemented her colouring. 'I do, too.'

Susan helped her out of the silver gown and folded it back into the modiste's box. The blue gown went on easily and floated against Violet's skin like a whisper. How would it feel as it slid from her skin and puddled on the floor? A chill of anticipation prickled over her. Soon, she would be wed and, not long after, she would be alone with Seth. In the privacy of his master suite in Dalton Place where most of Violet's belongings had already been relocated.

Susan put her hair into a series of twists with violets sprinkled throughout her dark tresses.

A soft knock came at Violet's door, and Felicity entered upon permission to do so. Her hair had been drawn into a wonderful coiffure that made her look rather grown-up and she held herself with the decorum of a lady. Well, if ladies carried fat cats in their arms, of course.

'Felicity, you look lovely,' Violet said with genuine delight.

Her shoulders lifted, clearly pleased with the compliment. 'As do you. And Hedgehog.' She scratched the cat under the chin and his vibrating purr filled the room. 'Do you recognise the silk?'

She stopped petting him long enough to point to his bonnet. It was the very same ice blue as Violet's gown. Violet's mouth fell open and Felicity grinned. 'The modiste had some scraps left over and I asked her if I might have them.'

'You made the bonnet?' Violet asked.

Felicity shrugged. 'Of course. I make all of them.'

The child's melancholy had lifted with the wedding preparations, though Violet suspected Felicity was dreading returning home, which was the source of her unhappiness.

Felicity cocked her head suddenly and raised her brows. 'I believe I hear music. Hurry or you'll be late for your own wedding.' With that, she rushed from the room, leaving the door slightly ajar in her haste.

Violet and Susan looked at one another and chuckled. 'I wonder how she can love that cat so much,' Violet mused.

'I believe...' Susan said slowly. 'She treats the cat the way she wishes she might be treated.'

Violet opened her mouth to protest the notion, but stopped. Ever since Felicity had arrived and Seth had demonstrated how best to speak to the girl, Felicity had been wonderfully behaved.

'I think you're correct,' Violet said softly.

'I believe you treat her exactly how she wants to be treated, my lady.' Susan fidgeted with a flower in Violet's hair and smiled. 'Now go downstairs where your handsome Earl awaits you.' Tears filled her maid's eyes and Violet had to turn away before she, too, began to cry.

Lord Hollingston waited for Violet by the double doors leading to the drawing room. His chest swelled with pride as she approached.

'You look lovely, Daughter,' he said.

She embraced him. 'Thank you, Father. And thank you for encouraging me to wed. I think I'm going to be very happy.'

'I truly hope so.' He kissed her cheek. 'I truly do hope so.'

He offered her his arm and led her into the drawing room where the vicar waited for them with the *Book of Common Prayer* in his hand. She scarcely noticed the man, or anyone else for that matter.

Seth waited at the end of the room with his

arms folded behind his back like the soldier he'd been for so many years. His unruly hair had been combed into submission, and he wore cream-coloured breeches with a gold and cream brocade waistcoat, finished off handsomely with his dark superfine jacket.

He watched her with affection shining in his expressive eyes and when he spoke the vows binding them together for ever, she felt the depth of his sincerity in his fathomless gaze. At last, when the ceremony was complete and his mouth brushed over the backs of her knuckles, the skin under her gloves tingled with anticipation.

In fact, *all* of her tingled with anticipation, for this man she had spent a lifetime wanting.

The time after the wedding ceremony had been spent in a blur of congratulatory toasts and well-wishes. But to Seth, nearly all his attention had remained focused on the exquisite beauty of his bride.

It had not escaped his notice how her ice-blue eyes continued to slide over to him, heating him from the inside out. How was it that even a glance from her could make his body go tense with eagerness?

After a hearty wedding breakfast had been consumed, several more toasts made and the cutting of the lovely frosted cake, finally it was time to take Violet to their home. They left Hollingston House amid a flurry of felicitations and entered the quiet hall of Dalton Place.

Seth wanted nothing more than to draw Violet up the curved staircase to his bedchamber and watch the silky gown flutter from her body. He wanted her naked and writhing with need beneath him. He wanted her to be *his*. Fully and completely. In body as well as in name.

He reined in his impatience as his Countess was introduced to the staff of her new home, though she already knew them all well from years of close familial acquaintance. Instead, he observed her, noting the genuine warmth on her face as she spoke to each member of his staff, remembering not only their names, but also those of their families and asked after them.

His blood stirred as he watched her, cherishing from afar the woman he would soon worship up close. She would be a wonderful mistress of Dalton Place, as well as Dalton Manor when they relocated to the country once Parliament let out. More than that, she would be an ideal mother. Her consideration and care with Felicity had demonstrated as much.

At last, the final servant had been properly introduced and they all began to resume their duties.

Violet turned back to Seth with a coy gaze that slammed straight into his groin. Her pretty mouth lifted at the corner. 'I saw you staring at me, my lord.'

He hummed in acquiescence—no sense in denying it—and offered her his arm.

She accepted his offer, her touch sensual as it
crept slowly over the crook of his elbow. 'Dare I
ask what you're thinking?'

'Dare me to show you and you've got yourself
a bargain.' He lifted a brow at her.

She sucked in a breath and glanced about.

'You needn't worry,' he assured her. 'We're
quite alone.'

She stepped closer, bringing with her the sweet
scent of violets that adorned her dark hair. 'I'd
rather be even more alone.'

He grinned. 'Who am I to deny my lovely
young wife her wishes?'

He led her up the stairs to his bedchamber,
closed the door and turned the key in the lock. His
heart slammed like a drum in great, heavy thuds.

She looked up at him with a coquettish smile.
'Now you'll show me what you were thinking?'

A kiss on the back of her gloved hand hadn't
been enough for him earlier. He'd wanted her full
lips under his, her curves pressed against him.

'With immense pleasure, my wife.' He pulled
her into his arms and lowered his mouth to hers
the way he'd longed to do.

She met his kiss and parted her lips so her
tongue brushed his. Fire shot through him, singe-
ing every nerve ending with the force of his blatant desire. He had held off on being alone with
her after their engagement until this very moment,
when he knew he would not have to hold back.

'Violet,' he groaned into her mouth. 'My beautiful Violet.'

She echoed his desire with a moan and ran her hands down his chest, plucking at the buttons of his waistcoat. He tipped her head back further and deepened the kiss as his hands met the cool silk of her gown and the lush curves beneath.

His palms skimmed over her hip, over her round rump and up to her full breasts. He wanted to hold every voluptuous part of her to him and marvel at the movement of her breasts while he took her in hard, steady thrusts.

A growl slid from somewhere in his throat. He dragged his mouth down to her neck where the sweet, powdery scent of her violet perfume fired through his senses like erotic gunpowder. His fingers fumbled with frantic need over the silk-covered buttons. The damn things were impossibly small and slipped beneath his fingertips before finally releasing from the narrow closures.

The task was rendered all the more difficult by the way Violet's hands roamed over his torso. She pushed his jacket down his shoulders, forcing him to briefly part from the buttons. Next came his waistcoat.

Damn it, how many bloody buttons were there?

He was somewhere midway down her back when her fingers curled around his shaft and his mind went utterly and completely blank.

He didn't recall undoing the rest of the buttons,

but he did remember the exact moment that he eased the delicate fabric from her shoulders with a simple caress and how it fell like a sigh to the ground in a shimmering pool of fine silk.

Her fingers abandoned their exploration while he took her in.

The short corset she wore was of a heartier silk, also blue where it cradled her breasts in offering to him with the globes of firm cleavage rising high on her chest. Good God.

He cradled her breasts in his hands and buried his face in their bounty. They were likewise perfumed with that quintessential violet scent. He grazed his mouth over her smooth, warm skin while his fingers teased at the edge of the heavy silk, drawing it down to free a single pink bud of a nipple.

It popped free of the binding and his mouth closed over it, his tongue flicking until the little nub was instantly hard against the tip of his tongue. Violet cried out and cradled his head, holding him to her generous breasts.

He continued to love her nipples while his fingers found the silken cords used to tie the bodice. He unknotted the dratted thing, unlaced it and shoved it aside so she wore only her chemise.

He was practically panting with need. His hands shook as he reached for the small ribbon that held the neckline of the chemise drawn closed.

Now. He would finally see her now. Love her now. Have her now.

And, oh, how he wanted her. With a lust that couldn't be slaked by a single night together. A lifetime might not be enough for him, especially with how she moaned and squirmed under his touch. She'd hidden that passion with the wallflowers for years and he would make her experience it to the fullest every day for the rest of their lives.

He took that simple ribbon and wound one end around his forefinger securely. His gaze slid to hers. The delicate muscles of her neck stood out and she watched him with what almost appeared to be shyness.

Despite the confidence she exuded, there was still self-doubt lingering on her face. Her forearms flinched where they hung awkwardly at her side, as though she longed to cross her arms over her chest and press the thin linen closer to her body so it couldn't be lifted off.

Her self-consciousness wouldn't be apparent to most, but a lifetime of knowing her made it apparent to him.

His sweet Violet. He would ensure she knew exactly how beautiful he found her, exactly how much she stoked the inferno of his desire.

Without dropping his gaze from her, he pulled gently on the ribbon wrapped around his finger and the bow at her chemise slipped free.

Chapter Twenty-Four

Violet had to will her heart to remain in her chest. As it was, she feared at any moment it might leap out through her throat or knock through her ribs.

No man had ever seen her disrobed. Not even Lord Fordson. He'd had her in a quick moment in the garden during the night of her debut.

Seth's dark gaze glittered with desire as he brushed his finger over her collarbone, stroking her skin with a feather-light touch as he loosened the neckline of her chemise. She fought to keep her hands at her sides when she longed for nothing more than to cross her arms over her chest to keep the flimsy fabric in place.

The neckline gaped around her shoulders and slipped down several inches. Seth's stare dropped lower.

It was in that incredibly vulnerable moment, the most awful thing trickled through her mind: her mother's words.

Men wanted women who were fashionably slender. Plump women were unseemly. A body like Violet's would never be considered attractive.

She sucked in a breath and her arms flew up before the chemise could ease down another inch, clutching it to her chest.

Seth didn't chastise her for her action, or demand she pull her arms away. Instead, he tilted her face up towards him. 'I've spent more moments than I can count fantasising about what you look like.'

She shook her head and hated the tears burning in her eyes. If he had indeed fantasised about her, she did not wish to ruin it with reality.

'I imagined your breasts are firm and lovely.' He skimmed his fingers over the fallen neckline of her chemise and her skin shivered at the caress. 'Enough to overflow from my hands.'

His touch swept lower to her waist. 'I imagined your hips are full and feminine, something to hold on to while I thrust into you.'

Her breath caught at the boldness of his words.

'And as for this…' He caught her bottom with both hands and pressed her to the very obvious erection rising hard between them. 'I want to clutch it in my hands while you ride me.'

His eyes held hers. 'Remember when I told you how seeing you in that gown on your debut made me want to kiss you?'

She nodded, unable to even speak.

His hips flexed against her rhythmically as he spoke, pressing his arousal into the softness between her legs where she thundered with need.

He was breathing heavily, his chest rising and falling with the evident longing he felt. 'I lied.'

Violet blinked at the unexpected words and turned away so he couldn't see her flash of hurt.

He released her bottom and gently turned her face back towards him. 'I didn't want to kiss you. I wanted this.' His hands ran down her body. 'I wanted *you.*'

He reached up and slid a pin from her hair. A liberated curl fell over her shoulder as the violet pinned in place tumbled to the floor.

'I wanted you so badly that I didn't trust myself to dance with you.' He drew another pin from her locks, then another. 'I've never experienced lust as powerful as that. It's why I left. I worried... I worried I wouldn't be able to control that longing.'

Her hair was loose around her shoulders now with a dozen dark purple flowers dotting the floor. She gaped at him, unable to fully process what he'd just told her.

'And you...you still want me?' she whispered. 'Like that?'

He growled and pulled her to him. He kissed her hungrily, thoroughly, so the breath fled her lungs and didn't bother returning. His kisses went

down her neck and his teeth nipped her earlobe.
A fresh wave of tingles skittered over her skin.

'I still want you that badly,' he said against her
ear. 'Even more. Even after all these years. Even
after all this time. Good God, Violet.' He took her
hand and carefully lowered it from where she held
her chemise. '*Feel* what you do to me.'

Touching his arousal had been different earlier, when it was of her own volition, when it was
not him guiding her to see her effect on him. She
pressed her fingers obligingly to the blazing heat
bulging against his placket. It was hot as a fever
and hard as steel.

He hissed out a breath from between clenched
teeth. '*You* do that to me.' He kissed down her
collarbone to the expanse of her chest and lower
still to where she still held her chemise with her
free hand. 'Let me see you, my beautiful Violet.'

She released her hold on the final bit of clothing and let it join the silk gown on the floor. He
stepped back to look at her and drew in a quiet
breath. Violet clenched her hands to keep them
from crossing back over her chest while his gaze
rose from the blue satin slippers to the white silk
stockings tied just above her knees, and up to
where there was nothing but, well, her.

'Violet.' Her name was little more than a groan
on his lips. He reached for her, kissing her, gliding his hands over her naked body. 'You're even
lovelier than I imagined.'

It was on the edge of her mind to question his compliments, but he stroked her with too much reverence, his ardour too convincing. And even when the last shreds of doubt clung to her mind, he gripped her to him and thrust against her with a soul-deep groan that bespoke of a desire that couldn't be feigned.

He truly did find her beautiful, not only in her fine gowns, but out of them. It made her want to be closer to him, for all of him to touch all of her. She arched herself against him and pulled free his cravat, then tugged up the hem of his shirt.

The daylight coming in from the windows shone like gold on his powerful torso, highlighting the carved muscles over his chest, his shoulders and arms, and flat, banded stomach. A tantalising line of dark hair trailed from his navel into his breeches.

The pulse of desire between her legs thrummed and made her heady with the need to release as she had the night they were caught by her mother, when his caresses had played so expertly over her that she'd been swept somewhere she'd never been before. Somewhere she wanted to go again.

Her hands ran over the heat of his skin, soft despite the hard strength beneath. The dark hair sprinkling his chest rasped at her palms as she explored his nakedness. He kissed her hungrily and nudged her back towards the large bed.

The room was masculine with dark wood and luxurious deep red velvet coverlets on the thick mattress. She allowed him to lay her back, stretched out over the rich velvet. He crawled over the top of her while still wearing his breeches and continued kissing her while his fingertips worked a slow path down her body.

She parted her legs in anticipation and his caress swept at the source of her longing. She cried out as he stroked her the way he'd done that one blissful, fateful night.

'I want to hear you climax for me again, my love,' he whispered.

Except he withdrew his fingers from her and instead shifted down her body to the foot of the bed where her thighs were still parted. Quickly, she pulled her knees together, but he tutted and gently edged them open once more.

Her breath came quick with nervousness, embarrassment and…and anticipation for what he might do next. He leaned over her sex and slowly, carefully, drew his tongue over her.

She gripped the sheets, unable to think, to move, to even breathe. The swirling licks and sucks he'd once employed on her nipples, he now performed between her legs. Fire and wet heat combined into complete and total bliss.

Somehow she managed to draw enough breath to cry out again and again until her voice was hoarse. He inserted a finger carefully into her, working the digit within her body even as he continued to lick, to tease.

When her release did finally come, it was hard and fast and sent her spiralling over the edge of a control she had no intention of reining in. Even then, he continued to kiss her intimately until the sensitivity overwhelmed her and left her hips jerking with each pass of his tongue.

He straightened with a somewhat arrogant grin. Somehow in the time since their wedding ceremony and now, the smooth combing of his hair had given way to its natural proclivity and was attractively mussed. Just the way she'd always liked it.

Heavens, but he was handsome. And he was hers. Her husband, her lover.

'I want you.' Her voice had gone husky with desire. 'Please.'

The grin slipped away, replaced with something far more serious that made her core clench. His hands went to his breeches and he began to unbutton his fall.

Lust hammered through Seth's body. It pulsed in his manhood as it sprang free from his breeches and ran molten in his veins. The musky scent of Violet's arousal nearly drove him mad with need.

The cries of her climax still hummed in his ears. He wanted to hear them again, to draw out more whimpers, more moans, more pleasure.

He pushed his breeches to the ground, along with his stockings and shoes. Her eyes swept down his body and lingered over his hardened shaft as her stocking-clad knees rubbed against one another, as if she could scarcely contain her own lust.

He braced himself over her with one arm while he guided the head of his arousal against the wet heat of her sex. The tip nudged against her, burying slightly within.

'Yes.' The word was sighed out on a long exhale and her legs spread wider as she pushed her hips towards him.

He flexed forward, edging deeper inside her. She sucked in a hard breath and moaned. Seth could only fist the coverlet in his free hand and clench his teeth to keep from spending inside her right then and there.

Her dark hair spilled over her creamy, smooth skin, her lips were red from his kisses, her cheeks flushed and her eyes bright with desire.

She was exquisite.

He withdrew gently and pushed into her until he was buried to the hilt. She gasped and he immediately paused, not wanting to cause her any discomfort. It had, after all, been six years since she'd been with a man.

'Don't stop,' she whispered.

It was an order he could easily follow. He moved inside her, slow at first, then in steady strokes in and out of her body. The sheath of her sex around him was a tight grip that squeezed with each movement. Every lift of her hips, every wriggle of her bottom.

Her full breasts gave a bounce with every thrust, jiggling as he increased his speed, as the friction between their bodies built and built and built. He tensed in preparation for release, but he held himself in place for a breath to still his own climax as his fingers reclaimed the bud of her sex.

He wanted her clenching around him when he found his release. His thumb circled over her. He needed only two passes over the sensitive nub before she threw her head back with the force of her pleasure. Her cries echoed around him, beckoning him towards his own release.

He gripped her hips and plunged hard into her as her orgasm spasmed around his shaft. He came with a roar, his seed spilling into her with each jerk of his hips that brought their pelvises pressing flush together.

He waited above her until their panting breaths slowed and then collapsed at her side. She remained on her back with her eyes closed, as though savouring the languid tranquillity of the moment. She opened her eyes and gazed up at him as a lazy smile spread over her lips.

He propped himself up on his elbow. 'I do hope this puts your worries about my attraction to you to rest.'

She rolled towards him. 'If it didn't, would you have to convince me further?'

He grinned. 'I might have to.'

'Then I fear I remain unconvinced.' She put a hand to her brow in a mock demonstration of distress.

He leaned towards her and kissed her full, pink mouth. 'You saucy minx.' He pulled her towards him. 'I love you, my beautiful Countess.'

Her coquettish expression turned shy. 'Do you truly?'

He pulled back and studied her. 'You know I do. I told you as much when I proposed to you the second time. Or does that officially count as the third time?' He considered. 'The proper second time,' he concluded.

She put a finger to her chin in contemplation. 'I believe it was the second time. Officially.'

He caressed her soft cheek. 'I shall always show you how I've always held you in such high esteem, how I value how different you are from every other lady of the *ton*, how my heart responds so viscerally when you're near. I thought you were lost to me six years ago when I left to fight for England. And now that you're my wife, I want you to know what you mean to me. Every moment of our lives.'

She drew a circle on the bedsheets with her fingertip and gave the action her whole attention. 'You've always been so handsome, so confident. It's a wonder you would ever love a woman like—'

He put a finger to her lips to still the words from falling free. 'A woman whose affection I am not sure if I'll ever be worthy of, but will still readily seek.' He grinned. 'I suppose there's still a bit of rogue in me after all.'

She peered at something on his shoulder and her brows furrowed. 'Were you injured?'

He glanced at the scar from a healed bullet graze. 'It was nothing of note.'

'I could have lost you.' She spoke softly, as though musing more to herself than speaking to him. 'You could have gone to war and never returned.'

'You could have danced with an honourable man who stole your heart and I'd never have had the opportunity to wed you,' Seth replied.

'Is it fate that kept us for one another?' Violet asked.

'If it is, I don't intend to question it.' He kissed her. 'I will, however, take full advantage of it.'

And he did. Throughout the day and well into the night. She was everything he'd ever wanted, everything he'd felt he never deserved. She was his and he would do everything in his power to ensure she always knew she was loved and well cared for.

For the first time in his life, this task felt like one he could perform with ease, for with a union as perfect as theirs, nothing could possibly go wrong.

Chapter Twenty-Five

Seth fell asleep some time in the night with Violet curled in his arms, both of them spent to the point of sheer exhaustion.

Ghosts, however, were not so easily placated. No sooner had his eyes closed and darkness pulled at him than the distant thunder of a cannon firing echoed through his mind.

Men in red uniforms ran forward around him, their bodies jerking with the slamming of bullets.

Someone shoved him—hard. The ground rose up, crashing into his side with such force it knocked the wind from his lungs.

Brent cast him a resolute stare before the cannonball crashed into him...

'You're in your bed at Dalton Place,' a soft voice said in Seth's ear. 'With your wife, Violet.'

Cool, gentle hands slid in comforting circles over his shoulder, drawing him from the dream.

He woke with a start and stared into the darkness at where Violet gazed down at him.

'It was only a dream,' she soothed.

'I know,' he replied, suddenly feeling rather ridiculous. Night terrors were something left back in the nursery.

But she didn't chastise him. Instead, she smoothed her hand over his brow, presumably brushing a bit of his unruly hair back. 'Do you have them often?'

He clenched his jaw.

'Then know that I will always be here to rouse you and soothe you.' She lay on his chest and embraced him, saying with her body what she had not yet said with words.

I love you.

He craved it with a ferocity he'd never before experienced. Those three words. The weighty impact behind them.

He wrapped his arms around her and let his senses savour all of her—the gentle violet scent still lingering in her hair, the warm silkiness of her nakedness against him, the beauty of her dark locks spilling over the white sheets. All of her washed away the horror of his dream and soothed his ragged nerves.

Whatever he had done in his life to earn such a treasure as Violet, he didn't know, but he was damn grateful for it. Sleep claimed him once more and carried him without interruption. That was, until the warmth curled around him shifted and slid away.

* * *

He opened his eyes and found a very naked, very lovely, Violet easing from the bed.

'I didn't want to wake you,' she said softly.

'I'm awake.' He reached for her. 'Come back to bed.'

'I can't sleep any longer.' She laughed.

He grinned. 'I didn't mean to sleep.'

A pretty flush blossomed in her cheeks. 'I wish I could.' Her gaze raked over his body where he lay on his side amid the tousled sheets. 'I truly do wish I could,' she said with apparent sincerity. 'But I'm afraid I promised to meet with Felicity and my mother at Gunter's for ices.'

'Nonsense, you're a newly-wed bride.' He sat up and reached for her again. 'Come back to bed, my love.'

'Felicity wanted Gunter's to celebrate. You know I can't let her down.'

Seth chuckled. 'I know. Has she continued to be well mannered?'

'Yes, thanks to your advice.' Violet went to the washstand, wet a cloth and rubbed it over her face and neck. 'If you hadn't shown me how to care for her, how to be sensitive to her need for attention, I don't know that she ever would be so properly behaved.' She paused in her washing. 'Would you mind, perhaps, if we invite her to the manor this summer?'

'I wouldn't mind at all,' Seth said with a smile.

'I think Hedgehog would get on nicely with the stable cat. Though sadly little Sadie has never worn a cap to speak of.'

'Well, not all felines can be so fashionable.' Violet set aside the cloth. 'Thank you, my lord.'

He wrinkled his nose. '"My lord" is so formal. I'm a second-born son regardless of my title now. Seth works nicely. Or the greatest lover there ever was.' He winked. 'That has rather a nice ring to it as well.'

'In that case, *the greatest lover there ever was*, I must ready myself to meet with Felicity and my mother, but I shall see you later this afternoon when I return.'

He pushed himself from the bed and retrieved a robe for her. 'I'll have Harold ready the carriage for you.' He approached her with the heavy robe slung over his forearm. 'Though you are forewarned, there's a bit of a jolt to his stops. He's one of my former soldiers who lost an arm. He's getting better, though my mother would disagree.'

Violet turned her back to allow him to aid her into the robe and glanced over her shoulder at him. 'I appreciate the warning.'

'It is only fair.' He turned her around to secure the sash at her waist and gave her a tender kiss. 'I shall see you when you return.'

She walked backwards towards the door adjoining their suites and blew him a kiss before slipping into her own bedchamber. Seth summoned

Gibbons to have Harold prepare the carriage while Bennet helped Seth prepare for a new day.

The valet entered the room with a twinkling smile. 'Felicitations on your union, my lord. I dare say Lady Violet is an excellent choice for you. Excellent.' He bent to retrieve Seth's cast aside jacket.

Seth relished the contented hum in his chest. 'Thank you, Bennet.'

The valet straightened with the clothing gathered in his arms and set it on the bed to tend to later. 'Shall we prepare you for the day with haste or with care, my lord?'

With haste or with care. Seth's way or Bennet's way. There was a difference of at least two hours between the two, but Seth had nothing else planned for the afternoon.

'Bennet's way,' Seth replied, and the valet's eyes lit with delight.

A fraction of a lifetime later, somewhere between the twentieth swipe of the razor and the thousandth, a rapid knock came from the door. 'Forgive me, my lord,' Gibbons said from the other side. 'This is most urgent.'

Bennet backed away and Seth sat upright, wiping the remainder of the shaving soap from his face. 'Come in.'

Gibbons rushed in immediately. The older man was in such a state, he didn't even close the door behind him. 'A Mr Nash is here to see you. My lord, he—'

'Finally.' Seth got his feet. Seth had been sending messages to the former Runner for the past week for news on Mr Pattinson's whereabouts with no response.

A dot of red on Gibbons' collar caught Seth's attention. 'Is that blood?'

'Mr Nash is quite unwell, my lord,' Gibbons said weakly.

It was then Seth noticed the butler's face had gone a peaked shade of grey. Alarm spiked through him.

'Where is he?' Seth demanded.

Gibbons wavered on his feet. 'The study.'

'Bennet, see to Gibbons.' Seth strode quickly to the open doorway.

Gibbons shook his head. 'I'd prefer you find a physician immediately, Bennet. Mr Nash has sustained grave injuries.'

Grave injuries? Seth's stride lengthened into a run as he raced down to the study. He shoved through the door and almost didn't see Nash where he lay slumped in a leather stuffed chair. A slash of bright blood showed on the yellowed shirt he wore under an old jacket.

'Nash,' Seth called.

The man's eyes flew open. 'Mr Pattinson,' the former Runner groaned. 'Back in London.' He winced through a pained breath. 'Means to stop you.'

Seth sank to his knees by the chair. 'Save

your breath, man. Let me see the extent of your wounds.' He lifted Nash's shirt and grimaced at the deep wound in the man's side.

Seth was no surgeon, of course, but he'd seen enough injured men and had even done his part to aid when he could. If the blade went between Nash's ribs, there could be irreparable damage to the lungs, or other soft organs. An injury that could prove fatal.

Seth tugged off his cravat and pressed it to the wound to staunch the bleeding. Nash hissed at the pressure against his injury.

'We've summoned a physician,' Seth said.

'Don't worry about me,' Nash gritted out. 'Protect your bloody family.'

Violet stepped out into the sunshine with Susan at her side. She was tempted to walk in the golden glow of warmth and breathe in the scent of fully bloomed flowers as she did so. That is, until she caught sight of Seth's carriage waiting for her.

It would be her first time taking the Dalton carriage, her first outing as the Countess of Dalton. Surely it wouldn't do to walk. A footman limped around the carriage and opened the door for her with a flourish.

She thanked Burton, who beamed at her in response, and stepped on to the small stair to climb into the small cabin.

A posy of violets waited on the cushioned seat

and scented the air with their delicate perfume. No doubt a gift from Seth. She smiled and touched a dark purple petal as the carriage pulled away.

'It was kind of him to think of you so, my lady,' Susan said.

'Indeed it was.' Violet leaned back on the padded seat back and smiled.

Seth.

Her heart seemed to whisper his name every beat. Seth, Seth. Seth, Seth. Seth, Seth. The way he had looked at her when he loved her, his eyes locked on hers as if their souls were as perfectly joined as their bodies.

I love you.

Those words had hovered on the tip of her tongue every moment they were together. Yet of all the confessions she'd already made to him, she found it the hardest to say.

She'd got to know him so much better last night than she had during the short period of their courting. Not necessarily through their intimate moments, though those certainly had been enlightening and highly enjoyable. It was also through the scars upon his body, placed there by war and fighting and danger.

The jagged white line on his shoulder from the graze of a bullet some time ago as well as other healed injuries. Several slashes that peppered his side and dotted his chest. Nicks along his forearms and hands and the bruise that had gone yellow along the top of his thigh.

She had thought never to see him again when he left her at her debut, but she hadn't ever considered it might be due to his death. Never had it been more apparent as a possibility than it was last night when she saw the physical effects on him from years of fighting. If some of those injuries had been slightly to the right or left, or up or down, they might have ended his life. He might never have come home.

The very thought gripped her heart with a fear she could not bear. It was then she knew she had to tell him she loved him. No matter how frail her heart, no matter how vulnerable it made her, she had to proclaim the truth of it as bravely as he had.

Seth was worth the risk. He would *always* be worth the risk.

Susan's brow wrinkled, and she sat forward to better look out the window.

'Is something amiss?' Violet asked.

'It's only that we seem to be driving in rather a roundabout way to go to Gunter's,' Susan replied, her attention fixed outside. 'And this does not appear to be Berkeley Square.'

Violet glanced out the window and a chill of apprehension trickled down her spine. Susan was right. It was not Berkeley Square outside, but an expanse of cobblestones with the visible, choppy water of the Thames visible in close proximity. Were they at the wharf?

The carriage drew to a smooth stop.

Goosebumps prickled over her skin.

'I was expecting a hard stop,' Violet said softly.

Susan frowned. 'I'm afraid I don't—'

The door flew open and a man filled the narrow opening. His dark hair was combed fashionably back to reveal a handsome face lined with wrinkles around his eyes. He wore a fine black jacket and a stark white shirt and cravat. The pale green of his waistcoat, however, was smeared with red.

Violet's heart nearly stopped as she recognised the mess to be blood.

'Who are you?' she demanded.

'We haven't yet had the honour, my lady.' The man inclined his head politely while keeping his gaze fixed on Violet. 'I'm Mr Pattinson.'

She continued to stare at him, looking for anything on his face that might indicate who he was or what he was doing. Pattinson. She rolled the name over in her mind. Why did it sound so familiar?

'Your family's solicitor.' He waggled his head. 'Former solicitor,' he amended.

Recognition dawned on her. Mr Pattinson was the man who had stolen Seth's mother's jewels.

'You have some gall,' she exclaimed. 'It takes a despicable man to swindle the jewels from a widow whose son had only recently died.'

'And it takes a despicable family to hide a man's misdeeds.' Mr Pattinson's upper lip pulled back to reveal fine, white teeth.

'I'm afraid I don't know what you're speaking of.' Violet spoke innocently even as she wondered if he referred to Seth's older brother.

'Defending him to the end, eh?' Mr Pattinson scoffed. 'Just like you wealthy nobs, thinking the rest of us are beneath you, to use for whatever you need us for and then discard us.' He reached into his jacket and withdrew a pistol. 'The time for the rich to crush those below them has come to an end.'

Susan gave a little scream and Violet put her hands up in silent plea. 'Please, you needn't use that.'

'Oh, I won't shoot you.' Mr Pattinson swung the pistol towards Susan. 'I'll shoot her.'

Fear spiked through Violet. 'Stop, please. What is it you want from me?'

The disgusted grimace on Mr Pattinson's face peeled up into a cold smile. 'Revenge.'

Chapter Twenty-Six

'What do you mean "protect my family"?' Seth demanded.

Nash's head lolled and his breath came in shallow gasps. 'Pattinson's daughter…'

'My lord, a message for you.' A servant rushed into the room, a young maid with blond hair who usually worked in the kitchens. 'Gibbons wasn't about and someone knocked at the door. I didn't wish to keep them waiting, so I opened it. When I did, I found this.'

She held out a folded piece of paper as Seth got to his feet.

He took it from her. 'Gather my family immediately. And tell Harold not to dare leave and have Lady Violet brought in. Post-haste.'

The woman hesitated at this new round of orders. Her gaze slid to Nash and widened.

'Now,' Seth commanded fiercely.

She leapt at the demand and bolted from the

room. With shaking hands, he unfolded the note. The script there was bold, the two lines stark black against the white background.

I have your sister. Meet me at the abandoned brick building by the wharf and come alone.

Seth jerked his head up. Caroline. Pattinson had Caroline.

He knelt at Nash's side once more. 'What does Pattinson want with my sister?' he demanded.

Nash shifted and gave a pained wheeze. 'His daughter. Dead. Your brother...' He grimaced. 'Syphilis.'

Seth's blood went cold. The man's broken sentence was plain enough to understand. William had given Mr Pattinson's daughter syphilis and it had been the cause of her death.

Seth's chest went tight with fear. Whatever Pattinson wanted with Caroline, it was not good.

Seth would do as he asked and come alone, but he would not arrive unarmed. He pushed to his feet and went to his desk. He jerked open the drawer and pulled out his pistol. It was heavy and cold in his hand, the familiar weight of death.

Footsteps pounded out in the hallway and his mother entered the study. 'Dalton, what is the meaning of this?'

Someone followed closely behind her. Confusion rattled Seth's brain and made him look up to stare at the woman behind his mother. Caroline.

Seth regarded his sister curiously. 'Caroline?'

'Yes, I'm here,' she said breathlessly. 'What is it, Seth? You've given us all quite a fright.'

He looked down at the note. Was it a jest of some kind? It was a bloody awful one if so.

Who the devil would claim to have Caroline when he did not?

The blonde maid returned to the room at a mad dash pace that stopped abruptly short upon her catching sight of the Dowager.

'Forgive me, my lord.' She kept a cautious gaze on Seth's mother. 'I could not find Lady Violet. It appears she'd departed some time ago.'

She paused a moment and dragged in a ragged breath, clearly winded from having rushed about with such haste.

Seth cursed to himself. If Violet was outside the town house, she could be in danger.

'That isn't all, my lord.' The maid's face fell and she put a hand to her chest.

'What is it?' Seth asked, his voice hard.

'Harold and Burton…' A sob broke from her throat. 'Harold and Burton are horribly injured.'

Seth braced himself on his desk at the news. The men who had fought at his side for years were injured. And if they had been attacked—

'What is the meaning of this?' Seth's mother demanded.

Seth looked down at the note in his hand as the terrible understanding dawned on him. 'Caroline, did you ever meet Mr Pattinson?'

Caroline blinked and shook her head. 'No.' She turned back to the maid who was openly sobbing. 'What happened to Burton and Harold?'

'A physician is on his way,' Seth said. 'Mr Nash requires assistance as well.'

Seth's mother followed his gaze and gave a choked cry.

'When the physician comes, have him see to Nash, Harold and Burton.' Seth checked the chamber of his pistol.

'Where are you going?' Seth's mother demanded.

'To the wharf.' He clenched his hand into a fist, balling up the note. 'Mr Pattinson thinks he has Caroline.'

Caroline's brow furrowed. 'Me?'

'Except there is now another dark-haired young lady in this home,' Seth said grimly.

Caroline gasped. 'Violet.'

Seth closed his eyes against the pain radiating from his very soul. 'Yes. Pattinson doesn't have you. He has Violet.' Seth tucked the pistol into the band of his breeches. 'And I'm going to get her back.'

Violet wriggled in an attempt to free her hands of their bindings. Not that she could be so easily liberated, not when the ropes were tied so tightly they sawed into her raw skin with every movement.

At least she had been told to tie up Susan and had been able to do so with looser bindings. Her maid sat in the chair Violet had been forced to strap her to. Sobs hiccuped from Susan and echoed in the large warehouse.

It was empty within, save for a stack of crates at the rear of the building. Mr Pattinson stood beside Violet, his arm locked on the crook of her elbow. She twisted her wrists.

His hand tightened on her. 'Enough struggling, or I'll shoot your maid.'

'What are you going to do with us?' She glared at him.

His pale gaze swept to the single small door leading into the warehouse. 'I'm going to kill your brother.'

Her brother?

Her confusion was fleeting when she recalled how he'd referred to being her family's solicitor. It wasn't because she was Seth's wife and now a Sinclair. It was because Mr Pattinson thought she was Caroline.

Well, she wouldn't correct him and she certainly wouldn't let him succeed in what he planned to do. She stopped moving as he'd demanded and glanced around frantically. There had to be something, anything, she could use as a weapon. The ground was filthy, a mess with piles of dirt and refuse.

And then she saw it: a rock. Just larger than the palm of her hand.

'I want no part of this.' Violet jerked her arm free from Mr Pattinson's grasp.

'You're already involved.' He snagged her arm again. As she had anticipated.

She yanked herself from his hold once more and used the momentum to topple over. She slammed hard to the ground and a puff of dust welled up around her. Quick as she could, she patted behind her for where she expected the rock to be. Grit collected on her fingertips, then she bumped something soft and wet. She wouldn't think too hard about what that could be.

Mr Pattinson uttered a gruff curse and reached down to pull her up. Violet floundered and kicked her feet on the filthy floor in an effort to free herself from his grip. More dust stirred up, but though it covered her actions of trying to locate the rock, it did little to aid in its recovery.

The solicitor grabbed her shoulders and hauled her upright. As she was dragged over the floor, she snagged something hard and rough. The rock.

She closed her fingers around it and hid it within her hand tied beneath the other, concealing it from view. Mr Pattinson gripped Violet so hard, she had to bite the inside of her cheek to keep from crying out.

'If you do that again, your maid suffers for it,' he growled. 'Do you understand?'

Violet nodded.

'No.' Susan's scream cut through the air with a suddenness that made both Violet and Mr Pattinson turn towards her.

Susan stamped her feet on the floor, sending up a cloud of filth as she rocked back and forth in her chair like a woman possessed. 'Don't you dare use me as a threat against my lady. You vile creature. We'll have you—'

The cocking of a gun sounded.

'Killed,' Susan finished saying. She gave a smug smile and settled back into the chair.

Seth appeared from behind her with a gun aimed directly at Mr Pattinson.

'If you miss me with that bullet, you'll hit your own sister,' the solicitor said.

'She's not my sister,' Seth growled. 'She's my wife.'

Mr Pattinson gaped at him. 'You aren't married.'

Violet took advantage of the man's surprise to wriggle her wrists once more. A bend, a twist, a flex. The rough rope ripped into her skin like fire.

'We were very recently wed.' Seth came closer. 'Yesterday. She's innocent in all of this, Pattinson. She's not from my family.'

The solicitor hesitated and slid a glance towards Violet who immediately stilled in her attempts to liberate her hands. She needed only to get one free. Just one.

'Did she know about your brother?' Pattinson demanded.

Seth ignored the question. 'I know about your daughter. Nash told me.'

'Nash.' Mr Pattinson spat upon the ground. 'That pathetic excuse for a man followed me all over England before I finally let him catch me.' The solicitor gave an angry hiss from between his teeth. 'Why couldn't you leave me to the jewellery? I wanted to get away from London, to start a new life. Why did you have to chase after me?'

Violet twisted her hand until her thumb joint strained against the rope. She was so close, just a smidge more and she would be free.

'You took advantage of my family while I was at war.' Seth narrowed his eyes.

'Your brother stole from my daughter.' Lines creased Mr Pattinson's brow and spittle flew from his mouth. 'First her innocence, then her life. He took everything from me. I couldn't stay in London, seething in loss and bitterness.'

He lifted his pistol and pointed it directly at Violet. 'Maybe you need to know what it feels like to lose someone you love.'

She had never looked down the barrel of a pistol before. It was a fathomless hole with seemingly no end. Ironic for something that could cut short lives with such finality. She pulled harder at her hand, until something popped and pain shot up her arm. A little whimper emerged from her throat, but it didn't matter.

She was free.

'Don't,' Seth's voice cracked. 'Take me and let her go.'

Mr Pattinson's gun cocked. 'You will know loss before you die.'

Violet tightened her grip on the rock in her good hand. Before she could swing it, Seth ran at her, shoving her to the ground. A fraction of a second later, an explosion boomed in her ears and she knew with sickening certainty that the gun had gone off.

Chapter Twenty-Seven

The thundering gunshot ricocheted around in Seth's brain, echoing off the chasms of the experiences that haunted him. Gunpowder burned in his nostrils and stung at his eyes. Ringing clanged in his ears, the high-pitched whine drowning out everything else.

Something else hung in the air. Coppery. Wet. Blood.

His mind spun. Waterloo. No—Violet. Something at his side ached and swirled into the mix of his confusion.

He staggered and it made the pain at his side sear in agony.

'Seth.' It wasn't the baritone of a soldier, but the pitch of a woman's voice. Violet's voice.

He turned in her direction as she lifted her hand and brought it down hard on Mr Pattinson's head. His eyes went wide as blood flowed from the wound, washing over his face, over his pale eyes. Like Brent.

Brent had pale blue eyes. They'd met Seth's just before—

Everything around Seth moved impossibly slowly, the way it had when the cannonball had collided with Brent's body. Pattinson glared at Violet and drew his gun back in an obvious attempt to strike her with it.

All at once, everything clicked into place and Seth's mind fell back on instinct. He wasn't an earl—he was a soldier facing his enemy. He took aim at Pattinson's face, braced for the kick of the weapon and pulled the trigger.

The force of his gun jolted his arms, a familiar sensation he was well prepared for. Pattinson's head snapped back and he dropped to the ground. Seth stared trance-like at the body slumped on the ground atop a growing puddle of blood.

'Susan.' Violet grabbed his arm as she ran past, breaking whatever spell death wove around him.

Together, they loosened Susan's ropes and freed the maid. Once she was safe, Seth put his attention fully on Violet, noting the dust peppering her dark hair and the smattering of blood on her neck and face.

'Are you hurt?' he asked.

She shook her head slowly, her eyes wide in the way one looked when they witnessed death for the first time. 'Oh, Seth, he was planning to kill us.'

Seth's back tensed with irritation. 'I should have shot him first.'

'It doesn't matter.' She shook her head. 'I

thought we were all going to die, that I'd never have a chance…' Tears filled her eyes and her lower lip trembled. 'That I'd never have the chance to tell you I loved you.'

He lifted his arm to put it around her shoulders when a sharp pain lanced through his side. One he had been acquainted with several times in his life. He'd been shot.

He glanced down at his side to assess the damage and grimaced at the hole torn through his red waistcoat, glistening with blood.

'Seth,' Violet exclaimed. 'You've been shot.'

A light-headed sensation fogged around his brain. 'So I have.'

It was more than his waistcoat that was wet with blood. So, too, were his black breeches. His white stockings were stained crimson and droplets splashed the filthy ground around even him. He regarded it with a momentary confusion. Where had all the blood come from?

He staggered and small hands caught him, keeping him upright.

'Seth?' Violet said, her words somewhere distant and faint.

He whispered her name and then the ground rose up to meet him as he collapsed.

Violet waited outside Seth's bedchamber door, her heart lodged firmly in her throat. The physician had been with him for well over an hour.

She paced down the hall, passing the worried faces of the Dowager Lady Dalton, Lady Caroline, Gibbons and even her own parents. Hedgehog sat at Lady Caroline's side, one eye partially obscured by a ridiculous yellow bonnet. Felicity had sent him there to be of assistance in keeping everyone's spirits elevated. Thus far, they all felt as dejected as Hedgehog looked.

Nash's injuries had been stitched closed and he was recovering in one of the guest rooms. Harold and Burton had both suffered head wounds and were also recovering in guest rooms. It was now Seth they were all worried about.

The physician finally emerged from the room. His mouth was set in a grim line, but then Dr Franklin's mouth was *always* set in a grim line.

Violet ran to him. 'Will he recover?'

Doctor Franklin studied her from the bent bridge of his nose. 'He will, but he will need a considerable amount of rest.' He sighed. 'Lord Dalton has been asking after you and won't be put off.'

Violet peered into the sunlit room behind the physician. 'May I go to him?'

Doctor Franklin stepped back to allow her entry into the bedchamber. 'By all means.'

Violet strode swiftly, but quietly, into the large bedchamber. The last time she'd been inside, she lay snuggled in the red-velvet bed with Seth, their bodies damp with sweat from sport and their naked limbs tangled in soft sheets.

He sat up in bed now with only a slight grimace. 'Violet. Thank God you're safe.'

'I am, thanks to you.' She sank gently on to the mattress beside him.

'As am I, thanks to you.' He winked at her.

A bandage was visible beneath the collar of his shirt. It appeared to wrap around his shoulder and waist. She reached her hand out to his. 'Is it terribly painful?'

He lifted a brow. 'You say that assuming I've never been shot before.'

She cast him a chastising look. 'Don't jest.'

'I'm not.' He smirked. 'I've been shot twice.' His gaze wandered to his side. 'Three times,' he amended. 'Stabbed through once and sliced at too often to count. It will take more than a solicitor to bring me down.'

She bit her lip. 'Was it true? What he said about his daughter?'

Seth rubbed his fingers over the back of Violet's hand. 'I believe it is. I wish he had come to me to speak of it rather than trying to kill you. All of this could have been avoided.'

'Is there anything we can do?' Violet asked.

'We can seek out his remaining family, if he has any, and offer restitution of some kind.' Seth's eyes deepened with a sadness Violet could feel in her chest. 'We will pay for his funeral costs as well.'

Seth's hand tightened on hers. 'I'm sorry I had to kill him, but I would do it again to save you.

I thought I'd lost you all those years ago when I went to war. When you looked so beautiful in that gown you thought I hated. I knew someone would marry you and I'd never have the opportunity.' He scoffed. 'Hell, I didn't deserve the opportunity being the kind of man I was then.'

'And I could have lost you several times over while you were off fighting for King and country.' Violet lay a hand on his shoulder. 'I think parts of us were missing the other.' She bit her lip. 'It sounds foolish, but before you returned home, I felt so broken. But with you here, I feel—'

'Whole,' he said.

She sucked in a breath. 'Yes. As though you're the piece of me I was missing.'

'And together we're stronger.' He gently stroked her cheek. 'I love you, Violet Dalton.'

Her throat went tight. 'And I love you, Seth Dalton.'

He grinned. 'I'd like to hear that again, if you please.'

Violet pulled in a soft breath. 'I love you, Seth Dalton. I love you, I love you, I love you and I'm sorry I was too great a coward to say it sooner.'

She kissed him lightly on the lips and imbued in that one innocent kiss all the love she held for him.

'I'll never put you at risk again,' Seth vowed passionately. 'I will never lose you again.'

She shook her head. 'We'll never lose each other. Now get some rest.'

'Only if you stay with me.'

She crossed her arms stubbornly over her chest.

He did likewise and winced.

Violet gave an exasperated sigh. 'Very well, but only so you'll sleep.'

She lay on the bed at his uninjured side with her hand resting on his chest, reassuring herself of every beat of his heart, every inhale of his breath. He was safe. He would recover. And their life together would go on. With both of them whole.

Seth only remained in bed for three days before he was too restless to be detained any longer. Much to the disapproval of the physician—the stodgy old goat—and every woman in Dalton Place, he refused to be bedridden any longer.

Granted he wasn't moving as swiftly as he did before his injury, but he'd sustained enough wounds to know it was only temporary. It was for that reason that he insisted the house be packed up for the family to relocate to Dalton Manor for the summer.

Violet's maid, who had recovered remarkably well from the ordeal of being abducted, not only orchestrated Violet's belongings being packed efficiently, but also rushed Bennet along. If left to his own devices, the valet would surely have taken a month to pack everything away.

'Are you checking on Bennet again?' Violet

asked from behind Seth where he stood in his bedchamber doorway. 'That poor man.'

'You have no idea,' Seth said drily. 'He would take two hours to shave my face if I let him. And I wish that was an exaggeration.'

'He only wants to make sure you're perfect.' Violet ran an assessing touch over his jaw and nodded. 'I don't believe it gets much closer than that.'

Seth put his arm around her and pulled her against his good side. He breathed in her delicate powdery scent and let his thoughts drift back to how that perfume was more enhanced along the sides of her neck when he'd kissed her there, when they'd spent the night loving each other.

More and more in the last few days, he found his memories wandering from recollections of violence, death and war. Instead, they were replaced with ridiculous moments of a cat named Hedgehog, tender ones with the woman he loved, and even amusing ones like when he'd fallen through the gap in the hedges between their homes.

Those were the memories he wanted in his mind. And he had a lifetime to build them with Violet.

'Your mother's jewels were all recovered with the exception of the bracelet found in Bath that you purchased.' Violet glanced up at him, as if she was worried he might not wish to discuss Mr Pattinson.

Seth nodded. 'I'm pleased they were all intact. And Mr Pattinson's remains were handled accordingly?' His chest ached with the loss of the man's life. Seth knew what he personally was willing to risk to save his sister and his wife. He could only imagine what he would do to avenge a daughter who had been wronged as egregiously as Pattinson's had.

'I handled it personally,' Violet said. 'Nash is seeking any additional living relatives, but is not hopeful.'

'He's already up and about?' Seth chuckled. 'And to think you were worried about me. The man was run clean through.'

'You tough men.' Violet rolled her eyes in playful exasperation. 'I'm told Harold and Burton are already back to work as well. Your mother claims Harold's stops are getting smoother now.'

'As long as Mother is happy...'

Violet tapped his arm in light chastisement. He chuckled and drew her against him more tightly. Soon they would be at Dalton Manor, away from balls and soirées and societal obligations—where the days would stretch out with leisure time and sunlit skies.

He looked forward to picnics and horseback rides through the property. All of them with Violet. And some day, perhaps even with their children.

'Dare I ask what that smile is for?' She tilted her head, studying him.

'I'm wondering how many children we'll have.' He pressed a kiss to her brow. 'You'll be the most wonderful mother. Felicity agrees with me. She's already requested six cousins.'

Violet's eyes went wide. 'Six?'

'We'd best get started.' Seth nudged her back against the door frame. 'The sooner the better.'

Violet bit her bottom lip and he knew she was weighing his injury against the call of desire. He knew well how he'd find her when she looked at him like that—wet and hot with need.

Someone cleared their throat behind Seth. 'Forgive me, my lord.'

Seth turned to find Gibbons intentionally averting his gaze. 'Lord Rawley is here to see you. I'm afraid he's rather insistent.'

Seth cast a regretful look at his beautiful wife and backed away. 'Yes, of course.'

'He's in the study.' Gibbons gave a light bow.

Seth thanked his butler, pressed a kiss to Violet's lips with a murmur of promise for later and made his way to the study. Rawley was not at the seat in front of the desk as Seth had expected. Instead, he was by the decanter of brandy with an empty glass in his hand.

He caught sight of Seth and quickly set it aside. 'Forgive me, I needed…' He straightened. 'I took your advice.'

Seth lifted his brows and wondered how Rawley had built up the temerity to go to Lottie's. He must truly like Caroline as much as he claimed to. Seth slowly walked to the decanter. 'Would you like a brandy?'

Rawley's cheeks went pink. 'I already had one.'

Seth smirked. 'When did you start drinking like Kentworth?'

'When I knew I had to come here.' Rawley padded the trembling fingertips of his hands together.

A smile crept over Seth's lips. Caroline had been beside herself with melancholy since Seth's decision that they remove to Dalton Manor until Parliament reconvened. She'd hoped to hear from Rawley, who had been disappointingly silent.

'Did you mean to ask me something?' Seth poured the man another brandy which Rawley took without hesitation.

In the entirety of his acquaintance with Rawley, Seth had never known the man to have more than one glass of any libation.

'I would like permission to…' The Viscount drew in a deep breath and drank a gulp of brandy. 'To write to Lady Caroline over the Parliamentary recess.'

'To write to her?' Seth tried to hide his disappointment. He'd been hoping for more. Far more.

Rawley swallowed. 'Yes. Please.'

Well, it was a start. 'You have my permission. You also may visit us at any time if you should desire to do so.'

Rawley smoothed a hand down his hair. 'That

is kind of you. I confess, I have rather a full schedule at my own estate.'

'Of course.' Seth patted his friend's shoulder in an attempt to put him at ease. 'The offer stands regardless. Caroline will be most pleased to hear from you.'

Rawley ducked his head and grinned to himself. 'Thank you.'

'Lady Caroline is here, if you'd like to join us for tea,' Seth ventured.

A sudden panic seemed to seize Rawley and Seth feared for a moment he would say no. Then an expression of determination set on his face. 'Yes. I should love to. Thank you.'

Seth rang for tea before the Viscount could change his mind. It had been years since Seth had been at Dalton Manor, but even with a lifetime of visits, he suspected this might be the happiest yet.

His mother's jewellery had been restored, Caroline would have the suitor of her choice to exchange letters with and Seth would have Violet at his side. He and Rawley made their way to the drawing room and met three happy faces: Caroline, the Dowager and Violet.

Seth sat beside his wife, revelling in the wonderful scent of her and how she made every internal inch of his chest seem to glow. He had been reluctant to return home to the duties of the earldom. Giving up his life as a soldier had felt as though he'd lost a piece of himself. Now, he realised it was not an amputation, but the end of a chapter. And while he didn't know where life would take him in the future, he knew those around him would make for a happy tale indeed.

Epilogue

September 1815—Dalton Manor

It had been years since Violet had held a picnic outdoors. Far too long to be certain. The white blanket was spread out over sunlit emerald grass and a silk awning was the only break in the endless blue sky overhead. A gentle breeze caressed their cheeks, keeping them cool in the shade despite the summer's heat.

The afternoon could not have been more perfect.

Felicity had joined them at Dalton Manor for the summer and now ran about with a large red ball with Hedgehog, wearing a straw bonnet, chasing after her. She was now a well-behaved child who always did her lessons without complaint—well, almost always—and relished the freedom to run about on the large estate.

'I ate outdoors often in my time in the military, but never was it a picnic.' Seth took a reverent breath and slowly exhaled, his mouth lifting into a smile. 'This is far more pleasant than my previous experiences.'

He had been relaxed since their arrival at the estate. Nightmares still plagued him from time to time, but they were fewer as the weeks passed. When they did come back to haunt him, he reached for Violet in the night and she held him until the worst of it had passed. While her chest ached to see him suffer from his memories, it soothed that hurt to know he found comfort with her.

The Dowager set a cup of lemonade on a small table beside her chair. 'I'm glad you're done with the business of war. I like you being home.' She glanced away, as she often did when emotion got the better of her. 'I like knowing you're safe.'

Caroline cast a glance towards the manor once more. 'Do you think Harold will be back soon?'

'Waiting on another letter?' Seth teased.

She squared her shoulders, but the flush to her cheeks answered well enough for her. The correspondence between Caroline and Lord Rawley had been consistent throughout the summer.

Violet grinned at Seth, who winked in return. After all, they had a wager about when Rawley might actually ask permission to wed Caroline. Seth optimistically suggested it might be towards the beginning of the Season, while Violet presumed midway through.

'There's a carriage in the distance,' Felicity

called out, abandoning her ball to instead race towards the manor.

Caroline got to her feet and made a show of dusting invisible bits of grass from her skirt. 'Well, I shouldn't let the child go alone.'

'Indeed,' the Dowager said with a secretive smirk as she got to her feet to join her daughter.

'We shall all go.' Seth rose and offered his hand to Violet, who accepted it and let him help her to her feet.

As soon as she was upright, however, the world spun about and nearly knocked her off balance. Seth's strong arms caught her. 'I'd tease you for having too much wine, but you haven't had a drop of it.'

Violet held on to him a moment longer than necessary. 'Just a bit of light-headedness.'

Felicity was already nearly at the manor and Caroline was halfway there with Seth's mother trailing behind them.

'We don't need to go to the house,' he said with apparent concern. 'We can remain here, if you prefer.' His gaze turned suspicious. 'You've had several light-headed spells lately. Is there...perhaps... something you care to tell me?'

Violet lost herself in the darkness of his gaze and felt herself yielding her hold on the secret she'd tucked against her heart for the better part of a month. 'I wanted to be certain first.'

He pulled in a soft inhale. 'And you are now?'

Violet nodded. 'It's been over two months since my courses. Sometimes issues can still arise—'

A wide grin split his face, silencing her caution. 'Not this babe.' His eyes sparkled with emotion and he put a tentative hand to her lower stomach. 'Not our child. Violet, we're going to be parents.'

She choked back a sob and nodded. 'We are.'

He lowered his head and kissed her over and over again until they were both somewhere between laughing and crying.

'The post came,' Felicity yelled in the distance.

Seth put his head to her brow. 'Perhaps the only one who might be more excited than me is Felicity. Though even then, I doubt it.'

Violet chuckled. 'I think we can all be equally elated.'

Seth folded his hand over hers and together they strode towards the house where the familiar carriage now stood. Harold waved his one arm at them in a jovial greeting as Burton limped over with a small bundle of folded missives in his hand.

Violet and Seth arrived in time to witness Caroline's joy at receiving a new letter from Lord Rawley and Felicity had her own letter from her siblings who had gone to their country estate for the summer.

'And one for you, my lady.' Burton handed her a letter.

She glanced down at the neat script and gave a cry of delight. 'It's from my cousin.' It had been an age since she'd last heard from Eleanor. In fact, not since the Duke and Duchess of Somerville had left for India where they'd unearthed the famed Heart of Fire ruby.

Violet read through the contents and spoke aloud as she did so. 'They're briefly in London before going to Egypt. How exciting! And they wish us both the same happiness they've found in marriage.'

The last part, however, she kept to herself. The bit about how Eleanor was so pleased Violet had gone to Lottie and news that Violet's farewell to the *Lady Observer* column had only helped to further Lottie's popularity with the *ton*. She even had her first male student now.

Violet glanced at Caroline's beaming face after she read that part and made a note to tell Seth later when they were alone. It appeared Rawley had indeed taken Seth's advice.

'They should like to come for a visit while they're in England,' Violet finished.

'Of course,' Seth said. 'It would be wonderful to see Somersville again. It's been far too long since we've had a chat.'

'My sister and brothers want to come, too.' Felicity hefted Hedgehog into one arm and held the letter up with the other. 'They would like to arrive next week.'

Seth shrugged. 'It's a large house. It can entertain a few more visitors.'

'Even Lord Rawley?' Caroline asked softly.

Violet stifled her gasp of happiness for her sister-in-law.

'Especially Lord Rawley.' Seth put his arm around Violet.

'I'd like to change my prediction,' Violet whispered.

'Oh, it's far too late for that,' he replied.

Caroline spun around and clutched the letter to her heart.

'Far, far too late, my love,' Seth repeated.

'I'd like to see her happy,' Violet said. 'Like us.'

'I don't know that it's possible for anyone to be as happy as us.' He turned slightly, putting his back to everyone as he pressed a quick, sweet kiss to her lips. 'And how that joy will double soon.' His fingers lightly caressed her lower stomach where their child grew in her womb.

'I love you,' Violet said with the whole of her heart.

'As I love you, my beautiful wife.' He took her hand in his and led her back to the picnic where a lovely trifle was waiting for them. And she knew in the depth of her soul that berry trifles would now always taste like sunny days on the Dalton estate with a child's laughter, giddy delight and eager anticipation for the future.

After all, life was sweeter with happy memories and they now shared those in abundance.

* * * * *

COMING SOON!

We really hope you enjoyed reading this book.
If you're looking for more romance, be sure to
head to the shops when new books are
available on

Thursday 20th August

To see which titles are coming soon, please visit

millsandboon.co.uk/nextmonth

MILLS & BOON

Coming next month

A FORBIDDEN LIAISON WITH MISS GRANT
Marguerite Kaye

How had they managed to become seated so close together? His head was bent towards her, as if he was confiding his deepest secrets or whispering sweet nothings, instead of talking about shipping lanes. While they spoke, their bodies were conducting another, altogether different conversation. There was a light in his eyes that she could not mistake. She was pretty sure it was reflected in her own eyes. She had forgotten what this felt like. She didn't remember it being anything like this, truth be told. In any case, this had nothing to do with love and everything to do with lust. The word, with all its dark and sinful connotations sent a delicious frisson down her spine. She was almost forty, and she was in lust!

Constance moved a little bit closer. 'I've never been on a paddle steamer,' she said, daring to put her hand on his knee. 'I'd love to sail on one. What's it like?'

The sharp intake of his breath made her think, for a split second, that she'd made a huge mistake. Then his hand covered hers. 'I'm afraid it's not as romantic as it sounds. It can be a bit noisy. In the engine room you can't hear yourself think, but some steamers have passenger decks and cabins that are much quieter.' He turned her hand over and began to draw circles with his thumb on her palm. 'Basically, the more you pay for your ticket, the more civilised your journey will be.'

She was having difficulty breathing. She couldn't believe this was happening. That she was actually encouraging it to happen. Don't think, Constance! The fates wanted this. Ridiculous excuse, but she didn't care. 'And is it dangerous?' she asked. 'That scar on your hand...' The hand that was working magic on hers. 'And that was only a model, you say?'

'A fully working model built to scale. I shouldn't have tampered with it. Serves me right for getting burned. Constance...'

'Grayson?'

'Talking of getting burned. Are we both in danger of doing just that?'

'I don't know. I hope so. I don't mean *burned,* but...' She broke off, unable to voice what she actually meant, not because she was mealy-mouthed but for fear of being wrong. 'What exactly do you mean?'

'I mean that I would like to make love to you, but I'm worried we might regret it,' he said softly. 'And if I've got it completely wrong then forgive me, but I thought...'

'You haven't got it wrong. And I wouldn't regret it.'

His eyes widened. 'You mean you want to...'

'Make love.' Her heart thumped. Her body thrummed. 'Yes,' Constance said. 'Though I can't believe I've just said that.'

Continue reading
A FORBIDDEN LIAISON WITH MISS GRANT
Marguerite Kaye

Available next month
www.millsandboon.co.uk

WE'RE LOOKING FOR NEW AUTHORS FOR THE MILLS & BOON HISTORICAL SERIES!

Whether you're a published author or an aspiring one, our editors would love to read your story.

You can submit the synopsis and first three chapters of your novel online, and find out more about the series, at **harlequin.submittable.com/submit**

We read all submissions and you do not need to have an agent to submit.

IF YOU'RE INTERESTED, WHY NOT HAVE A GO?

Submit your story at:
harlequin.submittable.com/submit

MILLS & BOON